A Children of the Pines Novel

Book One

By
Kelly Schweiger

First edition 2026

Dedicated to Toni Cary.
One of my first fans and a wonderful lady
who will be greatly missed.

Contents

Prologue 1

Previously in the World of Where the Pines Still Stand

1. The Shape of Things 3
2. Dark Clouds Building 17
3. The Board 27
4. In Good Order 34
5. What Can be Made 40
6. In Inches, Not Miles 50
7. The Ones Who Wait 62
8. A Place to Gather 76
9. We Learn by Watching 86
10. Habit 93
11. The Days Between 99
12. What is Passed Down 114

13. What is Given Away 131

14. When Someone Is Needed 142

15. What Has a Name 155

16. No Sign 170

17. First Words 177

18. The Line 188

19. Daylight 196

20. The Cost of Restraint 204

21. The Door Left Open 216

22. Bought Time 232

23. What Remains 241

Core Cast — Children of the Pines

The Lodge 256

The Harbingers 261

About the Author 262

Acknowledgements 263

PROLOGUE

PREVIOUSLY IN THE WORLD OF WHERE THE PINES STILL STAND

A year has passed since a massive coronal mass ejection struck the earth, collapsing electrical grids across the globe in a matter of hours. The modern world—its networks, machines, and quiet conveniences—went dark. Civilization was thrown backward overnight, returning people to a way of life not seen since the 1800s.

High in the Adirondack Mountains, the Callahan family survived the collapse by retreating to their remote mountain lodge. Years of preparation, hard-earned skills, and deep roots in the land carried them through the chaos that followed as cities faltered and supply lines vanished. The death toll was devastating.

In time, the Lodge became more than a refuge for the Callahans. Neighbors arrived. New friends stayed. Children filled the fields and trails between the trees. Together they began the slow, stubborn work of rebuilding a life without electricity, without modern comforts—trying to create a community worth protecting.

But the violent new world is beginning to change.

Beyond the safety of the mountains, whispers travel between settlements of a different kind of threat emerging. Not raiders. Not starving wanderers.

Something more organized.

Something driven by ideas.

Welcome to ***The Children Of The Pines.***

Chapter One

The Shape of Things

The world didn't end the day Quinn lost his hand. It just became harder to hold onto.

The sun shone bright and the sky was the perfect shade of blue. The Lodge never stood still.

The men dug the walipini greenhouse eight feet into the earth.

New fence posts went up along the south pasture.

Owen expanded the smokehouse while Morales worked on the solar array.

Every week something new took shape.

Quinn sat on the porch, his left arm ending three inches below his elbow. The stump was healing well, the skin still shiny, tight, and tender to pressure. Eight weeks had passed since the night he lost it and he was finally allowed to get out there and help more.

Quinn chose the barn because no one was supposed to be there.

The morning had the kind of chill that didn't bite so much as settle in. He stood for a moment just inside the wide doors, letting his eyes adjust, his arm tucked awkwardly against his body the way he'd learned to hold it when he wasn't thinking.

The stump ached. Not sharp. Just enough to remind him it was there.

A stack of empty feed buckets waited near the wall. Light work. Manageable. He told himself that as if saying it first might make it true.

He bent, hooked the first bucket with his good hand, then pressed the second against his forearm. The plastic slipped, clattered to the floor, and rolled away into the shadows.

Quinn exhaled through his teeth.

He retrieved it, slower this time. Pressed the rim against the inside of his forearm, careful of the scar. The skin there was tight and pale, the line of healing still faintly pink and very sensitive to pressure. He could feel the pressure now, not pain exactly, but a deep awareness, like leaning on a bruise that refused to fade.

The bucket slid again.

He swore under his breath and stood still, breathing, jaw locked. The barn was quiet except for the soft shifting of animals and the distant creak of the rafters settling. He tried again, pressing the rim against his forearm. The bucket slipped and clattered to the floor. Grace crossed the barn in three strides and caught it before it rolled away.

"That's enough."

The words weren't sharp. Just there.

Grace stood in the doorway, arms folded inside her coat, eyes steady. She hadn't announced herself. She never did anymore.

"I've got it." Quinn reached for the bucket again, movements stiff, deliberate.

Grace didn't argue. She didn't move to help. She just stayed where she was, watching the way he shifted his weight, the way his shoulders pulled tight like he was bracing for a blow that wasn't coming.

He got the bucket this time. Lifted it. Took two careful steps.

The ache flared, deep, spreading down into muscle that no longer had anything to finish the motion it wanted to make. His grip faltered. The bucket slipped.

Grace crossed the barn in three strides and caught it before it hit the ground. She set it back against the wall, upright, then turned to face him.

"You don't have to prove anything."

"I do." His voice came out rougher than he meant. "I can't just stand around."

She looked at his arm then. Not the way people used to look, quick and guilty, but fully. Like it was just another fact to be accounted for.

" I agree, you can't. Then do something that works. Not something that hurts."

He opened his mouth, then closed it again.

Grace stepped past him and picked up a length of rope from a nearby hook. She looped it around two of the buckets, tied them together with practiced ease, then handed the rope to him.

"Carry them that way. Balance them against your hip."

He hesitated, then took the rope. Tried it. The weight pulled, awkward but manageable. He took a step. Then another.

It wasn't graceful. It wasn't fast.

But it was forward.

Grace watched him go until he reached the far end of the barn and set the buckets down without dropping them.

When he turned back, she was still there.

"Tomorrow we'll figure out something better."

Quinn nodded. His arm throbbed. His chest felt tight. But beneath it all, something steadier took hold.

He had helped. It wasn't much.

But it was something.

Gemma swung down from the horse at the Lodge rail and handed the reins to Tobias, who looked as tired as she felt. Dust on his boots, coat smelling faintly of smoke and pine. They'd split the rounds again. Always did lately. It was the only way to cover everyone without running themselves into the ground.

"Gemma, I think we should ride together." Tobias hesitated, fingers tightening briefly on the reins. "I've heard rumors on my route. Folks not showing up where they're expected. A few places... just quiet. Bandits, maybe. Or worse."

"Dad, we can't cover enough ground that way," Gemma said. "And Doc's already swamped at the school. New people are moving in daily, and most of them aren't in great shape."

Tobias frowned, nodded. He didn't like it, but he understood. "Then we each take someone along. An escort."

Gemma snorted. He was waiting for the *I am perfectly capable* speech. Instead, she paused.

"That's probably the safest way to go," she said finally. "And if there's an emergency medical problem, there'll be someone to help—or get help." She considered it a beat longer. "I'll ask Hunter if he wants to ride with me on Wednesday."

Tobias blinked.

After a few seconds—enough time to realize his daughter hadn't argued, hadn't postured, hadn't needed permission—he cleared his throat and went back to business.

“The Burke place was quiet,” he said, sliding the leather through his fingers, checking the worn spots out of habit. “Mrs. Harris asked about you."

Gemma nodded as she shrugged out of her satchel, the weight of it familiar against her shoulder. "Tell her I'll be back in three days. And that cough sounds better."

Tobias smiled faintly. "You always say that."

"Because it usually is, she only coughs when I am around." She glanced toward the Lodge, where woodsmoke curled from the chimney and disappeared into the steel-gray sky. "Go get something hot. I'll catch up."

He didn't argue. Tobias rarely did. He headed inside, leaving Gemma alone in the sharp afternoon light.

The school was where she would be tomorrow. She'd been there yesterday, assisting Doc with a deep gash that would've been nothing before and was everything now. She'd handed him instruments, watched his hands, memorized the way he moved when supplies were thin and mistakes weren't allowed.

She'd learned more in the past year than she ever thought she would.

Gemma slung the satchel over her shoulder again, glanced at the chalkboard that was the twin of the one in the Lodge to see if she had any pressing jobs, and then went looking for Quinn.

She found him near the barn. He gravitated toward places where there was work to be done and fewer eyes to see him fail.

He stood with his back to her, shoulders tight, his left arm held close to his body. The sleeve of his coat hung empty past the elbow, pinned up neatly, as if order alone could make sense of it.

"Hey."

Quinn startled, then turned. His face eased when he saw her. "Hey."

She crossed the space between them and wrapped him in a hug.

"You're back," he said.

"Mm-hmm. Two splinters, one stubborn fever that's probably pneumonia, and a goat bite." She pulled back to look at him. "You?"

He shrugged. "Same as always."

Gemma's eyes flicked once to the line beneath his sleeve, then back to his face. She didn't ask how it was healing. She already knew. She'd checked it herself three days ago. Clean scar. Good color. No infection.

The body was doing what it could.

"You eating?"

"Later."

She studied him for a moment longer, then nodded. "I'll check on you tonight."

Quinn hesitated. "You don't have to—"

"I know." Her smile was gentle but firm. "I want to."

She squeezed his shoulder once more and turned away before he could argue.

Grace was down by the edge of the clearing, hauling something that looked heavier than one person should handle. Gemma watched her for a moment. The way she leaned into the weight, the way she didn't stop when it shifted awkwardly.

When Grace noticed her, she set the load down and wiped her hands on her coat. "You're back."

"Just got in." Gemma nodded toward the path that wound along the treeline. "Walk with me?"

Grace glanced once toward the barn. Then she nodded.

They walked in silence for a few minutes, boots crunching softly over twigs and pine needles covering the path. The pines stood close here, their shadows long and cool.

"He's not sleeping," Grace said finally.

Gemma didn't pretend to be surprised. "I know."

"He won't say it hurts." Grace's jaw tightened. "But he flinches when he thinks no one's looking."

"Pain's easier than grief. You can measure pain."

Grace kicked at a stone, sending it skittering off the path. "He keeps trying to do things the old way."

"He will," Gemma said. "For a while."

"How long?"

Gemma slowed, considering. "Until failing hurts more than changing."

Grace stopped walking. "Well...that is just awful."

"It's honest." Gemma stopped too, turning to face her.

Grace's eyes flicked toward the Lodge. "Sometimes I don't know what to do. If I help too much, he shuts down. If I don't—"

"He thinks you're giving up on him."

Grace nodded.

Gemma reached out and squeezed her hand. "You're doing it right. You stay. You don't rush him. That matters more than fixing anything."

Grace swallowed. "He doesn't see it that way."

"He will." Gemma's voice was steady. "Not today. But someday. He is not one to wallow, but this is far beyond the typical emotional weight to deal with. We need to think outside the box, make accommodations that will help him see what is possible."

They stood there, breathing in the cold pine air, the weight of the world pressing in around them.

"He lost more than his hand."

Gemma nodded. "I know."

Jo stepped out onto the porch and rang her dinner bell. "Lunch is ready... come and get it." She yelled out into the spring day.

It always made her smile to see everyone come from all directions. Eating together was a vital part of their lives. It kept them close, grounded, and informed. Seeing all of their faces around the enormous table brought sheer joy to her heart.

Her service dog Odin padded across the porch and lay in a sunny spot, his dark coat soaking up the warmth.

Jo glanced at the 'board', an old flip chalkboard that currently stood on the porch. Job rotations, important tasks, and information was all there. Everything looked correct so she turned toward the door.

"Alright Odin, you take a nap... I'll just keep on working." Jo said as she headed back inside.

Odin lifted his head, chuffed, then rose and padded to the door. He looked up at Jo and chuffed again.

"That's what I thought." She laughed and held the door for him.

Inside, the kitchen smelled of venison stew and fresh bread. Steam rose from the pot on the woodstove, and the long table had been set with mismatched bowls and spoons that had seen better days but still did the job. A fresh bowl of foraged early greens sat on the table. Sorrel, chickweed, and dandelion greens. There was rhubarb cobbler for dessert.

Gus came in first, stamping the dirt from his boots. He crossed to the wash basin without a word, scrubbed his hands, then bent to kiss her temple.

"Smells good, Jo."

"Better taste good. I had to stretch it with extra potatoes."

"Then it'll taste like home."

The others filtered in. Owen with sawdust on his sleeves. Gemma and Grace from the path. Quinn last, moving slower than the rest, his face carefully neutral.

Jo watched him take his seat at the far end of the table. He kept his left side angled away, his arm resting on his lap where it couldn't be seen.

She ladled stew into bowls and passed them down the line. Bread followed, torn into rough chunks and shared hand to hand.

Conversation rose around the table. Someone mentioned the fence line. Someone else asked about the Harris place. Laughter broke out over something Tobias said, though Jo missed the setup. Tobias talked about the rumors he had heard on his rounds, and there was a grumble of concern.

She kept half an eye on Quinn. He ate with his right hand, steady enough, but his portion sat mostly untouched.

Odin padded over and rested his chin on Quinn's knee.

Quinn's hand dropped to the dog's head, fingers curling into the thick fur. His shoulders eased, just a fraction.

Jo caught Gus's eye across the table. He nodded once.

They didn't need to say it. The work of healing wasn't done at the table. But it started here.

Gus gathered the younger children after lunch, his voice carrying over the clatter of bowls being stacked.

"Everyone put on your boots and jackets. We're going on a little walk-about in the woods."

The announcement sparked immediate chaos. Max and Rosa bolted for the mudroom, Jake hot on their heels. Edwin and Marisol raced past, already arguing about who got the good stick last time. Little Lucy toddled after them, determined not to be left behind.

Gus crossed to where Grace and Quinn sat at the far end of the table. He rested one broad hand on the back of Grace's chair.

"I was hoping you two would help me out with these whippersnappers."

Grace's face lit up. "Whippersnappers?" She laughed, bright and genuine. "What are you doing, Pop?"

"Taking the kids out for some schooling in the forest. Thought I'd see if Gemma and Rowan want to come along too."

Grace glanced at Quinn. His jaw tightened, and he shifted in his seat, left arm still tucked close. The refusal sat plain on his face before he even opened his mouth.

Gus caught it too. He leaned forward, voice dropping a notch, steady and without pity.

"I think it's important for you older ones to share your knowledge. Easier for the little ones to digest coming from their older cousins instead of their old Pop."

Quinn's gaze flicked to the window, then back to the table. His right hand drummed once against the worn wood.

Finally, he nodded.

Grace's smile bloomed, softer this time, relief threading through it. "Yeah. We'll come."

Gus clapped Quinn's shoulder once, brief and firm, then straightened. "Good. Meet by the south trail in ten."

He moved off toward the stairs, already calling for Gemma and Rowan.

Grace stood and nudged Quinn's elbow. "Come on. Before Rowan claims all the teaching glory."

Quinn huffed, almost a laugh, and pushed back from the table. His steps were slower than Grace's, but he followed.

Jo watched them go, her hand resting on the edge of the sink. Odin pressed against her leg, warm and solid.

She didn't smile. Not yet.

But she felt the small shift, the way light found its way through cracks.

Gus called it a walk-about, which made the little ones think it was an adventure and made Quinn think it was a chore.

He lingered at the edge of the porch, tugging his jacket on with practiced awkwardness, jaw tight as he watched Gus gather the younger kids. Boots thumped against weathered boards. Questions spilled out of them like seeds thrown to the wind. Grace noticed, of course. She always did. She didn't say anything, just stepped closer and bumped his shoulder lightly with hers, grounding him without forcing him to look at her.

"I don't feel like doing this."

Grace smiled, small and knowing. "I know."

That was enough.

They set out along the familiar trail that curved away from the Lodge and into the trees, Gin drifting behind them. She carried a rifle slung easy, eyes always moving, but there was curiosity in her too. The way she slowed to touch bark, the way she listened when Gus spoke. She was security for the group, but in reality she really wanted to learn about her new home.

"Alright," Gus stopped near a stand of young birch. "This isn't a hike. This is learning how not to starve or freeze if you get turned around. Rule one: what's the forest give you first, late spring?"

"Green stuff!" Lucy piped up.

Gus nodded. "Aye. And which green stuff won't make your stomach regret your life choices?"

Quinn answered before he meant to. "Dandelion. Whole plant. Leaves, flower, root if you're desperate."

The kids turned toward him like sunflowers.

"Really?" Edwin asked, eyes wide.

"Really." Quinn gestured with his good hand toward the ground. "You just look for the jagged leaves. Like a lion's teeth. Don't mix it up with anything milky unless you're sure. But sorrel are the best..." pointing at a patch of wood sorrel, "lemony and delicious. We had both at lunch today."

Gus shot him a sideways glance, beard twitching with a smile he didn't comment on.

They moved deeper, Gus pointing out young spruce tips, explaining how they could be chewed raw or steeped into tea. Sadie knelt beside him, absorbing everything, asking quiet, sharp questions about preparation and storage. She took notes in a small, battered notebook, glancing up now and then to watch Quinn as he talked. Gemma watched cataloging him where he hesitated, where he didn't. Pop was a genius sometimes.

Grace walked beside Quinn, matching his pace when he slowed, quickening when he didn't.

When Max got a thorn in his hand, Quinn gently dug it out, pretending not to notice Max's quivering lip.

Quinn smiled at him. "The forest doesn't always advertise its teeth."

That earned him a thoughtful look from Gemma, something like respect settling into place.

They stopped near a stream, water running cold and clear over stone. Gus had the kids crouch and listen. "What do you hear?"

"Water," Jake said.

"Birds." Max said

"Wind." Marisol said

Quinn closed his eyes without realizing it. He could hear more than that: the way the water broke around rocks, the soft scuttle of something small in the underbrush, the hush that meant nothing large moved nearby. His shoulders eased, just a fraction.

Rowan noticed. His sister always noticed.

"How do you know when it's safe?"

Quinn opened his eyes. "You don't. Not completely. But you learn the patterns. When the woods go quiet all at once, that's when you pay attention."

Grace watched him as he spoke, really watched him, and saw the way the words came easier out here. The way the loss didn't sit quite so loud in his mind when the forest recognized him back.

They turned back as the light shifted, the younger kids chattering now, comparing leaves and bark and arguing over who'd spotted what first. Marisol ran ahead, then doubled back.

"Quinn, you're really smart."

He blinked, caught off guard. "I just pay attention."

She nodded, satisfied with that, and ran off again.

Gin fell into step beside him as they walked. “You grew up learning this?”

“Yeah.”

She glanced at his arm, then quickly away. “Good to have people who know the land.”

Quinn swallowed, then nodded. “Good to still be useful.”

Gin stopped walking. “You never weren’t.”

Quinn just shrugged and walked on.

Gin looked at Grace, who smiled softly and fell in beside Quinn again.

By the time they reached the Lodge, Quinn realized something unsettling and fragile all at once: his chest didn't hurt the same way it had when they left. The ache was still there, but it wasn't everything.

Grace caught his eye on the steps and smiled, soft and steady.

For the first time in a while, Quinn smiled back without forcing it.

From the porch, Jo watched him and felt the old, unwelcome certainty settle in her bones that peace never arrived without asking for something in return.

Chapter Two

Dark Clouds Building

The old pickup rumbled to a stop on the gravel drive, dust rising in the afternoon light. Marcus was already halfway down the porch steps, Gus close behind with Jo leaning on her cane near the rail. Odin sat alert at her knee.

Gunny swung out of the cab with a grin that split his weathered face. "Hello, Callahans!" he bellowed.

His voice carried across the yard, drawing heads from the barn and the garden. Hunter straightened from where he'd been working on the new solar panel array they had scavenged with Morales, both men exchanging a glance before heading over.

"What's the word, old man?" Marcus clasped Gunny's hand, firm and brief.

"Better than last week." Gunny released his grip and nodded to Gus, then tipped his head toward Jo. "Ma'am."

"Nate." Jo's eyes crinkled. "You staying for supper?"

"If you're cooking, I'm staying."

Gus snorted. "You'd stay if we were boiling boot leather."

"Damn right I would. I bet Jo's boot leather is delicious." Gunny turned back to Marcus, voice dropping half a notch. "Road's clearing faster than expected. We got three more families settled near the school. Baker's crew finished the smokehouse yesterday."

Jo shifted her weight on the cane. "Any trouble?"

"None worth mentioning. Couple scuffles over supplies, but nothing that needed more than words." Gunny glanced around the property, taking in the new fence posts, the goats grazing near the barn, the tidy rows in the garden where Gemma knelt with Marisol. "You folks don't slow down, do you?"

"Can't afford to," Gus said simply.

Gunny nodded, something almost fond settling into his expression. He'd spent enough time here now to know the rhythm of it: the early bells, the shared meals, the way everyone had a task and nobody shirked it. Gin had designed and built a gunsmith shop and was planning to teach everyone on her favorite topic, weaponry. Morales had rebuilt half the solar setup and was eyeing the water pump next. Hunter spent his mornings on the radio or escorting Gemma on her rounds and his afternoons learning to hunt with Tobias, Owen, or Franklin.

Even Kosinski had stayed when Wallace's group headed north to Vermont, choosing the Lodge over anything else.

Gunny understood why.

"Got some mail for you too," he said, reaching into the truck bed. "And news from the northern settlements."

Marcus's expression sharpened. "Good news or the other kind?"

Gunny pulled a canvas sack free and slung it over his shoulder. "Bit of both. Let's go talk for a spell."

The steam rose from four mugs as Jo set them on the table, her hand steady despite the weight of what hung in the air. A year. Hard to believe The Day had carved twelve months out of them already. So much lost. So much found. The world had fractured, reshuffled itself into something brutal and strange, and here they sat, still breathing, still fighting to do more than just survive.

From the far end of the Lodge, voices drifted through the open door of the old formal dining room. Clare's patient tone, Ellie's laugh, Mary correcting someone's arithmetic. The library and classroom now, shelves of salvaged books and handmade slates where crystal chandeliers once hung. The children's recitation rose and fell like a hymn.

Jo placed a plate of cornbread on the table and waved off the half-hearted protests. "Hush. You'll eat."

Marcus reached for his mug without argument. Gunny grinned and helped himself to a wedge of bread. Gus just shook his head, but his hand found Jo's wrist as she passed, a brief squeeze of gratitude.

"Alright," Marcus said, leaning back in his chair. "What's the SitRep, Gunny?"

Gunny swallowed, wiped crumbs from his beard, and his expression sobered. "Wallace radioed in last night. Says they've got spotty comms with what's left of the military out west."

The room stilled. This was the first real news they have had in a year.

"California, Washington, Oregon, Nevada. All under enemy control." Gunny's voice didn't waver, but his jaw tightened. "They stopped the advance for now. Stalemate. But the reports..." He paused, met Marcus's eyes. "Seventy to ninety percent loss of life. US alone."

Jo's breath hitched, sharp and small. Gus's knuckles went white around his mug.

Marcus just shook his head, slow and grim.

"Seventy," Jo whispered.

Father Tom closed his eyes, sorrow etched on his face.

"At least." Gunny's tone was flat, military. The kind of voice that delivered bad news and moved on because there was no other choice. "Could be more. Hard to know when the country's gone dark with little to no way to communicate."

Gus set his mug down hard enough that coffee sloshed. "And the rest of the world?"

“Worse, probably.” Gunny tore another piece of cornbread but didn’t eat it. “Europe’s silent. Asia, South America—same story. A few pockets holding on, but it’s scattered. Wallace says the brass thinks centralized government is done. What’s left is regional. Tribal.”

“Like us,” Jo said quietly.

“Like us,” Gunny agreed.

Marcus rubbed a hand over his face, the weight of a career’s worth of strategy pressing against something too big to plan for. “What about the enemy? Any intel on who they are? What they want?”

Gunny shook his head. “Nothing solid. Wallace says they’re working it, but everyone’s stretched thin.” He paused. “We’ve expanded local communications. Settlements checking in weekly. Sharing what they can.”

He looked down at the table.

“One didn’t check in this week.”

Jo waited.

“Could be nothing,” Gunny added. “Could be equipment. Could be weather.”

He didn’t sound convinced.

The children's voices rose again from the classroom, a chorus of arithmetic and spelling. Normal. Steady. A tiny thread of hope stitched into the ruin.

Jo straightened, her grip firm on her cane. "Then we keep doing what we're doing. We teach. We plant. We protect what's ours."

Gus nodded. "We live well."

Marcus's mouth twitched, almost a smile. "That simple?"

"That simple," Jo said.

Jo's arm rested light through Gunny's, her cane left behind at the Lodge steps. She pointed toward the half-dug greenhouse foundation, Owen and Hunter bent over measurements, then gestured to the new root cellar taking shape beyond the barn. Spring dirt still clung to the edges, fresh turned and waiting.

"That'll double our storage come fall," she said. "And the smokehouse the school crew finished last week is solid. We can cure twice what we managed last winter."

Gunny nodded, watching the steady rhythm of work. Normal. Purpose. The things that kept people from unraveling.

Then his gaze drifted to the barn, where Quinn stood near the open door, one-armed, fumbling with a rope halter. The stump of his left arm pressed close to his ribs as if he could hide it. Grace appeared beside him, said something quiet, and took the halter without fuss.

"How's Quinn doing?" Gunny asked, voice low.

Jo followed his line of sight and the warmth in her expression dimmed. She sighed, slow and weighted.

"He's making progress. The arm's healing well. Grace is an absolute blessing." She paused, choosing words carefully. "But emotionally, he's struggling. Feels useless. Like a burden."

Gunny had seen it before. Too many times. Young men who'd lost pieces of themselves and couldn't see past what was gone. The body healed faster than the mind. Always did.

"And Boone?" he asked, careful.

Jo's head turned sharp, surprise flickering across her face.

"He's doing better now. The fury and grief have dulled some." She looked back toward the barn, thoughtful. "It's hard. Those two did everything together. Always competing, especially when it came to harvesting timber. Now they're having trouble navigating the change. Quinn won't ask for help. Boone doesn't know how to offer it without making it worse."

They stopped at the edge of the greenhouse excavation. Marcus glanced up, nodded once, then returned to his work.

Jo studied Gunny's face, her hazel eyes sharp beneath the spray of freckles. "You're very observant, Nate."

He shrugged, tucked his hands into his pockets. "I've been taking care of young men for a long time. Building them up. Putting them back together when they break." His jaw tightened. "I've seen it all. Horrific injuries included. Helped families and soldiers adjust to a new reality more times than I care to count."

Jo patted his arm, warm and firm, then rose on her toes and pressed a quick kiss to his weathered cheek.

"That's one of many reasons you're a good man," she said quietly. "And a wonderful addition to our family."

Gunny felt the knot in his chest loosen, just a fraction. Family. Still a strange word after all these years alone.

"Appreciate that, Jo."

She smiled, tugged his arm gently, and they started walking again.

After a lively dinner the family scattered. Gunny crossed the great room and dropped onto the couch beside Quinn and Grace. He smiled at them both but turned his attention to Deb and Gin, who sat on the opposite couch wrestling with skeins of yarn.

"What on earth are you ladies doing there?" Gunny asked, smirk tugging at his mouth.

Both women glared at him. The look only made him laugh harder.

"We are learning to crochet," Gin said, frowning at the wad of knotted yarn in her lap like it had personally insulted her.

"Ohhhhhhhh, I see." He grinned, teeth showing.

"I don't see you crocheting," Deb grumbled, "so until you do, zip it."

Gunny turned to Quinn, elbowed his right arm gently, and laughed. "Touchy, huh?"

Quinn's mouth twitched. Not quite a smile, but close.

Grace leaned into Quinn's shoulder, her knitting needles clicking soft and steady. She kept her eyes on her work but her voice carried warm amusement. "They've been at it for two hours. I offered to help. They refused."

"I'm a Marine and she is a cop," Gin muttered, tugging at a loop that only tightened further. "We don't need help with yarn."

"Clearly," Grace said, needles never slowing.

Gunny shook his head, still grinning, then glanced sideways at Quinn. The kid sat quiet, shoulders angled inward, left arm tucked against his ribs. His gaze stayed on the fire, distant but listening.

"You ever crochet, Quinn?" Gunny asked, easy and light.

Quinn blinked, pulled back into the room. "No, sir. Gran taught all of us to sew, although my Dad said it isn't pretty.""

"Me neither. Looks like torture to me."

"It is," Deb said flatly, holding up a tangled mess of green yarn. "Absolute torture."

Gin snorted. "Speak for yourself. I'm getting it."

"You are not. You have made yarn vomit."

"I am getting it and this is just my method."

Grace's needles paused just long enough for her to glance up, eyes bright with laughter. She caught Quinn's gaze and something passed between them. Quiet. Steady.

Quinn's shoulders eased, just a fraction, and the ghost of a smile touched his face.

Gunny leaned back into the couch, arms folded, and watched the fire crackle. The room hummed with life. Laughter. Warmth. Small victories in a world gone cold.

He'd take it.

Gemma was up early. Only Jo stirred when she entered the Lodge. Her grandmother sat by the fireplace, a blanket across her lap and a mug cradled in both hands. book on her lap, and Odin sprawled at her feet, one ear twitching at the sound of the door.

"Good morning, Gran." Gemma crossed the room and kissed the top of Jo's head.

"My, you are up and around early." Jo gestured to the teapot on the side table. "Do you have plans or couldn't you sleep?"

Gemma nodded at the offer and reached for a clean mug from the shelf. She poured, the steam curling into the cool air. "Both, actually. I am headed out to do rounds and I could not sleep. I knew you would be awake, so I came over." She settled into the chair beside Jo, wrapping her hands around the warmth. "It is an adjustment with almost everyone back in their own homes instead of crammed in here."

Jo sighed, long and soft. "But the house feels so empty. I am glad for the frequent sleep -overs."

Gemma laughed, the sound low and easy. "It's not like we aren't in and out of here all day, for most meals, and we live across the yard."

Jo laughed too, shaking her head. "I know, I know. But mornings like this used to be chaos. Someone always needed something. A bandage, a biscuit, a hug." She sipped her tea, gaze drifting to the fire. "Now I sit here with my book and it's quiet."

"You love quiet."

"I do." Jo smiled, but it didn't quite reach her eyes. "Doesn't mean I don't miss the noise, the life."

Gemma studied her grandmother's face, the lines deeper in the firelight, the auburn braid streaked heavier with white than it had been a year ago. She reached over and squeezed Jo's hand. The swollen knuckles pressed warm against her palm.

"We're still here, Gran. Right across the yard."

"I know." Jo squeezed back. "Go on, then. Do your rounds. But take some of that bread and cheese from the counter. Oh, and maybe some jerky. You'll need it. Who is your escort?"

Gemma grinned, rose, and crossed to the kitchen. She wrapped two thick slices of bread in a cloth and tucked them and the jerky and hard cheese into her pack. Odin lifted his head, watching.

“That would be me, ma’am,” Hunter Hunter said, knocking as he opened the door.

“Haven’t I told you there’s no need to knock?” Jo said, laughing despite herself. “This place is grand central. Just come on in.”

Hunter flushed, earnest as ever.

"We'll be back before supper," Gemma said, slinging the pack over her shoulder.

Jo waved them off and turned back to her book. Odin resettled his chin on her foot as the door clicked shut, leaving the great room still.

Her smile faded.

She stared at the page without reading, thumb motionless where she'd been about to turn. Something sat wrong in her chest—not the familiar ache of her joints, but something deeper. The kind of feeling she'd learned not to ignore. The kind that had woken her at three in the morning before the fire that took their first home. The kind that had made her stock the root cellar a full month before The Day.

Dark clouds building.

Odin whined softly and pressed closer.

Jo looked toward the window. Morning light lay pale across the yard. Everything looked the same as yesterday.

That didn't comfort her at all.

Chapter Three

The Board

Nobody went anywhere alone anymore. Not after the Coalition.

When the kids played in the yard, someone stood watch. When Tobias or Gemma made house calls, someone rode along. The duty rotated and Hunter had drawn the assignment four times now. He wouldn't mind drawing it every time. Gemma was good company, sharp and steady, and she never treated him like the green boot he still felt like most days. It didn't hurt that she was beautiful either, though he kept that thought locked down tight. ,

She hefted her saddlebags and he stepped in to help, lifting the weight so she could buckle the straps. The worn leather heavy with supplies she'd packed the night before. He handed up her medical bag and she secured it behind the saddle, fingers quick and practiced.

"Thanks." She patted her horse, Cookie's neck and led him toward the door.

"Gran will tell Dad, you know he would panic because he didn't know we were leaving early." she said, swinging into the saddle. She pointed, "I also left a note on the board."

They walked the horses down the drive, hooves muffled on packed dirt. The watchtower loomed invisible in the dark pines to their left, yet Gemma lifted a hand as they passed. A low bird call answered. "Donovan," she thought and aloud she commented, "His Blue Jay is terrible." Hunter chuckled in agreement.

The mountain road opened before them, pale and winding. Gemma tilted her face toward the sky, and Hunter caught the edge of her smile.

"I think it's going to be a beautiful day," she said softly. "The sky is so clear."

He looked up. Stars still pricked the western dark, but the east glowed faint and clean, no clouds, no haze. Just the promise of light spilling over the ridges. He stole a quick glance at Gemma and said, "Yeah, it is."

Mr. Jenkins rounded the corner of the house, a pail of milk in one hand, his face creased from work but clean-shaven. He spotted them and lifted his free hand.

"Good morning, Gemma. Hunter." He smiled wide. "Come on in."

Inside, warmth hit them like a wall. The woodstove radiated heat, and the smell of cornmeal and butter filled the small room. Tommy Jenkins sat at the table, a bowl of mush in front of him, spoon halfway to his mouth. He was maybe six, gap-toothed and wiry, and he loved Gemma. But when Hunter stepped in behind her, Tommy's eyes went wide as saucers.

A grin split his face.

"Hunter!" He nearly knocked the bowl over scrambling to his feet.

Hunter grinned back. "Hey, bud."

Maddie Jenkins sat on a high stool at the counter, her casted leg propped on a foot stool.

"Just in time," she said. "Would you like some mush? Or tea?"

"Tea would be wonderful, thank you," Gemma said.

"Same here." Hunter nodded. "Appreciate it."

They never ate on rounds. Food was too scarce, too precious. People offered because hospitality still mattered, even now. Gemma and Hunter accepted tea because refusing everything felt wrong. Besides it was pine needle tea, and pine trees were one thing they had an abundance of.

Maddie set two mismatched cups on the table and poured. Steam rose slowly and fragrant. Gemma wrapped her hands around the warmth and glanced toward the back room.

"How is everyone today?" she asked. "How's Bobby?"

Maddie's smile dimmed just a fraction. She wiped her hands on her apron and sat across from them.

"Bobby's still feeling poorly," she said, "He's still asleep, up any minute now."

Gemma hid her smile behind the cup. "Mind if I take a look at him? And check on your leg, Mrs. Jenkins?"

"Please." Maddie stood. "I'd feel better if you did."

Gemma crossed to the small crib where two-year-old Bobby lay sleeping. Even in the dim candlelight, his color looked wrong. Too pale beneath the flush, his breathing rapid and shallow. She bent and pressed the back of her hand to his forehead.

Hot. Too hot. Five days.

She began her examination, careful to keep her movements slow, unhurried. Sick children sensed haste the way animals did. It only made them tighten, made everything worse.

"Hey, buddy," Gemma said softly, brushing her knuckle along his cheek. "I'm just going to listen, all right?"

He didn't answer. He barely lifted his head.

That alone tightened something in her chest.

She slipped the stethoscope beneath his thin shirt, warming the metal first against her own wrist. His breathing was fast. Too fast for sleep, too fast for rest. But not labored in the dramatic way you expected. No harsh wheeze. No barking cough. Just shallow pulls, one after another, like he was afraid to take a full breath. She closed her eyes and listened.

The sounds were wrong.

Not absent. Not crackling. Just uneven. Duller on the right.

Gemma shifted him gently, listening again. His ribs flared with each inhale, subtle but unmistakable.

"How long has he been breathing like this?" she asked quietly.

Maddie swallowed. "Since yesterday morning. Maybe the night before. I thought it was just the fever."

"Any coughing?"

Maddie said. "Mostly at night. It's dry."

Gemma straightened slowly, keeping her voice calm. "Has he been drinking?"

"Some. Not much today."

She glanced toward the doorway where Tommy hovered, eyes wide and scared. "Has Tommy been sick at all?"

Maddie shook her head quickly.

She met Maddie's eyes. "I don't think this is just a cold."

The woman stiffened. "Is it his lungs?"

"Yes," Gemma said honestly. "But not the kind you hear right away. It's the quiet kind."

She sat back on her heel, thinking. "I think it might be pneumonia. It doesn't always sound bad at first. It doesn't always look bad. But it doesn't get better on its own."

The word landed heavy in the small cabin.

"Is it catching?" Maddie asked, fear sharp now.

"It can be," Gemma said. "Not like the fast-spreading sicknesses. But enough that we need to be careful."

She reached for her bag. "I want to start treating him today. Keep him warm, not too warm, and keep him drinking. I'm going to check on him again tomorrow. If his breathing gets faster, if his lips look dusky, or if he stops wanting to wake up, you send someone for me, my Dad, or Doc immediately. Do you understand?"

Maddie nodded, tears slipping free now.

Gemma gave Bobby one of her remaining doses of Azithromycin. It was all she had and not enough. She handed Maddie a tiny vial of Tylenol, almost the last of her stash. If it was what she thought, she needed more.

"What do I do?" Maddie asked, voice choked with worry.

"Use that. Keep Tommy away for now. Wash your hands often. Push fluids, even a tablespoon at a time. Give him this every four hours until it is gone. Keep water boiling on the woodstove to get some moisture in the air." Gemma said as she repacked her bag.

Quiet illnesses were the most dangerous kind.

And this one had already stayed too long.

Gemma scrubbed her hands at the well pump outside the Jenkins cabin, the cold water biting into her skin. She worked her nails with a small brush under the stream, methodical, thorough. When she finally straightened, her face had gone tight.

Hunter watched her from where he stood with the horses. "Is it bad then?"

She looked at him, and whatever guard she kept up during calls had dropped. He saw it plain now.

"Yes." The word came out flat. "And it's contagious."

She dried her hands on a rag from her bag, fingers stiff with cold. "The community has so few antibiotics left. I hope I'm correct and didn't just waste a dose we can't afford to waste."

They rode in silence for a stretch, the trail narrow and hemmed in by birch and pine. The sun climbed higher, threading light through the canopy.

Finally, Gemma spoke again. "I'm trying to decide if we should detour to the school and ask Doc to take a look. We started early enough, I think we have time."

She turned toward him then, her eyes searching his. The worry sat plain in her expression, raw and unguarded in a way he didn't see often.

Hunter studied her for a moment, considering. She was young. Eighteen maybe and carrying the weight of calls like this, with no backup, no hospital, no Xrays or tests, no margin for error.

"You're very good at this, Gemma," he said quietly. "Like some kind of savant. I can't believe how much you know at your age."

Her mouth twitched, but she didn't look away.

"I think you're most likely correct," he continued. "But I also think you'd rest easier if you had Doc confirm it."

She exhaled slowly, her shoulders dropping just a fraction. "You're right. I also hope he has some antibiotics to share."

"Always am," he said lightly, earning the barest flicker of a smile.

"Don't push it, Boot."

He grinned. "Wouldn't dream of it... Ma'am."

Gemma laughed and nudged Cookie forward, adjusting her course. "School, then. We'll stop by and see if Doc can spare an hour."

Hunter followed, noting the worry hadn't left her face entirely

Chapter Four

In Good Order

Gemma chewed her bottom lip raw on the ride back. The trail wound through birch and hemlock, dappled light falling across her shoulders, but she didn't notice any of it. Bobby's breathing played on a loop in her head. The dull thud on the right side. The way his tiny ribs pulled in with each breath like something was squeezing him from the inside.

She opened her mouth. Closed it. Shifted in the saddle.

A mile later she drew a breath to speak, then let it out in a long, shapeless sigh.

She started to say something again. What came out was a low mumble, half-formed, swallowed by the breeze.

Hunter leaned across the gap between their horses and punched her arm. Not hard. Just enough. His grin was loose and easy, the kind that made his whole face open up.

"You having a heart attack over there? Aneurysm? Stroke?" He ticked them off on his fingers. "Because I gotta tell you, Gemma, we ain't got a hospital."

She blinked at him. A sound escaped her throat, somewhere between a laugh and a groan.

"Should we leave them saddled, Gemma?" George asked, already stroking Cookie's neck.

"Yes please, George. We won't be long." She swung down, steadying herself as her boots hit the dirt. "Maybe see if they want some water though, all right?"

"Sure thing." Aciden flashed a smile and led Storm toward the trough.

Gemma pulled her medical bag free and slung it over her shoulder. Hunter fell in beside her as they crossed the yard toward the school building. The morning air had warmed, but the chill hadn't left the ground yet. Their boots crunched over frost-brittle grass.

Inside, the hallway smelled of woodsmoke and old paper. Voices drifted from the classrooms, children reciting something in unison. Gemma led the way to the back stairwell, descending into the narrow passage that dropped below grade. The sub-basement.

After the Coalition attack, Doc had moved the clinic down here. Safer for the sick and injured, he'd said. Easier to protect if it came to that again.

The door at the bottom stood ajar. Gemma knocked twice and pushed through.

The room beyond was cool and dim, lit by two oil lamps mounted on the stone wall. Shelves lined one side, stocked with supplies that would've looked sparse a year ago but felt generous now. A few cots sat around the room, neatly made. In the center of the room, Doc Ramirez bent over a small table, stitching the hand of a teary boy while his mother rubbed his back in slow circles.

"Almost done, Jon." Doc's voice stayed calm, steady. "You're doing great."

Jon sniffled but didn't pull away. His mother murmured something soft, and the boy nodded.

Gemma and Hunter waited near the door, silent. Doc finished the final stitch, snipped the thread, and wrapped the boy's hand in clean gauze. He tied it off with practiced efficiency and patted Jon's shoulder.

"Keep it dry. Come back in three days so I can check it."

Jon nodded, wiping his nose with his good hand. His mother thanked Doc twice, voice thick with relief, and ushered the boy toward the stairs.

Once they'd gone, Doc straightened and turned. His gaze flicked between Gemma and Hunter, reading them the way he always did.

"Miss Callahan," he said, wiping his hands on a rag. "Boot."

"Doc." Gemma stepped forward, setting her bag on the table. "Sorry to drop in unannounced."

"You're never unannounced." He tossed the rag aside and leaned against the table, arms crossed. "What've you got?"

She hesitated, just for a breath. Then she told him.

Doc listened without interrupting, his expression unreadable. When she finished, he nodded once.

"It does sound like Atypical Pneumonia. But...you want a second opinion."

"I do. Otherwise I won't sleep."

He studied her for a moment, then glanced at Hunter. "You two got time to ride back out there now?"

Gemma sighed with relief.

"Horses or truck?" Hunter asked.

"I'll grab my kit." Doc was already moving, reaching for a worn leather satchel on the shelf. He slung it over his shoulder and gestured toward the door. "Let's go."

Outside, the air smelled clean, sharp with pine. George brought a roan gelding around while Aeiden held Cookie and Storm steady.

Doc mounted without a word, settling into the saddle like he'd done it a thousand times before. In the last six months he probably had.

Doc watched Gemma's posture, the way she sat straight but relaxed, her hand light on the reins. She was smart to come for confirmation.

That kind of caution kept people alive now.

Without bloodwork or imaging, pneumonia could slip sideways fast. Bacterial, viral, aspiration, it all sounded the same through a stethoscope. And if it turned septic or the boy's airway closed up, there'd be no vent, no ICU, no backup.

Just them.

The Jenkins place came into view through a break in the hemlocks, woodsmoke curling from the chimney in a thin gray ribbon against the pale sky.

"Two soldiers!"

Tommy launched himself off the porch like a bottle rocket, bare feet slapping the cool dirt as he tore across the yard straight at Hunter and Doc. His arms windmilled with the kind of reckless joy only a kid could muster at the sight of two men on horseback.

The cabin door swung open and Mr. Jenkins filled the frame. "Thomas Allen Jenkins, you hush that hollering. Your brother's sleeping."

Tommy's face scrunched into a knot of pure indignation. The pout lasted all of two seconds before his heels started bouncing and the grin crept back, impossible to contain.

Hunter swung down and ruffled the boy's hair. "Hey, bud. Brought reinforcements."

Doc dismounted and knelt to Tommy's level, extending a fist. Tommy bumped it with solemn precision, then grabbed Doc's hand and tried to drag him toward the porch. Doc let himself be led, satchel bouncing against his hip.

When the bedroom door opened, Doc emerged with Gemma close behind. They walked together toward the porch, heads bent toward one another, voices low and urgent.

“You agree?” she asked.

“I agree we shouldn’t wait,” he said. “But we’ll need to watch how he responds."

Hunter watched them through the window glass. The oddest pair of colleagues he had ever seen. An ex-military surgeon who looked more like someone who would have skipped the draft, with his long hair falling past his collar and a shaggy beard that hadn't seen a razor since before The Day. And beside him, a tough teenage girl in scuffed work boots and a flannel shirt two sizes too big, standing her ground like she'd earned every inch of it.

Doc came back inside and crossed the room to Hunter. He gripped Hunter's hand and shook it once, firm.

"Gotta get back. Visit more, Boot. I need someone to pick on."

Hunter snorted. "Yes, sir."

Doc ruffled Tommy's hair on the way out, mounted the roan and pointed it down the road toward the school without looking back.

Hunter found Gemma near the split-rail fence, arms folded tight across her chest, staring at nothing.

"You ready?" He walked up behind her, keeping his voice easy.

She turned. Her face was a storm cloud, jaw set hard, color high on her cheeks.

He took a step back. "Gemma?"

A curt nod. Nothing else. She stalked to Cookie, grabbed the pommel, and swung up in one sharp motion, then reined the horse in the opposite direction from Doc and kicked forward.

Hunter scrambled for Storm, got a boot in the stirrup, and hauled himself into the saddle. He urged the horse into a trot, closing the gap until he pulled alongside her.

"Gemma? What happened?"

She didn't look at him right away. Her fingers were white on the reins.

"Doc thinks I might be right about Bobby." Her voice came out flat, stripped of everything. "But he said it could also be a really severe virus. Or Bobby could be immunocompromised. And we won't ever know."

Hunter opened his mouth. Closed it.

Her eyes were glassing over, bright and furious, and she blinked hard against it, chin lifting the way it always did when she refused to let something win.

Then she clicked her tongue, gave Cookie a sharp kick, and the mare lunged into a fast trot down the trail toward the next visit.

Chapter Five

What Can be Made

Tobias returned from his rounds shortly before Gemma, and Hunter should have been back. Morales rode beside him, rifle slung across his back, scanning the tree line out of habit.

They pulled up to the barn. No sign of Cookie or Storm.

Tobias frowned, glanced toward the eastern trail. Late, but not worrying late. Not yet.

"I'll put the horses up," Morales said, reaching for the reins. "You go do your thing."

Tobias nodded, handed them over with a tired smile. "Thanks."

He headed toward the house, boots crunching on gravel. The sun hung low, painting the porch in amber. Somewhere near the woodshed, he heard the steady thunk of an axe. Quinn, probably. The boy had been driving himself hard the last few weeks, trying to figure out the best way to split wood with one hand.

Tobias understood. Grief didn't take a schedule. Neither did shame.

He rounded the corner and spotted Quinn at the splitting stump, a log braced upright, the axe lifted high in his right hand. The swing came down clean. The wood cracked apart.

Quinn bent, picked up the halves with his right hand, and stacked them. Reached for another log.

Tobias stopped a few paces back, waited until Quinn straightened.

"You've got a good rhythm going."

Quinn startled, turned. His left arm hung close to his side, the stump tucked against his ribs. His face was flushed, damp with sweat despite the cool air.

"Didn't hear you."

"Wasn't trying to sneak." Tobias stepped closer, nodded at the growing pile. "That's a solid stack."

Quinn shrugged, looked away. "Keeps me busy."

"It does." Tobias leaned against the stump, casual. "Gemma's running late. Thought I'd check in."

"She's fine."

"Probably. Still." He paused, let the silence settle. "You eaten yet?"

Quinn shook his head.

"Neither have I. Come on. I'll heat up something while we wait. Maybe I could take a quick look and see how the arm is doing since I haven't checked on it in a while."

Quinn hesitated, jaw tight. Then he set the axe down and wiped his hand on his jeans.

"Yeah. Alright."

They walked toward the Lodge together, the last light slipping behind the ridge.

Tobias breathed easier when Fergus's bark echoed from the drive, followed by the familiar clopping of hooves on hard ground.

Quinn glanced toward the window. A small smile tugged at the corner of his mouth. Relief, maybe. Or just the comfort of knowing Gemma had made it home safe. Those two had been inseparable since the day he was born, more siblings than cousins.

"This looks great, Quinn," Tobias said, setting the gauze aside. "I think we can do away with the bandages."

Quinn's head spun around. His eyes widened.

"No bandages?"

"It's been ten weeks. The wound is healed and it's not as sensitive." Tobias wiped his hands on a cloth, met Quinn's stare with calm certainty. "So yes. No bandages."

Quinn sat frozen, staring at the stump as though seeing it for the first time. Raw. Exposed.

The front door swung open before he could answer.

Gemma and Hunter came through, shoulders sagging, faces drawn. Hunter pulled off his cap and shoved it in his pocket. Gemma dragged a hand through her hair, streaks of dust clinging to the braid.

"Long day, huh?" Tobias stood, moved toward the hearth. "Everything okay?"

"Very long." Gemma dropped onto the couch, let her head fall back against the cushion. "We even went to the school for Doc. The Jenkins' littlest one has atypical pneumonia."

Clare appeared from the kitchen, tray balanced in both hands. Tea, biscuits, jam. She set it on the low table without a word.

Hunter's face lit up. "Oh, you are a lifesaver." He reached for a biscuit, slathered it with jam. "That jerky and bread was tasty, but it does not keep you full for twelve hours."

Gemma's gaze drifted across the room and landed on Quinn.

He sat rigid at the table, his right hand resting on the edge, his left arm cradled against his ribs. Something in his face had gone tight. She knew that look. Upset, but trying not to show it.

Tobias stepped between them, oblivious. "What did Doc say? Agreed with your diagnosis and treatment?"

"He did." Gemma's voice softened. "Started him on the azithromycin this morning. Doc gave his mom a few more doses and said to keep fluids going, watch for respiratory distress. We'll check back in two days."

"Good call." Tobias smiled, nodded. "Oh, and good news. Quinn is officially bandage free."

Quinn had wanted privacy for that moment. Not an announcement in a crowded room. Not something tossed out like weather talk while everyone munched biscuits and sipped tea.

She caught his eye across the space. Offered the smallest nod.

Quinn looked away, jaw working. His fingers curled against the table edge.

Gemma shifted forward, reached for the teapot. Poured two cups, handed one to Hunter without breaking the quiet.

Out in the shop, Boone, Beth, Owen, and Franklin huddled around the workbench. Each held pieces they had worked on for the last two weeks. Sawdust hung in the lamplight. The wood stove crackled low.

Franklin set the metal down first, laying it carefully on the scarred workbench like something that might bruise if handled wrong. A smooth, silvered sleeve of shaped steel, dulled and brushed rather than polished, wide at one end and narrowing slightly toward the other. The work was precise but not decorative. This part was meant to bear weight. You could tell just by looking at it.

At the wider end, a joint had been fitted. Simple. Solid. Different tools could lock into place. No gears. No springs. Just metal seated into metal with the confidence of something built to last.

Beth added the padded sleeve next. Canvas on the outside, soft, worn cotton on the inside, layered with wool batting between. It was made to last through whatever came its way.

Owen placed the wooden pieces beside the metal. A short-handled mallet head. A flat, squared tool meant to brace boards. A smooth, worn wooden grip shaped to sit snugly into the metal coupling. The wood wasn't new. Edges rounded so nothing would catch or splinter. It looked like it belonged in a hand, even without fingers.

Then Boone brought the leather.

The harness was thick and well oiled, the color of old honey and smoke. Wide straps crossed in an X, reinforced where strain would pull hardest. Buckles were heavy but familiar. The kind used on tack and packs. Easy to adjust. Easy to trust. The leather cuff that would cradle Quinn's arm was lined and shaped, curved to hold without biting, with room for swelling and movement.

Beth ran her fingers along the canvas sleeve. "Think it'll chafe?"

"Not with the wool," Franklin said. "And we can add more if it does."

Owen tested the connection between the wooden grip and the metal joint. A quiet click. A firm tug. It held.

Boone lifted the harness, inspected each buckle, each seam. He pulled the straps taut, checked the stitching where weight would press hardest. Nothing gave.

"It's not pretty," he murmured.

"It's not supposed to be." Franklin touched the edge of the metal sleeve. "It just needs to work."

When assembled, it wasn't elegant.

It was *honest*.

The metal sleeve would fit over what remained of Quinn's forearm, secured by the leather brace and straps that anchored the weight back across his shoulder and chest. When a tool was locked into the end—a hook, a hammer head, a flat brace—it would extend just far enough to be useful without pretending to be a hand.

No attempt had been made to replace what was gone.

Instead, they had built something new.

Something that said: *You can still work. You can still help. You are not finished.*

Beth stepped back, crossed her arms. Her jaw tightened. "He's gonna hate it at first."

"Probably." Boone set the harness down with care. "But he'll use it."

Owen nodded once. "When do we show him?"

Franklin glanced toward the door. Voices drifted from the Lodge. Laughter. The clatter of dishes being cleared.

"Tomorrow," Boone said. "After breakfast. Before he has time to think himself into a corner."

Gemma stepped in then, and the four adults startled. She looked past them and saw what lay on the work table. She smiled broadly. "So that is where you guys have been sneaking off."

"We don't sneak." Franklin grinned. "We perform covert ops."

Gemma shook her head, laughing, and walked closer. The pieces lay arranged on the scarred bench. The metal, the leather, the wooden grips. She touched the canvas sleeve, traced the small, tight stitches Beth had sewn. It was wonderful. Clever, with the attachments that locked and shifted.

"Can I make a suggestion?" Her voice turned serious.

"Of course." Boone straightened.

"Uncle Boone, you should show this to him alone. In private." She met his eyes. "Please don't make a huge production out of it. I think he will be open to it and see the potential more easily if he is away from our huge family."

Boone exhaled slowly. Nodded once.

"Tomorrow," he said. "Just him and me."

The others nodded in agreement.

The workshop smelled like oil and sawdust and cold iron, the way it always did. Quinn stood just inside the door, not sure why Boone had called him out here, his shoulders tight the way they'd been for weeks now. He'd learned to keep them that way—braced, ready—for what? He didn't know.

Boone wiped his hands on a rag and nodded toward the bench.

"Come here, son."

No ceremony. No crowd. Just the two of them, the way hard things were always handled.

Quinn stepped closer and saw it laid out in pieces: metal, wood, leather. He recognized the shapes before he understood them. His breath caught anyway.

Boone didn't rush him.

"We've been watching you," Boone said finally, voice low, careful.

Quinn's jaw tightened. "I'm fine."

"I know." Boone meant it. "But I also know what it looks like when a man's angry at his own hands."

That landed harder than anything else had.

Boone picked up the metal sleeve first. "Franklin helped shape this. Owen too. Built it strong enough to take weight. Strong enough for farm work." He turned it slightly so Quinn could see the joint at the end. "Interchangeable. Hook. Hammer. Brace. Whatever you need."

Then he reached for the leather cuff.

"This part..." His voice shifted, just enough. "Your mother did."

Quinn leaned in without realizing it.

The inside of the sleeve was padded, thick but soft, the fabric stitched clean and even. Beth's work was unmistakable: impossibly small, careful stitches, reinforced where skin would rub, shaped to cradle instead of bind. She'd chosen cloth worn smooth with washing, something that wouldn't bite or chafe.

"She measured you while you slept," Boone said quietly. "Didn't want to make a show of it. Said you'd had enough of people looking."

Quinn swallowed.

Boone lifted the finished prosthetic and held it out. Not pushing it into Quinn's space, just offering it.

"We could see how frustrated you were," Boone said. "How you kept trying to do things one-handed that were never meant to be done that way. You weren't lazy. You weren't giving up."

His eyes met Quinn's. Steady. Certain.

"You were fighting your own body."

For a long moment, Quinn didn't move.

Then he reached out with his remaining hand and took it.

The weight surprised him. Not heavy, exactly, but real. Useful. Boone helped him slide the sleeve on and adjust the leather straps, snug but not tight. The padding settled against his skin, warm already, as it belonged there.

When Boone stepped back, Quinn flexed instinctively and stopped.

It wasn't a hand.

But when he lifted his arm, the tool moved with him. When he banged it against the bench, it held.

Boone watched his son take it in, every line of his posture shifting just a little.

"You don't owe anyone anything," Boone said. "Not work. Not strength. Not proof."

Then, softer: "But if you want to help again, we figured you should have the means."

Quinn nodded once. He couldn't speak yet.

Boone clapped a hand on his shoulder, firm, grounding. "Your mother wants you to eat. Says you can test it out later."

He paused at the door, then added, "She also said if it rubs or pinches anywhere, you come straight to her. And...no being stubborn about it."

A corner of Quinn's mouth twitched.

When the door shut behind Boone, Quinn stood alone, staring at the possibilities he now had strapped to his arm.

Quinn pushed through the back door of the Lodge and stepped into noise.

Voices layered over each other—Max arguing with Edwin about something that didn't matter, Rosa singing under her breath while she carried forks to the table, Jake's laugh punching through it all like a bell. The smell hit him next: eggs fried in bacon fat, sausage crackling on the griddle, coffee sharp enough to wake the dead.

Grace and Gemma stood at the long table, serving the little ones. Marisol reached for toast; Lucy spilled milk and didn't notice.

Gemma glanced up first.

She paused mid-scoop, spatula still over the skillet, and her whole face softened. Not pity. Not relief. Just recognition.

She nudged Grace with her elbow and tipped her chin toward the door.

Grace turned, dish towel slung over one shoulder, and her eyes went straight to Quinn's arm.

The prosthetic sat solid against him, leather dark where it crossed his shoulder, metal dull in the morning light filtering through the windows. The straps followed the line of his back like harness gear, something built for work

He looked as though something had been given back, even if it wasn't the same thing that was taken.

Grace's smile started slow, then broke wide across her face—genuine, bright, the kind that made her eyes crinkle at the edges.

Quinn saw it and smiled back.

A real one. The kind that reached his eyes and made his shoulders drop just a fraction.

Quinn crossed to the table, snagged a plate with his good hand, and nodded at Gemma when she passed him the skillet.

"Hungry?" she asked.

"Starving."

Gemma handed him a fork without fanfare and turned back to the stove.

Grace poured him coffee, set the mug down where he could reach it easily, then went back to wiping Lucy's milk off the bench.

Just breakfast, the way it was supposed to be.

And for the first time in ten weeks, Quinn ate like he meant it.

Chapter Six

In Inches, Not Miles

Mr. Jenkins didn't knock.

He pounded on the Lodge door hard enough to rattle the hinges, breath tearing out of him in ragged pulls. Boone was already moving by the time the second blow landed, pulling the door open to cold night air and a man pale with fear.

"It's Bobby," Jenkins gasped. "He won't wake right. His lips...they're blue."

That was all it took.

Gemma was down the porch stairs with her bag before Boone could even ask another question. Tobias was right behind her, pulling his coat on one-handed, and Jo appeared from the kitchen, hair braided back, her own bag in hand, eyes sharp and awake in the way only mothers and medics ever were.

"Gunny's truck," Jo said. "Now."

The engine roared to life in the darkness. Boone leaped into the bed with a rifle across his knees. Gunny running from the barn to see who was stealing his truck. Boone waved and they sped down the road. The headlights carved a narrow tunnel through the trees as they tore down the dirt road, gravel spitting beneath the tires. Gemma sat in the back seat, already laying out supplies on her lap by feel: antibiotics, fever reducer, a small vial of honey, dried mullein leaf wrapped in cloth, a bundle of thyme and yarrow she'd grabbed from the hook by the door.

"He was drinking earlier," Jenkins said over his shoulder, voice breaking. "Then he started breathing fast. Then slow. His lips—"

"I know," Gemma said gently. "You did the right thing."

The cabin came into view like a crouched animal at the edge of the woods, one dim lantern burning inside. Maddie met them at the door, wild-eyed and shaking.

"He's cold," she said. "But burning. I don't understand."

Gemma didn't answer. She dropped to her knees beside the pallet and touched Bobby's cheek.

His skin was hot, but his hands were cool. His lips had a dusky, unmistakable blue tinge, and when his chest rose it did so shallowly, too fast, ribs pulling in with every breath.

"Okay," Gemma said, steady but loud enough for the room to hear. "Maddie, we need water. Gran, I need blankets and heat. Now."

She pressed her fingers to Bobby's wrist. His pulse fluttered under her touch, rapid and thready.

Dehydrated. Hypoxic. Running out of reserves.

Gemma lifted his chin slightly, opening his airway, listening again to his chest. The sounds were worse now—still quiet, but uneven, strained. The kind of breathing that meant his body was burning fuel faster than he could replace it.

"We're behind," she said, not accusing, just stating fact. "But not too far."

Tobias knelt beside her, already prepping an IV kit. "I'm going to run this wide open for a bit," he said quietly, finding the vein in Bobby's small arm with practiced efficiency.

Jo slid in beside Gemma, already wrapping Bobby in warmed blankets, rubbing his feet briskly to coax circulation back. Maddie returned with water and a spoon, and Gemma mixed honey and a pinch of salt into it, tipping it carefully to Bobby's lips.

"Come on, sweetheart," she murmured. "Just a little."

He swallowed once. Then again.

Color didn't return immediately, but his breathing eased a fraction.

Gemma crushed the azithromycin tablet and dissolved it, coaxing it down in tiny amounts. She followed it with acetaminophen, measured by instinct and experience rather than numbers.

Then she reached for the herbs.

She poured hot water over mullein and thyme, the steam rising sharp and green. "This won't fix the infection," she told the parents quietly. "But it can help his lungs open, help him cough without exhausting himself."

She held the warm cup near Bobby's face, letting him breathe in the vapor, watching carefully for any sign of distress. Jo twisted mullein into a tight bundle.

"Once we get his breathing to slow a little, we can burn this and let him breathe the smoke," Jo explained. "It'll help keep his lungs open."

Minutes passed. Then more.

Slowly—agonizingly slowly—the blue at his lips softened. Not pink. Not yet. But less frightening.

His breathing dropped from frantic to merely fast.

Gemma sat back on her heels, finally letting herself exhale.

"He's still very sick," she said. "This isn't over. But he's responding."

Maddie collapsed against Jo, sobbing quietly into her shoulder.

Gemma wiped her hands on a cloth, heart still hammering. "We'll stay. All night if we have to. He doesn't fight this alone."

Outside, the forest held its breath.

Inside the small cabin, surrounded by lamplight, blankets, and the combined knowledge of old remedies and hard-earned medicine, a two-year-old clung—barely, stubbornly—to life.

Morning came in thin and gray, seeping through the cabin windows instead of announcing itself. The worst of the night had passed in inches, not miles, but it had passed.

Bobby slept now. Not the fitful, fevered drifting from before, but a deeper, heavier rest that tugged at his small chest with each breath. His color was better—not right, not yet—but no longer frightening. When Gemma pressed her fingers to his wrist, the pulse was still fast, but much stronger. There was moisture in his mouth. He stirred when she touched him.

Headed in the right direction.

She let herself sit back, spine against the wall, exhaustion and the inevitable adrenaline dump finally crashing over her like a wave.

"He's going to be alright."

No one spoke for a moment. Maddie just covered her mouth with both hands and nodded, tears sliding silently down her face.

Jo brewed more tea and coaxed fluids. Tobias dozed in a chair, waking every time Bobby shifted. Gemma checked him again at first light; lungs still tight, fever still there, but easing. Enough to let them leave instructions instead of fear behind.

By the time they stepped back outside, the forest smelled like damp earth and pine needles warming in the sun.

The ride back to the Lodge was quiet. Not tense anymore—just bone-deep tired. Jo leaned her head against the window. Tobias stared out at the road like he was counting trees. Gemma cradled her bag in her lap, fingers still stained faintly green from herbs.

Gunny was waiting on the porch when they pulled in, mug in hand, wrapped in a coat that looked older than most of the trucks that could still run.

"Well." He took a slow sip. "You three gonna tell me where you took my truck all night, or do I have to assume you finally decided to run off and join the circus?"

Jo laughed; an exhausted, startled sound that turned into a yawn halfway through.

"Borrowed," Gemma corrected. "With intent to return."

Gunny raised a brow. "Uh-huh. Looked an awful lot like joyriding to me."

Tobias climbed out and stretched carefully. "Kid's gonna make it."

Gunny's expression softened immediately, the teasing draining out of it like water through sand. "Good. That is very good to hear." Then, after a beat he mumbled, "Still stole my truck."

They shuffled inside, boots abandoned by the door, the smell of coffee and frying bacon wrapping around them like a blessing. Someone had left breakfast warming on the stove—eggs, bread, something sweet baking low and slow.

Gemma barely made it to the table before her legs gave out and she sat, forehead dropping to her folded arms.

"Eat," Jo said gently, sliding a plate in front of her. "Then sleep."

Gemma picked up a fork. Chewed without tasting. Swallowed because her body demanded it.

Across the table, Tobias did the same, methodical and silent.

The Lodge settled around them, holding them the way it always did—through the long nights, the small victories, and the quiet, hard-earned mornings that followed.

Gus stood near the kitchen door looking at his grandchildren and feeling an overwhelming sense of peace. He bent and lifted little Luke up, which made the one-year-old giggle. Luke loved to tug at Gus's beard; it was his favorite activity. Clare, Mary, and Ellie walked by with huge baskets of wet laundry.

"Headed out to hang laundry. Judith is in the kitchen, will you be around for a bit to help keep an eye on the kids while she makes lunch?" Clare asked as she went by.

Gus smiled, "Of course! Is your mother around?"

"She was in the clinic earlier, and then she said she was going up to the greenhouse. She is babying those new seedlings." Mary said with a chuckle.

Jo had almost made it to the greenhouse before the world tilted.

It wasn't sudden—not at first. It began the way it always did, a faint narrowing at the edges of her vision, like someone slowly drawing a curtain. Her heart kicked hard once, then again, too fast for the easy morning pace she'd been keeping.

Odin stopped.

Not hesitated. Stopped dead, paws planted, body rigid at her side. His head lifted, ears forward, then he leaned into her leg with a soft, insistent press.

"I'm fine," Jo murmured automatically, reaching down to brush his head.

Odin huffed, sharp and displeased, then moved in front of her, blocking her path. He looked back at her, amber eyes locked on her face, tail low and stiff.

That was when the dizziness surged.

Jo's breath hitched. The greenhouse glass flared white in the sunlight, painfully bright, and her knees went weak beneath her before she could brace.

"Odin," she started.

He barked. Once. Loud. Commanding.

The ground rushed up to meet her.

She didn't hit hard. Odin stayed pressed against her, steady and solid, her shoulder sliding down his flank as she folded to her knees and then to her side, breath coming too fast, heart hammering like it was trying to outrun her body.

"Mom!" Clare's voice cut across the yard.

Mary dropped the sheet she'd been folding, fabric billowing into the grass as she broke into a run. Ellie was right behind her, already shouting for help.

Jo lay still, one hand curled in Odin's thick fur, using him as an anchor while the world spun and narrowed. Her ears rang. Her vision tunneled.

"I'm okay," she tried to say, but it came out thin, barely a whisper.

Clare was at her side in seconds, dropping to her knees. "Don't move." Already assessing: skin color, breathing, the telltale way Jo's pulse fluttered too fast beneath her fingers.

Mary slid her jacket under Jo's head. "POTS?"

Jo nodded once or at least she thought she did.

Ellie crouched near her legs. "I'll get water. Salt?"

"Yes," Clare said. "And Dad."

Odin didn't move. He stood braced over Jo's torso, a living wall, growling softly when Mary shifted too close, then settling when Jo's hand tightened in his fur.

"That's it," Clare murmured. "You're all right. He caught it early."

The dizziness eased in slow waves. Jo focused on her breathing, on the feel of the ground beneath her, on Odin's steady warmth and weight pressed against her side. Her heart rate began to settle, grudgingly, like a child refusing to behave.

Ellie returned with a mug and a small pouch. Clare mixed salt into the water and lifted Jo carefully.

"Small sips."

Jo obeyed, grimacing slightly, but grateful. Color crept back into the world. The greenhouse came back into focus. The laundry line. Familiar faces etched with concern.

"Sorry," Jo said hoarsely.

Mary snorted softly. "Don't you dare apologise."

Odin finally relaxed, sitting beside her with a heavy sigh, his shoulder still pressed against her like a reminder.

Clare glanced at him and shook her head in quiet awe. "He knew before any of us did."

Jo leaned her head back against the grass, closing her eyes once more—not from dizziness this time, but relief.

"I know." Her fingers threaded through Odin's fur. "That's why I try to listen when he tells me to stop."

The back door banged open, spilling laughter and boots and voices into the quiet kitchen. Donovan shouldered through first, rifle slung easily over his back, face flushed beneath his cap. Declan came next, grinning wide, both hands gripping a canvas game bag that sagged with weight.

Edwin and Jake followed, breathless and triumphant, slingshots still tucked in their belts.

Gin brought up the rear, shaking her head but smiling despite herself.

"Look what we got, Gran!" Jake crowed, practically vibrating.

Jo turned from the stove, one hand still braced against the counter. Odin lifted his head from where he'd settled beside her chair.

Declan hoisted the bag onto the worktable with a satisfying thump. "Seven squirrels, two grouse, and Donovan nailed a woodchuck."

"Clean shots, too," Gin added, leaning against the doorframe.

The twins exchanged a look, pride flashing quick and bright between them.

"We learned from the best," Donovan said, glancing toward Gin with a crooked grin.

Gin crossed her arms, impressed despite herself. "You keep shooting like that, you'll outpace half the recruits I trained."

Donovan's grin widened, and words tumbled over themselves, "Remember when that moose chased us and tried to stomp us, and Dad and the Uncles saved us, and we had to butcher that huge thing?"

He was laughing now, eyes bright with the memory.

Declan snorted. "Tried to stomp you. I ran faster."

"A moose?" Gin straightened, eyebrows climbing. "You're joking."

The boys shook their heads in unison, grins splitting their faces.

"Big bull," Edwin said solemnly. "Huge rack. It was right here in the yard."

"And then we spent two days cutting it up," Jake added. "There was so much meat we ran out of bags. Until the meat all burned up in the fire."

Sadie walked in and added, "and we had to use the brains to tan the hide. We made gloves, jackets, and moccasins."

Gin stared at them, then at Jo, who nodded calmly.

"Welcome to the mountains," Jo said, voice dry. "Where the wildlife fights back and nature has an attitude."

Gin laughed, short and sharp, shaking her head again. "You people are unreal."

The woodshed smelled of fresh-cut pine and cold earth. Three men sat on overturned crates near the open wall, watching the operation unfold with the studious attention of generals reviewing troops.

Gus stretched his legs. Zeke whittled a stick into nothing. Buck leaned back against a post, arms crossed, chewing a toothpick.

Max and Jake worked together, grunting as they rolled a thick log toward the splitting stump. Hunter caught it with his boot and steadied it upright. Quinn swung the axe, the modified bracket locked tight against the prosthetic sleeve. The blade bit clean through. Two halves toppled.

The younger kids darted in like sparrows, snatching pieces and racing toward the growing stack along the shed wall.

Rosa crouched beside a chunk too big for her arms. She wrapped both hands around it and pulled. It didn't budge.

"Help me, Marisol."

Marisol and Sadie jogged over. Each grabbed a side. Together they hauled it toward the pile.

Edwin shook his head. "Rosa, pick smaller pieces."

She stuck her tongue out at him.

Lucy stumbled past with an armload of twigs that obscured her face. Jake laughed and guided her by the shoulder before she walked into the wall.

Gus leaned over and scratched Fergus behind the ears. The old hound's tail thumped twice, lazy and content.

"Zeke built it."

Zeke looked over at his friend and grinned, gap-toothed and wicked.

"You steered it."

Buck perked up. He'd learned over the months that when these two got going, a story worth hearing wasn't far behind.

"We found some scrap wood." Gus settled into the telling like easing into a warm coat. "Second winter we spent here at the Lodge. We were still living in one of the cabins."

"Made a sled," Zeke said, warming to it.

The kids slowed. Max paused mid-roll. Hunter lowered the axe. Even Rosa stopped whining.

"It went fast," Gus said.

"Too fast." Zeke nodded, solemn as a preacher.

"Hill was steeper than we thought."

Zeke leaned forward. "Tree came outta nowhere."

Buck's eyes went wide. "Did you crash?"

Gus smiled. "Missed it."

Zeke nodded. "Barely."

Hunter set the axe against the stump. Quinn wiped a sleeve across his forehead. The kids drifted closer, drawn like moths.

Buck frowned. "What happened to the sled?"

Both men answered at once.

"Still goin'."

Silence.

Buck blinked. "What do you mean, still going?"

Gus pointed past the shed, through the trees, toward the far ridge where the land dropped away into shadow.

"That way."

The kids erupted.

"No way!"

"You're lying!"

"Is it really?"

Zeke shrugged. "Ain't seen it since."

"Might be in Mexico by now," Gus mused.

Jake's mouth hung open. Max crossed his arms, skeptical but intrigued. Rosa giggled. Edwin looked like he was doing math in his head.

Hunter grinned and picked up the axe again. "Y'all are full of it."

Zeke winked. "Prove it."

Fergus yawned and lay his head back down.

Quinn shook his head and lifted another log onto the stump. Grace appeared in the doorway with a water jug, took one look at the scene, and rolled her eyes.

"Back to work," she said.

The kids scattered, laughing now, energy renewed.

Gus and Zeke exchanged a look.

Mission accomplished.

Chapter Seven

The Ones Who Wait

The library hummed with high voices and stomping feet. Someone shrieked, someone else giggled, and something wooden clattered across the floor.

In the great room, the older teens claimed the space around the hearth. Firelight painted shadows across worn furniture and patched quilts draped over chair backs. Grace sat on the couch beside Quinn, needle moving steadily through a wool sock stretched over her fist. Rowan perched on Quinn's other side, leaning forward with elbows on her knees.

Across the coffee table, Declan and Donovan sprawled in mismatched chairs, voices low and conspiratorial.

"We could check the old oak near the ridgeline," Declan said. "Dad saw a comb there two summers back."

Donovan countered. "We need somewhere with good cover. Maybe the hollow by the creek?"

Rowan tapped her chin. "What about the pine grove past the barn? Plenty of deadfall for hives."

The twins exchanged a glance, weighing it.

Hunter lay on the floor near the fire, long legs crossed at the ankle, a battered copy of *The Art of War* propped on his chest. He turned a page without looking up.

"How is Gran feeling now?" Grace asked, to nobody in particular.

"Annoyed people want to know how she is." Rowan laughed.

Out on the porch, the Middles gathered in a tight circle, dice clattering across the planks. Lily's voice carried through the open door, dramatic and commanding.

"The dragon exhales, and fire engulfs the bridge. Roll for damage."

Groans erupted. Someone protested. Lily's grin was audible.

At the table, mugs steamed with chicory and dandelion root. Voices murmured, soft and unhurried. On the rockers outside, Gus and Marcus watched the game unfold, occasionally trading low commentary.

Gemma pounded down the stairs. She hit the landing hard, slid on wool socks, and skidded to a stop in front of the couch. Papers fluttered in her raised hand.

"Who wants to help me study?"

Grace's needle paused. Rowan glanced up. The twins twisted in their chairs.

Quinn leaned forward, mouth opening.

Grace's hand clamped onto his thigh. She shook her head, small and sharp.

Quinn's jaw snapped shut. He looked at Rowan, brow furrowed.

Rowan's glare could have stripped bark.

Gemma's smile faltered. "Anyone?"

Hunter closed his book and set it on the end table. He rose in one smooth motion and reached for the papers.

"I could help." His drawl softened the offer. "What are we studying today?"

Gemma's face brightened. She looped her arm through his and steered him toward the study tucked beneath the stairs.

"Doc will quiz me on last week's material. I want to blow his socks off with my brilliance."

Their voices faded behind the closing door.

Grace drove her elbow into Quinn's ribs.

"Whoa." Quinn rubbed his side, bewildered. "What was that for?"

"How are you this dumb?" Rowan asked, voice flat.

Lily passed through, Marisol on her heels, both carrying bowls of popcorn toward the porch. Lily snorted.

"Even I understand what's up, and I'm just walking through."

Marisol giggled.

Quinn looked between Grace and Rowan, utterly lost.

He looked at the twins, but they looked equally lost.

Grace sighed and returned to her darning. Rowan slapped the back of his head like only a sister could, before heading for the kitchen.

The wagon creaked into view, groaning under the weight of bodies and laughter. Gunny sat up front beside Zara, reins loose in his weathered hands. Father Tom perched on the bench behind them, his collar bright against the faded black shirt. Rita and Margaret braced themselves in the bed, children wedged between supply crates and rolled blankets.

The last half mile always felt longer than it was.

Before the wheels stopped turning, Ty vaulted over the side, dirt spraying beneath his boots. Ming and Jenny followed, more graceful but no less eager. George hit the ground running.

From the barn, Max caught sight of the wagon and hollered. Jake, Edwin, and Marisol dropped whatever they'd been doing and raced up the slope, voices carrying ahead of them.

The jumble of children met in the yard and scattered like buckshot. Someone produced a leather ball. Teams formed without discussion. Shouts rose into the cold air.

The older girls peeled away from the chaos and drifted toward the picnic table where Rowan, Fiona, and Lily already sat. Mia plopped down beside them, grinning.

Gus and Jo waited on the porch, side by side. Odin sat at Jo's knee, ears pricked forward. Gus had his thumbs hooked in his belt, face open and easy.

Until he saw Gunny's expression.

Hunter appeared from the direction of the toolshed, wiping grease from his hands. He straightened when he spotted the Gunnery Sergeant and snapped a quick salute.

"Sir."

Gunny waved him off, irritation and affection mixed in equal measure.

"Come on, Boot. Relax." He jerked his chin toward the Lodge. "Let's get a beverage, son. We all need to chat."

Father Tom climbed down from the wagon, brushing dust from his sleeves.

"Yes," he said quietly. "We need to chat."

Gus and Jo looked at each other. The ease slid off Gus's face. Jo's mouth pressed into a thin line.

"Do we need everyone?" Jo asked, already turning toward the door.

"Grab Marcus." Gunny's tone left no room for argument. "You can all fill everyone else in later."

Gin rounded the corner of the porch, rifle slung over one shoulder. She grinned when she saw Gunny and clapped him hard on the shoulder.

"Hey there, Salty."

Gunny's scowl deepened, but the corner of his mouth twitched.

"Watch it, Ginger." He tried to sound menacing. "You are not too old to spank, young lady."

Gin's fist came in fast. Gunny sidestepped, and she missed by an inch.

"Still quick," she admitted.

"Still ornery," he shot back.

A cabin door slammed across the clearing. Marcus and Deb emerged, walking shoulder to shoulder up the worn path. Marcus read the porch in three seconds flat. His stride didn't change, but his jaw tightened.

Deb touched his arm. He nodded once.

They climbed the steps together.

Gunny looked at the assembled group and blew out a long breath.

"Inside," he said.

Jo opened the door.

Jo and Gin carried a pot of tea and a plate heaped with thick slices of oatmeal bread with butter to the table. The steam rose between them, cutting through the chill that had followed everyone inside. Jo set the pot down with care, filled cups without asking, then settled into the chair beside Gus. She looked up, met Gunny's eyes.

"Spill it."

Gunny looked at Father Tom and said simply, "Father, if you will."

Jo blinked. Her gaze swung to the young priest.

"Father?"

Father Tom cleared his throat. His hands rested flat on the table, fingers spread wide like he needed the solid wood beneath them.

"I am not sure that I am not insane, to be honest." He paused, swallowed. "You see, as usual, I heard confessions and had Sunday school before Mass. The children love it so much." His voice softened there, just for a breath. "This week, however, several children did not attend. I was concerned that they might be ill, so I sought them out afterwards. When I could not find them or their mothers, I went to find Zara."

Zara sat forward, elbows braced on the worn wood.

"Less than a week ago, a group moved into the campgrounds down by Little Bear Lake. We have been watching them carefully, and they are quiet. There are maybe thirty adults all told. Quite a few children, too." She exhaled through her nose. "They did not seem dangerous, just a little odd. They all wear these rough linen tunics and robe belts of different colors."

Gunny stood. He paced to the window, back again, restless energy rolling off him like heat from a stove.

"They call themselves the 'Harbingers.'" He bit the word off like it tasted foul. "The leader is this greasy, smooth-talking fellow they call Oracle. Yeah, Oracle." His lip curled. "He is slicker than goose-shit, I bet anything that he is some kind of zealot."

Marcus leaned back in his chair, arms crossed. Deb's hand found his forearm.

Gunny scrubbed a palm over his face.

"Still, as Zara said, we kept a really close eye on them. The only weird thing is that we now have four women who have taken their children and joined them. Tunics and all." He shook his head, jaw tight. "How could anyone who has gone through what those women have, willingly join a group that is not well armed and is basically a dictatorship. I don't get it."

Silence dropped like a stone.

Gus shifted in his seat. Jo's knuckles stood out pale where she gripped her mug.

Father Tom's voice came quiet, careful.

"People seek meaning when everything else is stripped away. They seek peace and stability. Comfort and peace are severely lacking in the world right now."

"Meaning." Gunny spat the word. "They are seeking control of their world. That charlatan is offering them certainty in a world that has none left. But why? What is he getting out of it? There has to be something."

Gin stared at the table, her usual smirk gone.

Marcus spoke for the first time, voice low and steady.

"Four families."

"Four," Zara confirmed.

"And you think more will follow."

It was not a question.

"Yeah. I do." Gunny said as he turned from the window and frowned.

Father Tom's fingers curled against the table edge.

"I tried speaking with two of the mothers yesterday. They would not even look at me. Just kept their eyes down and said they had found purpose. That Oracle had shown them the way forward." His voice cracked, just a fraction. "These were women who came to Mass every Sunday. Who laughed with their children. Now they speak like they have been hollowed out and filled with someone else's words."

Deb's hand tightened on Marcus's arm.

"What kind of purpose?"

"Service, I bet." Zara's tone was flat. "Devotion. Purity through obedience? I did notice I did not see anyone old. Not even late middle-aged. They were all younger than... thirty max." She reached for her tea, took a long swallow. "The belt colors must mean something. The Oracle wears purple."

"Purple," Jo repeated. Her gaze shifted to Gus. "Like royalty."

"Like a king," Marcus said quietly.

"Or a God," Father Tom sighed sadly.

Gunny dropped back into his chair, the wood groaning under his weight.

"That is what worries me. Structure. They work in shifts, tend fires, gather wood, and cook meals. Everything runs too smoothly. And the way they look at him when he speaks." He shook his head. "Like he hung the damn moon."

Gin's voice cut through, sharp.

"What about the men?"

"Far fewer than the women," Zara said. "Maybe a dozen. Young too, mostly. Strong backs. Oracle keeps them close, has them patrol the camp perimeter like guards."

"Guards," Gus echoed. His fingers drummed once against the table. "For what? Protection or control?"

"Both, probably." Gunny exhaled hard. "And people are lining up to be part of it."

Father Tom leaned forward, shoulders hunched.

"I failed them. I should have seen this coming. Should have done more to reach them before he did. This world is ripe for this type of manipulation."

Jo's voice came firm.

"You did not fail anyone, Father. People make their own choices, even bad ones."

"Especially bad ones," Marcus added.

Silence settled again, heavier this time. Outside, children's laughter drifted through the walls, bright and oblivious. The contrast twisted something in the room.

Deb spoke, her voice careful.

"Do we know if anyone has been hurt? If he is forcing them to stay?"

"Not that we have seen," Zara said. "But we have not been inside the camp.

Gunny planted both palms on the table.

"Look, I do not like this. Any of it. But we can not just storm in there and drag people out. They went willingly. And unless he starts breaking laws or threatening folks, there is not much we can do except watch."

"And wait," Marcus said grimly.

Jo's fingers wrapped around her mug, the ceramic warm against her palms.

"Then we watch closely. And we make sure everyone here knows what is happening. No surprises. No one wanders down there curious and gets caught in whatever web he is spinning."

Gus nodded.

Father Tom's gaze dropped to his hands.

"I will keep trying. Keep reaching out. Maybe if they see a familiar face, hear a voice that is not his..."

"Do it," Gunny said. "But do not go alone. Take someone with you. Someone armed."

The priest looked up, startled.

"You think it is that dangerous?"

"I think," Gunny said slowly, "that we do not know what it is yet. And that is reason enough to be careful."

The fire snapped and settled as the household gathered. Every chair, bench, and stair tread held someone. Quinn sat cross-legged near the hearth, Grace perched on the arm of the couch beside Rowan. Gemma leaned against the bookshelf, arms crossed. Tobias stood behind Jo's rocker, one hand resting on the back. The younger children had been sent to bed, but the teens and adults filled the space with quiet, waiting tension.

Gunny stepped forward, hands clasped behind his back.

"There is a situation developing up at Little Bear Lake. Some of you may have heard talk already. I want to make sure everyone hears it straight."

Gus moved to stand beside him, thumbs hooked in his belt.

"A man calling himself The Oracle has set up camp. Started small a few weeks back. Now he has got maybe forty people with him. Youngish women mostly. A handful of young men acting as guards."

Marcus took over, voice clipped.

"He is organizing them. Uniforms, shifts, structure. Preaching about purpose and meaning, peace and love in all this chaos. People are buying it."

Gemma's jaw tightened.

"Buying what, exactly?"

"Whatever he is selling," Gunny said. "Salvation. Belonging. A way forward when everything else has collapsed. Classic cult setup."

The word hung in the air, ugly and sharp.

"I don't know what their end game is, no matter what kind of group they are, I think we need to pay close attention." Zeke said briskly, "We have had some months of relative quiet, and I like it."

Boone shifted in his seat near the window.

"So what is the threat? Is he raiding? Taking supplies?"

"Not yet," Gus said. "No obvious threat, but he is pulling people in. Women who had families, lives. Now they walk around with their eyes down, spouting his words like scripture."

Owen's brow furrowed.

"Can we pull them out?"

"No," Marcus said flatly. "They went willingly. Unless he starts forcing people to stay or threatening violence, we have no grounds to intervene."

"But we watch," Gunny added. "Close. And we make sure no one from here goes wandering up there out of curiosity or desperation."

Grace's voice cut in, sharp.

"What about people coming to us? If someone wants out, do we help?"

"Absolutely," Gus said. "We take them in, no questions asked. Same as we always have."

Tobias's fingers drummed once against the rocker.

"What if he starts expanding? Pushing beyond Little Bear?"

"Then we push back," Marcus said. "But carefully. We do not start a fight we do not need. And we do not give him a reason to paint us as the enemy."

Quinn's voice came low, steady.

"So we wait. And we watch."

"And we stay ready," Gunny confirmed. "No one travels alone. No one goes near that camp or the followers unless they have got backup and a damn good reason."

Jo spoke from her rocker, quiet but firm.

"And we keep doing what we have been doing. Teaching. Sharing. Building community the right way. So if anyone is looking for hope, they know where to find it without needing a prophet to hand it to them."

Gunny's mouth twitched, almost a smile.

Silence settled again, but this time it carried weight. Understanding. The fire crackled. Outside, the wind brushed through the pines.

Gus straightened.

"Questions?"

No one spoke.

"All right then. Stay sharp. Stay together. And if you see or hear anything that does not sit right, you bring it to us. Understood?"

Heads nodded across the room.

"Good," Gunny said. "Now get some rest. Tomorrow is still coming whether we like it or not."

The Oracle sat on an overstuffed cushion at the center of the longhouse, firelight glinting off the polished stones arranged in a circle around him. His hair fell in waves past his shoulders, dark and carefully kept. He wore simple, soft linen, white and clean, a stark contrast to the patched and faded burlap-like tunics worn by everyone else in the room.

Six women sat closest to him. Maidens, he called them. Their hands folded in their laps, backs straight, eyes fixed on him with a kind of reverent stillness. They smiled when he spoke, yes, but the smiles seemed detached, vacant like reflections on still water.

"You see," The Oracle said, voice smooth as honey poured slow, "the old world collapsed because it had no center. No truth. People chased emptiness and called it freedom."

One of the women nodded, eyes wide.

"But here," he continued, gesturing to the room, "we have found clarity. Each of you has been chosen to carry the light forward."

Another woman, younger, maybe nineteen, leaned forward slightly. Her name had been Hannah. Now she was called Devotion.

"What do you need from us today, Oracle?"

He smiled, warm and patient.

"Only what you have already given. Your trust. Your presence. Your willingness to let go of the fear that binds so many others."

Devotion's smile widened, though her eyes remained flat.

"We are grateful."

"I know you are," he said softly.

Behind the circle of women, three young men stood against the wall. Guards, though they carried no weapons openly. Their faces held the same eerie calm, the same manic devotion. One of them, broad-shouldered and maybe twenty-five, stepped forward.

"The perimeter is clear, Oracle. No movement from the south."

The Oracle inclined his head.

"Good. We must remain vigilant. Some would see our peace as weakness.""They do not understand," Devotion murmured.

"No," The Oracle agreed. "But they will. In time."

He rose, movements deliberate and graceful, and the women shifted as though pulled by invisible strings. He crossed to the window, gazing out at the cluster of cabins and tents that had sprung up around Little Bear Lake. Smoke curled from cook fires. Figures moved between shelters, quiet and orderly.

"We are growing," he said. "Each day, more come seeking refuge. We must be ready to receive them."

Devotion stood, her voice hushed.

"What would you have us do?"

He turned, backlit by the window, face cast in shadow.

"Continue as you have. Welcome them. Let the children make friends with the children of those who are lost. Show them the peace we have found. Perhaps we will visit the town and offer to trade? Let them see that here, they are not alone."

The women nodded in unison.

One of the guards cleared his throat.

"There was talk in the camp. Some group up at the school in the next town over. They are organized, too. Taking in families."

The Oracle's expression did not change, but something flickered in his eyes. Brief.

"Let them," he said. "They cling to the structures that failed them. We offer something greater."

He returned to his cushion, settling with the ease of a man who had never doubted his place in the world.

"Go now. Rest. Tomorrow we will gather again."

The women rose as one, bowing slightly before filing out into the night. The guards followed, leaving The Oracle alone by the fire.

He stared into the flames and smiled.

Chapter Eight

A Place to Gather

Zara leaned back in the cracked leather chair that had once belonged to some middle school administrator who probably never imagined their office would become a war room. The desk between her and Jillian was buried under hand-drawn maps, inventory sheets, and a coffee mug that hadn't held actual coffee in close to a year. Chicory root and dandelion, maybe. Coffee, no.

Jillian shifted the baby to her shoulder, the little boy's head lolling against her collarbone, his wispy blonde hair catching the light from the window. She tapped her pen against the clipboard balanced on her knee, scanning the columns of names and addresses.

"I think Rita's team will be searching and clearing the homes on the west side of town the rest of this week." Her voice stayed low, barely above a murmur, the way mothers learned to talk when a child was ninety percent asleep and that last ten percent hung by a thread. "Then we can send the cleaning crew over to prep them for new arrivals."

Zara pulled one of the maps closer, tracing the grid of streets with her finger. Pencil marks dotted the blocks already searched. X's through the ones deemed unusable. Small circles around the ones ready for habitation.

"How many does that give us on the west side?"

Jillian glanced at her clipboard. "Seven houses in decent shape, Rita thinks. Two need work. One had a pipe burst, so the downstairs is a loss, but the upstairs bedrooms are sound."

"Seven is good. That could house three, maybe four families each if we double up the rooms."

"Twenty-some new people, give or take." Jillian's pen tapped twice. "We've got the bedding for it. Barely."

The baby stirred, one small fist curling against Jillian's neck. She patted his back in a slow rhythm until he settled.

"That is great." Zara folded her arms and let herself smile. A real one. The kind that had been rare for a long time. "Boomer and Harlan have a crew working on our perimeter fence. Two-thirds of the way around the occupied area here in town already. I hear they are building a stockade fence up at the Lodge too."

"Boomer doesn't sleep, does he?"

"Marines." Zara shrugged, as if that explained everything. It mostly did. "Harlan's the same. Those two have their crew running like a well-oiled engine. "

The baby made a soft sound, a half-whimper that faded into nothing. Jillian shifted him again, careful and practiced.

"How many new families came in last week?"

"Three. The Porters from down near Speculator, a couple with a teenager from over by Piseco, and a single mother with twin girls. Six and a half, maybe seven years old." Zara pulled a sheet from under the map. "All vetted by Rita's people. All willing to work."

"Good. We don't need passengers."

"No, we do not."

Zara looked out the window. Beyond the glass, the school's front lawn had been transformed. Garden beds lined the walkways. A chicken coop sat where the flagpole used to be. Two women carried baskets of laundry toward a line strung between maple trees, and a cluster of children chased each other around the old playground equipment, their laughter carrying faintly through the walls.

A few months with nobody trying to kill them and take their things. It felt almost dangerous to say it out loud, like naming the peace might break it.

"We're getting somewhere, Jillian."

Jillian looked up from her clipboard, pen finally still, and the baby finally asleep. She gestured to one of the teenage girls who was walking by, and she came in and scooped up the little bundle, heading for the nursery.

"Yeah. We are."

Jillian gathered her clipboard and slipped out, leaving Zara alone with the quiet and the maps. She leaned back in the cracked chair and listened to the sounds filtering through the open window. Hammering from the west fence line. A rooster that didn't understand time zones. And underneath it all, the steady hum of people doing what needed doing.

The teens had been the surprise nobody saw coming.

Not that anyone doubted them, exactly. But the speed at which they'd shed the last skin of childhood and stepped into real work, real responsibility, had caught even Zara off guard. Kids who a year ago had worried about algebra tests and social media now hauled water, mucked stalls, and kept younger children fed and entertained without being asked. They'd been forced to grow up with the sharp edge of a world that no longer had room for slow blooming. And somehow, most of them were handling it.

Some better than others.

Zara stood and moved to the window, resting her hands on the sill. Down past the garden beds and the laundry line, the livestock area spread out behind what had once been the school's athletic storage building. Fencing cobbled together from salvaged cattle panels and split rails penned the goats on one side and the pigs on the other. The horses occupied a lean-to barn that Boomer's crew had thrown up in four days flat.

Three boys moved among the animals with the easy comfort of people who'd done it long enough that their bodies knew the routine before their brains caught up. Ty, her son, fifteen and all elbows and jaw now, carried two buckets toward the horse trough. George walked beside him with a bale of hay balanced on one shoulder, talking with his hands despite the load. Aeiden trailed behind, pulling a small wagon of grain sacks, pausing to scratch the ear of a brown goat that pressed its face through the fence slats.

And at the center of all three boys, white as a snowdrift and nearly the size of a small pony, Samson padded along with the calm authority of a dog who understood his post. The Great Pyrenees pup was growing fast. He shadowed the boys whenever they worked near the animals, positioning himself between the livestock and whatever direction trouble might come from. He had good instincts. Better than some of the adults, if Zara was honest.

On the far side of the livestock area, the girls had their own domain. Jenny scattered feed for the chickens, tossing handfuls with a practiced arc while the birds swarmed her boots. Meg herded a line of ducks back toward their enclosure with a long stick and a patience that belied her fourteen years.

Six teenagers, ages fourteen to sixteen. Hormones like wildfire and emotions that could swing from laughter to fury in the space of a breath. Zara and Gunny had talked about it more than once, sitting on this same porch after the kids were in bed.

"They need jobs," Gunny had said. "Real ones. Keep their hands busy and their heads straight."

"And supervision," Zara had added. "Not a warden. Someone who gets them."

They'd found that someone in Eve Carpenter.

Eve had run a farm outside of town before the world tipped over. Raised eight children of her own, buried one, lost her husband ten years ago, and still got up every morning ready to fight the day barehanded if it looked at her wrong. She was sixty-something, built like a fence post, and had a voice that could stop a charging bull or a sulking teenager with equal effectiveness.

She stood now at the gate of the pig pen, arms crossed, watching the boys work. Nothing escaped her. Not the way George favored his left wrist, which meant he'd tweaked it again and hadn't said anything. Not the half-second too long that Ty's eyes lingered on Jenny across the yard. Not the way Meg blushed when George was around. Not the fact that Aeiden had skipped the second grain bin, probably thinking she wouldn't notice.

"Aeiden, you forget how to count?"

The boy's shoulders tightened. He turned the wagon around without a word and headed back for the bin he'd missed. Eve watched him go, then uncrossed her arms and leaned on the fence rail, her expression settling into something close to satisfaction.

She did not miss a trick.

Zara watched Eve redirect Aeiden with nothing more than a question and a look. No raised voice. No lecture. Just the quiet certainty of a woman who'd spent decades managing creatures far more stubborn than a sixteen-year-old boy.

Aeiden pulled the wagon back to the second grain bin, loaded a sack, and hauled it to the goat pen without complaint. His jaw was set, but he did the work. That was the thing about Eve. She didn't need obedience born from fear. She just made it clear that cutting corners wasn't worth the energy of the argument that would follow.

Ty finished filling the horse trough and wiped his hands on his jeans, glancing toward the chicken yard. Zara caught the look. So did Eve.

"Ty Malard, those stall mats aren't going to sweep themselves."

Ty snapped his head back toward the lean-to barn like he'd been caught with his hand in someone else's rucksack. George snorted and shoved him toward the door. The two disappeared inside, and a moment later, the scrape of a broom against rubber mats drifted through the open bay.

Zara shook her head and turned from the window.

She gathered the maps from the table and rolled them into a leather tube that had once held architectural plans for a building no one would ever finish. The inventory sheets she stacked and tucked into a folder. Jillian's handwriting filled every margin, notes, calculations, and question marks where the numbers didn't add up. They never quite added up. That was the trick of this life now. You did the math, came up short, and figured out which shortage you could survive.

The hallway outside the war room smelled like pine cleaner and woodsmoke. Someone had mopped the floors this morning, and the windows along the corridor let in panels of gray light that made the old linoleum shine. Zara passed two classrooms that had been converted into sleeping quarters. Curtains made from bedsheets divided the space into sections. In one room, a woman she recognized as Diane Holbrook sat cross-legged on a cot, mending a pair of child's overalls with stitches so small they were almost invisible. Diane looked up and offered a nod. Zara returned it.

Three new families. Eleven people total, including five children under ten. They'd arrived over the past two weeks in ones and twos, referred by contacts along the trade routes Gunny had established. Each family had been vetted. Interviewed by Zara and Rita separately, then together. Background checks were basically having someone vouch for you; there are no databases anymore. Skills assessed. Willingness to contribute was confirmed, not with promises but with demonstrated work during a trial period.

It wasn't a perfect system. Nothing was. But it was better than opening the gates and hoping for the best.

Zara descended the stairs to the main floor, where the old cafeteria had become the community's central hub. Long tables filled the space, some set with plates for the next meal, others covered with projects in various stages. A group of younger children sat at the far end with Clare, who had ridden over from the Lodge that morning. She held up a picture book and pointed at the illustrations while small faces followed her finger with wide, hungry eyes.

Reading hour. One of the few things that still felt normal.

Zara poured herself a cup of chicory from the pot near the serving window and leaned against the counter. The liquid was bitter and thin, nothing like real coffee, but it was warm, and it gave her hands something to hold.

Outside, Eve's voice carried faintly through the walls. Steady. Patient. Relentless.

Good. Someone had to be.

The dishes had been cleared and the cafeteria emptied of all but a handful of stragglers. Zara sat at the end of the nearest table with Rita, Gunny, and Clare, cups of mint tea cooling between them. The conversation had drifted from fence posts to firewood stores to the trade route schedule Gunny was mapping for the next month. Clare had her notebook open, jotting figures for the school's lesson supplies while she half-listened.

Zara noticed Ty and George hovering near the serving window. They whispered back and forth, George nudging Ty forward, Ty nudging back. They'd been circling for a solid two minutes.

"What's up, gentlemen?" Gunny asked as the two finally approached the table.

"Well," Ty began. He straightened his shoulders the way he always did when he was trying to look older than fifteen. "We had an idea and wanted to see what you thought."

All four adults turned to face them. Clare set down her pencil. Rita leaned back in her chair. Gunny folded his arms across his chest.

Both boys went stiff under the collective gaze. Ty rubbed the back of his neck. George studied the floor like it held the answer to something important. Ty opened his mouth, closed it, glanced at George, who shrugged, then Ty tried again but only got out a single syllable before clearing his throat.

Gunny's patience held for about six seconds.

"Spill it, boys. We're all ears."

"We want to set up a market. Like a giant yard sale but more proper and organized." Ty said it fast, the words running together like he was afraid he'd lose his nerve if he slowed down.

George jumped in, his hands already moving as he talked, excitement loosening his tongue. "We thought we could pick a spot and fence it in. Have guards posted. Then we let people pay something to set up a booth or a table to sell their stuff. Trade, barter, whatever people have."

Ty nodded and picked up the thread. "Then we could have a gate. Only let vetted people in. Check them before they come through, the same way we do for new families. I think it would help a lot. People out there have things they need to move, skills they could offer, but there's no central place for any of it."

Gunny's arms uncrossed. He leaned forward and rested his elbows on the table, the hard lines around his mouth softening into something that looked dangerously close to a grin.

"And it would be a hub for information."

Ty blinked. "Yeah. Exactly."

Zara stood from the bench and pulled Ty into a hug before he could dodge it. He went rigid for a half second, the way teenage boys do when their mothers show affection in front of other people, then his shoulders dropped, and he let it happen.

"This is a great idea, boys." Zara released him and looked between them. "We'll set up a meeting with you to work out the details. Logistics, location, security protocols. Are you two going to help get this going?"

"Yup." George grinned. "All six of us thought we could work on it together. We already talked it through pretty good. We spoke to Mrs. Eve about our idea, and she said she would help out."

"All six of you, huh?" Rita asked. Six teenagers who'd been hauling water and mucking stalls three months ago were now pitching community infrastructure ideas after dinner. Something was taking root in these kids that went beyond chores and survival tasks.

Clare picked up her pencil and tapped it against her notebook. "You'll need rules. Written ones. For vendors, for visitors, for disputes over trades gone sideways. People get ugly over a bad deal faster than you'd think."

"We can do that," Ty said.

Gunny pushed back from the table and stood. He extended his hand to Ty, then to George. Both boys shook it, standing a little taller when they let go.

"Get your six together. Bring me a proposal. Location options, layout sketch, list of what you'd need to build it out." Gunny held up a finger. "And I want Eve at that meeting."

"Yes, sir."

The boys walked out of the cafeteria with their chins up and their steps quick. Zara watched them go, then sat back down and wrapped her hands around her tea.

Rita was still watching the empty doorway. "Those aren't kids anymore."

Chapter Nine

We Learn by Watching

They built the Market the way most things were built now—slowly, deliberately, and with a lot of looking over shoulders.

The field chosen sat just east of the school, far enough away that the noise wouldn't bleed into lessons, close enough that no one would be walking blind to get there. It had once been a softball diamond. The backstop still stood, bent and rusted, and the bleachers had long ago been scavenged for lumber. What remained was flat ground, good drainage, and a sightline you could trust.

Gunny walked it first, boots sinking slightly into spring-soft earth, hands clasped behind his back. Eve followed a few paces behind him, eyes on the treeline, cataloging blind spots and footpaths the way other people counted fence posts. Zara stood with Ty, George, Jenny, Meg, Lori, and Aeiden clustered around her, each of them holding folded papers already smudged with dirt and pencil marks.

Ty was the one who spoke first.

"We figured we'd fence it on three sides," he said, unrolling his sketch on the hood of the truck. "Leave the south open for flow, but put the gate there. One way in, one way out."

George leaned in. "We can string bells along the fence. Like the perimeter ones. If someone cuts through instead of using the gate, we'll hear it."

"And tables?" Zara asked.

Jenny answered without hesitation. "Vendor tables go in rows. Wide aisles. No tight corners. No blind pockets."

Meg pointed to a square she'd drawn near the edge. "Kids' area. Nothing fancy. Chalk, rope games, maybe a ball. We keep it where everyone can see."

Eve grunted, which for her was high praise.

Gunny studied the layout for a long moment, then nodded once. "You've thought this through."

Ty swallowed, shoulders squaring. "We've been thinking about it for weeks."

"Good," Gunny said. "Because if we're doing this, we're doing it right."

They broke ground that afternoon.

Not with machines—those were reserved for things that couldn't be done any other way—but with shovels, post-hole diggers, and hands that were already calloused from months of work that mattered. Fence posts went in first, sunk deep and tamped tight. Salvaged wire followed, then split rails where they had them. By dusk, the bones of the place were visible. Not pretty. Solid.

The Rules came next.

They didn't write them all at once. That would've been a mistake. Instead, they talked them through, argued, crossed things out, and rewrote them cleaner. Zara insisted they be posted clearly, in plain language. Rita insisted there be consequences spelled out, even if no one liked reading them.

By the time the ink dried, there were twelve.

1. **All vendors must be vetted/vouched for.** No exceptions.
2. **All trades are final.** Disputes go to the Market Stewards, not fists.
3. **No weapons drawn inside the fence.** Peace-bonded or checked at the gate.
4. **Children stay in designated areas unless accompanied.**
5. **No recruiting, preaching, or proselytizing.**
6. **No hoarding.**
7. **No coercion.**
8. **No unapproved guards.**
9. **Market Stewards have final say.**
10. **Bell means freeze.** Everyone stops.
11. **Bell twice means leave.** Immediately.
12. **Anyone breaking the Rules will not return.**

Ty read them aloud, voice steady. When he finished, no one spoke for a moment.

The kids nodded. They understood that now, in a way they wouldn't have a year ago, that without rules, trouble breeds.

Market Day dawned clear and cold.

By midmorning, the field had filled with people. Tables went up, planks balanced on sawhorses, doors pulled off hinges and laid flat, crates stacked just high enough to feel official. Goods appeared in careful piles: jars of honey, knitted hats, dried herbs, hand tools, salvaged books, jars of nails counted out like treasure. Someone had brought apples, shriveled but still sweet. Someone else had a wheelbarrow full of firewood, cut clean and stacked tight.

At the gate, two Stewards stood watch. Not guards, everyone was careful about that word, but familiar faces with rifles slung and eyes open. Bells hung on the posts, dull brass and iron, tested twice before the first visitors were let through.

Inside the fence, it felt almost... normal.

Children found each other the way children always had. Fast. Instinctive. They didn't ask where you were from. They asked what you had. A ball changed hands. Chalk scraped against a board someone had propped up. Laughter rose and fell like birdsong.

That was when the first unfamiliar faces slipped in.

They were children, mostly. Clean, well-fed, dressed in simple clothes that didn't quite match anyone else's. Linen tunics, soft belts tied at the waist. Neutral colors. No patches. No bright scraps scavenged from old lives. They moved in small clusters at first, eyes scanning, measuring.

Marisol noticed them before anyone else did.

She was halfway through a game when she paused, ball tucked under her arm, and frowned. "Do you know them?"

Jake squinted. "No. New, maybe."

"Everyone's new," Edwin said, already shrugging it off.

The unfamiliar kids didn't push in. They waited. Watched. Smiled when someone looked their way. When a ball rolled toward them, one of the girls picked it up and handed it back with a soft, careful motion.

"Do you want to play?" she asked.

Her voice was gentle. Older than she looked. The kind of voice adults used when they were being patient.

Marisol hesitated. Just a beat.

Then she nodded. "Okay."

They fell into the game easily. Too easily. The new kids didn't argue over rules. Didn't shove. Didn't cheat. They praised small things—good throws, clever catches, even mistakes that led to laughter instead of tears.

"That was brave," one boy said when Edwin missed a catch and skinned his knee.

Edwin blinked. No one had ever called that brave before.

Nearby, Clare watched from the edge of the field, her brow knitting. She couldn't put her finger on it—nothing was wrong, exactly—but something felt... curated. She made a mental note and turned back to her storytime when a younger child tugged her sleeve. She had been bringing the vast majority of the kids down to the school for some group lessons and some playtime once a week. They certainly did not want to miss the great excitement of the first Market. So much so that nearly everyone from the Lodge had come down to attend. They even set up some tables to sell items.

Looking across the chaos of the children's area, Clare noticed that near the gate, a woman stood alone.

She didn't carry goods. She simply stood, hands folded, watching the children with an expression that might have been warmth—or calculation. Clare noted that when Zara's gaze flicked toward her, the woman inclined her head politely and stepped back, melting into the flow of people before Zara could say anything to her.

By the time the bell rang for midday break, the unfamiliar children were already woven in.

Names were exchanged. Small confidences shared. A girl with dark braids told Meg, "We don't have chores where I live. Grown-ups take care of things."

Meg laughed, a quick sound. "We have chores. Everyone does."

The girl smiled. "That sounds tiring."

Meg shrugged, uncertain. "It's just... normal."

The girl tilted her head, considering that. "Normal can change."

No one heard it but Meg.

By afternoon, the Market hummed. Trades were made. Rules held. The Stewards never had to ring the bell twice. When the last table was packed up and the sun dipped low, people drifted away tired and satisfied.

The unfamiliar children left quietly, gathered by adults in matching linen, hands resting lightly on shoulders. No one stopped them. Why would they?

From the porch of the school, Zara watched the field empty.

"It went well," Jillian said beside her, baby tucked against her chest.

"Yes," Zara agreed.

But her eyes lingered on the path leading north, toward Little Bear Lake, long after the last figure disappeared into the trees.

Some things didn't announce themselves.

They arrived smiling.

Chapter Ten

Habit

By the second Tuesday, the Market felt less like an event and more like a habit.

That, Zara decided, was both its greatest strength and its quietest danger.

They learned the rhythm quickly. Tuesdays and Fridays. Early setup, midday rush, late-afternoon taper. The bell stayed silent more often than not. People knew the Rules now. They moved through the gates with a kind of practiced ease, pausing for checks without complaint, greeting the Stewards by name.

The Lodge sent a group every Market day. Sometimes it was Gus and Marcus, sometimes Jo with baskets of bread and dried apples wrapped in cloth. Often it was Gin, rifle slung casually over her shoulder, boots muddy before she even hit the gate.

And almost always, there were children in tow.

Some came to help—Marisol with her careful hands cradling baskets of eggs wrapped in straw, Sadie with bundles of dried herbs tied with twine she'd learned to knot from Rowan, and Fiona perched on an overturned crate with her sketch pad turned ledger, keeping tally for trades that needed counting or weighing or sorting into fair exchanges. It was a place the world felt briefly stitched together instead of fraying at the edges, held by threads too fragile to name but strong enough, for now, to keep people from drifting back into the silent dark of their own four walls. They felt like a community.

Edwin made a beeline for the chalkboard every time, Rosa trailing after him with her hair half-fallen out of its braid. Marisol hovered close, watchful in the way older girls learned to be without being told.

Gin noticed. She pretended she didn't.

On the first Friday, she volunteered for security. She took up a position near the south gate, leaning against the fence with her arms crossed, eyes scanning the crowd. She looked bored. Anyone who knew her better knew that meant she was clocking everything.

She caught Edwin mid-sprint and hooked a finger into the back of his jacket before he could barrel straight into a stack of crates someone had left carelessly near the edge of the lane. The boy's momentum jerked him backward, his boots skidding on the packed dirt.

"Easy there, Speed Racer," she said, steadying him with a hand on his shoulder. Her grip was firm but gentle, the kind that stopped motion without bruising pride.

He grinned up at her, missing two teeth on the bottom and proud of it in the way only an eleven-year-old could be. "Sorry, Gin."

She ruffled his hair without thinking, the gesture automatic in a way that would've surprised her six months ago. "Try not to die before lunch, yeah? Jo and Father Tom would kill me."

Rosa giggled from somewhere behind her brother, one hand clutching the ragged end of her braid. Marisol smiled, small and careful, the way she always did around adults; she wasn't quite sure how to behave.

Gin watched them run off toward the chalkboard, their voices carrying back on the air, then shifted her stance so she could keep the whole area in her peripheral vision. The board was visible from here if she angled right. So were the supply sheds. And the gap in the fence line, someone really ought to patch that, locked in hard.

It was there, near the edge of the kids' area where the ground sloped down toward the old fire ring, that the Harbinger children gathered.

They didn't announce themselves. They never did. They simply... appeared. A girl with dark braids brought a loaf of bread one Tuesday, breaking it cleanly and passing pieces around without ceremony. Another brought a small crock of honey, dipping sticks for anyone who wanted a taste.

They shared easily. Freely. As if food were not something to be counted and measured.

"That's really good," Rosa said around a mouthful of bread.

The braided girl smiled. "You can have more."

Marisol hesitated. "We're supposed to ask first."

The girl's smile didn't fade. "It's already offered."

That seemed to satisfy her.

They played rope games and clapped rhythms that no one else knew. They sang softly while they jumped, voices blending in a way that made Clare glance up from her table more than once. The songs weren't loud.

They weren't catchy. But they lingered, slipping into memory like a tune you couldn't quite place.

By the third Market day, names were exchanged.

By the fourth, secrets.

Not big ones. Little things. Who snored. Who missed their dad. Who hated turnips, no matter how many ways you cooked them. The Harbinger children listened more than they spoke. When they did speak, it was with a calm that felt older than their years.

"We don't have lessons like this," one boy said, watching Edwin struggle through a math problem chalked on the board. "We learn by watching."

Edwin squinted at him. "Watching what?"

"People," the boy replied, as if that explained everything.

Gin drifted closer, pretending to check the fence line. She caught the exchange, filed it away, and said nothing.

At lunch, she stationed herself near the kids' area, pulling dried meat from her pocket and offering it to Rosa first, then Marisol, then Edwin.

"Trade you for that apple," she told Edwin, nodding at the one tucked into his pocket.

He handed it over solemnly. "It's a good apple."

"I trust your judgment," Gin said, biting into it.

She watched the Harbinger children out of the corner of her eye as she chewed. They ate together, always together. No scraps left behind. No crumbs wasted. When one of the Lodge kids dropped a piece of bread in the dirt, a Harbinger girl picked it up, brushed it clean, and handed it back without comment.

Rosa frowned at that. "It fell."

"So do a lot of things," the girl said gently.

Rosa didn't know what to say to that.

By late afternoon, the crowd thinned. Tables emptied. The Stewards stretched sore backs and loosened shoulders. Gin walked the fence one last time, boots crunching on gravel, eyes sharp.

As the Harbinger group gathered their children, Gin caught the braided girl watching her.

Not staring. Observing.

Gin met her gaze, expression flat.

The girl inclined her head the same way the adults did.

Gin's jaw tightened.

On the walk back to the Lodge that evening, Edwin rode ahead, in the wagon Rosa chattered to Clare and Marisol quiet but alert.

"They're nice," Edwin said as he rode beside the wagon. "The kids from the lake."

"They don't yell," Rosa added. "And they always have food."

Marisol sighed. "They don't play like us."

Gin glanced down at her. "How so?"

Marisol shrugged. "Like they already know how it's supposed to go."

Gin grunted softly. She shifted her rifle so she could turn toward Marisol.

"Anything else?" Gin asked

Marisol shrugged, "I am not sure. They really are nice. They just don't talk like other kids."

"Market again Friday?" Edwin asked.

"Market again Friday," Gin confirmed.

She watched the trees as they rode, the path familiar, the sound of the kids' voices threading through the evening air.

Threads, she thought, were easy to miss.

Until you realized how tightly they'd been woven.

Chapter Eleven

The Days Between

The days between Markets were longer now.

Jo felt it most in the mornings, when the bell rang and the children didn't scatter the way they used to. They lingered. Finished chores slower. Looked toward the tree line as if something might step out of it once the work was done.

She told herself it was spring. New families. New rhythms.

Still, she watched.

This particular Market day, Clare, Mary, Jo, and Zeke were joining Gin and her assortment of children on the wagon ride to town.

Mary was going to teach an art class, and Zeke had a box of carved, wooden toys to trade. Jo was convinced Zeke couldn't go another minute without getting involved with the Market. Every single person, no matter how new to the community, knew his name.

Clare and Mary headed straight to the classroom so classes would be finished before the market got busy.

By midmorning the school had settled into its familiar hum. Chalk on slate. The low murmur of reading voices. The smell of damp earth and woodsmoke drifted in through the open door. Eve moved among the livestock pens, sharp-eyed and efficient. She worked with the kind of practiced economy that came from raising too many children and tending too many animals to waste motion on anything unnecessary.

Nothing was wrong.

That was the problem.

Everything was too quiet, too settled. The kind of stillness that made the hairs on the back of Jo's neck stand up even when there wasn't a reason for it. She'd learned not to ignore that feeling.

Jo had wandered into the barn with Odin padding alongside her, the big dog's nails clicking softly on the packed earth floor.She was impressed with how much work had been done here at the school barns. ANother addition was going on for Market animals. She moved slowly between the pens, taking in all the new kids and lambs. Spring had been good to them this year. The animals were healthy and well-tended. She could see the care in every clean water bucket, every fresh scatter of hay.

"Well, hello there. Can I help you with something?" Eve asked.

Jo turned to see a stout woman with a messy, greying bun that had mostly given up the fight against the day's work. Bright blue eyes peered out from a face creased with laugh lines and weather. She wore a pair of worn coveralls that had been patched more than once, the kind of mending that spoke of making things last because you had to.

"Just admiring the little ones," Jo said, leaning her cane against the pen rail and reaching down to scratch behind Odin's ears. "I've got a terrible soft spot for the kids, but the lambs are sweet, too. I'm Jo Callahan."

Eve's eyes widened slightly, and she wiped her hand on her overalls before extending it, a grin spreading across her weathered face. "Jo Callahan, huh? Well, I'll be damned. You're pretty famous around these parts, you know that? I just arrived about a month ago. Been meaning to introduce myself proper, but every time I think I've got a minute, something needs doing." She gestured broadly at the pens. "I oversee the livestock and the teens that work here, too. Keeps me on my toes. My name is Eve. Eve Carpenter."

They shook hands, Eve's grip firm and calloused, the handshake of someone who knew the value of honest work. Jo liked her immediately.

The conversation unspooled easily after that, the way it did between two women who'd lived long enough to know what mattered. They talked about children, the particular challenges of raising them in a world that kept shifting under everyone's feet. They traded stories about homesteading, comparing notes on everything from the best way to keep raccoons out of the chicken coop to which herbs grew best in partial shade. And of course, eventually, they circled around to the Apocalypse itself, the way all conversations seemed to these days. Not dwelling on it, just acknowledging it the way you'd acknowledge weather or seasons. Something that happened. Something you lived through.

Clare stood at the window with her arms crossed, watching Leah help one of the younger girls sound out a passage from a battered copy of Charlotte's Web. The girl's finger traced the words, lips moving, and Leah nodded encouragement with the kind of patience Clare had spent years trying to teach. The scene should have warmed her, and it did, mostly.

But her eyes kept drifting past the glass. Gin had noticed it too. Clare could tell by the way the other woman positioned herself, always with a sightline toward the eastern tree line, always with that deceptive ease that masked something more deliberate. Gin never said anything directly. She just stayed close.

The shift came just before lunch. School was let out, and the Market was starting to get busy.

The Harbinger children appeared without announcement, as if they had simply been there all along. They waited at the edge of the yard, not crossing the invisible line Clare had drawn in her mind between school and not-school. They sat on fallen logs or stood with their backs to the trees, hands folded, patient.

They brought food.

Not Market food. No tables, no counting. Just things meant to be eaten easily: thick slices of bread wrapped in cloth, apples cut in half, small jars of broth still warm enough to fog the glass.

"You look tired," one of the girls said to Meg, offering her a piece of bread.

Meg hesitated. "We still have lessons."

"We'll wait," the girl replied, smiling.

And they did.

Clare watched from the doorway as Meg glanced back toward the schoolroom, then at the bread. The girl held it out the way someone might offer a hand to a stranger on a steep trail. No urgency. No pressure. Just an open palm and a face that said, Take your time.

Meg took the bread.

Clare marked the moment in her mind the way she used to mark attendance. Present. Noted. Filed.

She found Gin twenty minutes later.

"They're back," Clare said.

Gin didn't look at her; she just nodded. "Saw them come through the birches about an hour ago. Three today. Same ones as Tuesday."

"They bring food every time."

"Good food, too." Gin stretched and turned to Clare. "That bread's better than anything we've turned out of the cafeteria kitchen. Somebody over there knows what they're doing with a sourdough starter."

Clare leaned against the fence rail. A splinter bit into her palm, and she let it.

"The kids look forward to seeing them more than they look forward to lessons or anything else."

Gin squinted at her. "Kids have always preferred recess to arithmetic. That's not new."

"This feels different."

Eve set the scrub brush on the edge of the trough and wiped her hands on her coat, tipping her head toward Clare and Gin. Jo nodded, and the two older women walked over. Eve studied Clare for a long beat, the kind of look that peeled back politeness and searched for what sat underneath.

"You're not wrong to watch," Eve said. "Generosity without cost makes me itch. Always has. But I've also seen hungry people share their last potato with a stranger because that's just who they were. So."

"So which is this?"

Eve's mouth thinned into something not quite a frown.

"Couldn't tell you yet. But I used to say the same thing to my kids when the neighbour's dog started showing up with scraps." She held Clare's gaze. "Find out where those scraps are coming from before anybody gets attached."

When the bell rang for the midday break, the Harbinger children stepped forward, easy as breathing. There was no rush. They passed food hand to hand, never watching who took more or less. A girl with dark braids broke a round loaf into pieces and set them on a cloth spread over a stump. A smaller boy produced a jar of something golden, thick as syrup, and drizzled it across the bread without being asked.

George leaned against the fence, chewing thoughtfully. "You always eat like this?"

"Together," a boy answered. "It's easier."

"Who makes it?" Jenny asked.

The boy shrugged. "Whoever's there."

Jenny turned the bread over in her hands, examining it the way she examined everything. She bit into it. Her eyebrows lifted, and she said nothing more.

Nearby, Clare pretended to reorganize a stack of books on the outdoor shelf, her attention fixed on the cluster of kids. Nothing about it broke a rule. There was no preaching, no trading, no adult voices raised in authority. Just children sharing food and space.

Too smoothly.

She'd taught school for ten years before the world fell apart. She knew what organic friendship looked like between kids. The shoving, the whispered alliances, the rotating feuds that burned hot for an hour and dissolved by afternoon. This wasn't that. These children moved like a flock. Not following a leader, but turning together, sensing each other's shifts without looking. It was beautiful in the way a well-rehearsed performance was beautiful, and it unsettled her for the same reason.

A younger school child tugged at her sleeve. "Can we stay out longer today?"

Clare smiled. "A little."

She watched the Harbinger children closely then. They didn't encourage the request. They didn't discourage it either. They simply stayed. One girl sat cross-legged in the dead grass and began braiding a cord from strips of cloth, fingers quick and sure. Two of the boys tossed a ball with Edwin and Jake, matching the rhythm of whatever game had already been underway. They slid into the gaps like water filling low ground.

Later, when the kids drifted off in small groups, one of the Harbinger boys asked casually, "Do your parents come get you?"

"Sometimes," Meg said. "Most of us live right here."

"And the others?"

Meg nodded toward the road. "They come on Market days. From the Lodge."

"That's far," the boy said.

"It's fine now that the weather is nice," Meg replied, a little too quickly.

The boy nodded, filing the information away. His face gave nothing. Not interested, not satisfied. Just a small adjustment behind the eyes, the way a person marks a tree blaze on a trail they plan to walk again.

Clare set her books down. The stack was already neat. Had been neat the first three times she'd straightened it. She pulled her coat tighter and crossed the yard toward Gin, who stood with one boot on the bottom fence rail and both hands wrapped around a tin cup.

"He asked where they came from," Clare said quietly.

Gin sipped. Didn't turn. "Which one?"

"Older boy. Twelve, maybe thirteen. The one who always stands a half step behind the others."

"I see him." Gin's jaw worked for a moment. "Asked me something similar last week. Where do the horses go at night? Phrased it like he was curious."

Clare's stomach tightened. "He's mapping us."

Gin finally looked at her. The humor that usually lived around her mouth was absent.

"Maybe. Or maybe he's a kid in a strange place trying to figure out who's safe." She drained the cup. "Problem is, both of those look exactly the same."

Tuesday came cool and bright.

The wagon creaked its way down the road, wheels complaining over ruts. Gin walked alongside it for the first stretch, rifle slung low, boots steady. Edwin sat up front, elbows on his knees, eyes tracking the treeline. Marisol held Rosa's hand, Rosa swinging their arms as she hummed under her breath.

Gin recognized the tune.

One of the Harbinger girls had been singing it last Friday. A simple thing, no real words, just a melody that looped back on itself like a creek finding its own bend. Rosa had picked it up inside of an hour and hadn't stopped since.

Gin didn't comment.

At the school, the Market went up with practiced ease. Tables, bells, Stewards at the gate. The Rules posted clearly as always. Everything looked exactly as it should.

Edwin hopped down from the wagon before the brake was set, already scanning for familiar faces. Rosa slipped free of Marisol's grip and ran straight toward the chalkboard, where the Harbinger children were already gathered. Three of them today. The girl with the braids, the quiet older boy, and a younger one, Gin hadn't seen before. Small, sharp-boned, with a cap pulled low over his ears.

Gin shifted her position without thinking, placing herself closer to the kids' area. She told herself it was habit.

The new boy stayed near the older one's elbow. He didn't speak. His eyes moved from face to face with the careful patience of someone studying a room before sitting down in it. Gin knew that look. She'd worn it herself, first week of boot camp, sizing up every bunk and every body between her and the door.

Rosa reached the chalkboard, and the braided girl knelt to greet her. She produced a small bundle wrapped in cloth and unfolded it to reveal three pieces of flatbread, each one stamped with a pattern of pressed herbs.

"Made them this morning," the girl said.

Rosa took one and turned it over in her hands like it was a seashell. "It's pretty."

"You can eat it." The girl laughed, soft and brief. "The pretty part tastes good too."

Marisol arrived a step behind her sister, breathing harder from the chase. She looked at the bread, then at the girl, then at the new boy standing silent behind them.

"Who's he?"

"River," the older boy said. Just that. No last name, no explanation.

River lifted one hand in a wave that barely cleared his hip.

Edwin wandered over, hands stuffed in his jacket. He studied the new kid the way he studied everything. Directly, without apology. "You been here before?"

River shook his head.

"He's learning," the braided girl offered. "Same as we did."

Edwin accepted this with a nod. He picked up chalk and drew a lopsided grid on the board. "You play tic-tac-toe?"

River stared at the grid. Then he picked up a piece of chalk and drew an X in the center square. His hand was steady and precise.

Edwin grinned.

Gin leaned against a fence post ten yards off, watching the game unfold. The braided girl distributed the rest of the bread. Rosa ate hers in small bites, humming again. Marisol sat on an overturned crate with her knees drawn up, quiet, her gaze shifting between the Harbinger kids and the gate where adults milled and traded.

That girl noticed things. Gin appreciated it.

The older Harbinger boy, Thorn, drifted to the edge of the group. He wasn't watching the game. He was watching the Stewards. Counting them, maybe. Or timing their rotations. His face held the same flat calm it always did, pleasant and closed as a shuttered window.

Gin pulled a piece of jerky from her pocket and bit off a strip. Chewed slow. Kept her eyes soft and her posture loose.

She wasn't fooled.

But she also wasn't certain, and that was worse. Because with certainty, you could act. Suspicion just sat in your chest like a stone, growing heavier with every Market day that passed without incident. Suspicious of what? She couldn't put her finger on it, but she did not dismiss what her gut was trying tell her.

The afternoon light shifted, casting long shadows across the Market grounds. The crowd thinned as traders packed up early, eager to beat the rain that threatened the walk home. But the children stayed.

A Harbinger woman knelt near the chalkboard as Rosa approached, her skirt pooling on the packed dirt. She didn't reach out. Didn't call. Just waited, hands resting open on her knees, until Rosa stopped in front of her.

"Hello," she said softly.

Rosa beamed. "Hi."

"Would you like some honey?" The woman held out a small stick, amber and glistening, tilted so the light caught it.

Rosa looked back at Gin, the question plain in her wide brown eyes.

Gin nodded once.

The woman handed over the honey stick, then leaned back on her heels, giving Rosa the full width of the space between them. No grabbing. No coaxing. No hand on the shoulder. She simply waited, patient as a stone in a streambed, while Rosa licked the stick and smiled at the sweetness.

Gin watched every movement. The woman's hands stayed visible. Her voice stayed low. Her body stayed open and unhurried. Gin couldn't fault any of it.

That bothered her more than if she could.

Edwin drifted over, breathless from a game of tag that had sprawled across half the Market yard. His cheeks were flushed, and his jacket hung open despite the spring evening's chill. He planted himself beside Gin and looked up.

"They don't make kids choose what to do," he said, as if sharing an interesting fact he'd collected. "They already plan it."

Gin glanced down at him. "Plan what?"

He shrugged. "Stuff. Like, who plays with who. Which game goes first. Who brings what food." He scratched his nose. "It's not mean or anything. It's just already done before we get here."

Gin chewed on that. "How do you know?"

"Because I asked River if he wanted to play freeze tag and he said he was supposed to do the chalk game first." Edwin wrinkled his brow. "Supposed to. That's a weird word for playing."

"Yeah," Gin said. "It is."

Edwin scratched at the dust on his knee, thinking.

“River says weird stuff like that a lot,” he added.

“Like what?” Gin asked.

Edwin shrugged.

“Like when we were talking about old Mr. Carter. You remember old Mr. Carter? He hadn’t been seen for weeks.”Edwin said

“Yes. He was getting pretty bad,” Gin said. “Couldn’t even chop kindling anymore.”

River walked by and paused, overhearing Gin’s comment.

“Teacher says, sometimes,” he said calmly,“communities have to consider their burdens.”

The word sat oddly in the air.

Gin’s eyes lifted.

Edwin jumped up and grabbed River as he ran off again, pulled back by a shout from Jake near the fence. Gin didn't move. She turned the words over in her mind the way Rosa had turned over that stamped bread. Supposed to. Burden.

Marisol watched River run back toward the Harbinger children.

They didn't argue about what to play next. They simply moved to the next game together.

Marisol stood a little apart from the others, perched on the same overturned crate she'd claimed earlier. She hadn't joined any game. She held a stick of her own, drawing absent shapes in the dirt between her feet, but her gaze wasn't on the ground.

She was watching.

The braided girl said, "We share because sharing makes us whole."

River repeated it a beat later, word for word, same cadence, same small nod at the end.

A younger Harbinger girl said, "The fire keeps us. We keep each other."

Thorn murmured agreement from the edge of the group, and two others echoed him.

Marisol's stick went still.

She watched Rosa lick the last of the honey from the stick and lean sideways into the Harbinger woman's arm. The woman didn't pull Rosa closer, but she didn't move away either. She just let Rosa settle against her, and something passed over Rosa's face. Calm. Deep and instant, like a candle blown out. Rosa's thumb drifted toward her mouth, a habit she'd dropped months ago, and her eyes went half-lidded.

Marisol's stomach tightened.

The phrases came again. We share because sharing makes us whole. The same words from a different mouth, delivered like a song everyone had already memorized. The answers never stumbled. Never hesitated. The children spoke them the way you'd recite a prayer you'd said a thousand times, smooth and sure.

Something was wrong.

Marisol didn't know how to say it yet. The feeling sat in her chest like a swallowed seed, small and hard and wordless. She looked toward Gin, who stood with her arms crossed and her jaw set, watching the same scene from ten yards off.

Their eyes met.

Marisol looked away first.

The Market passed without incident. Trades were made. Laughter rose and fell between strangers finding familiar ground. The bells stayed quiet. Gin made her final loop of the fence, checked the south gate latch, and nodded to the Steward on duty. Everything accounted for. Everything in its place.

When it was time to go, Rosa frowned.

"Can we stay longer next time?" Small fingers curled into Gin's jacket, tugging once.

Gin crouched, one knee on the cold ground, and met her eye. Rosa's face was open the way only a five-year-old's could be. No guile in it. Just want.

"We'll see. We don't want to head home in the dark, do we?"

Rosa accepted that. She let go of the jacket and let Edwin lift her into the wagon bed, where a folded blanket waited. But her gaze slid back toward the trees, past the last row of vendor tables and the trampled grass, to where the Harbinger group was already gathering at the far edge of the field. The children fell into step without being called. No one shouted names. No one chased a straggler. They simply moved, a quiet current flowing back toward the trail to Little Bear Lake, and the braided girl walked at the center with her hands folded in front of her like she was carrying something precious and invisible.

Rosa watched until the trees swallowed them.

Gin checked the hitch, ran her palm along the horse's flank, and climbed up to the bench seat next to Zeke. The rifle went across her knees. Zeke clicked his tongue, and the wagon lurched forward, wheels squelched through muddy ruts as the school fell behind them.

Dusk settled in blue layers around the ridgeline. The air tasted like iron and pine. Somewhere deep in the timber, a barred owl called, and another answered from farther off, the sound hollow and round as a stone dropped into still water.

Edwin sat in the wagon bed with his back against the side rail, knees drawn up. He'd been quiet since they pulled away. Gin could see him in the corner of her eye, turning something over in his head the way he turned over the dials on that radio of his, careful and methodical, searching for a signal.

"They don't ask where you're going," he said thoughtfully.

Gin kept her eyes on the road. "Who doesn't?"

"The Harbinger kids. When the market's over, they just leave. They don't say goodbye. They don't ask if you'll be back." He picked at a thread on his sleeve. "River said they don't need to, because everyone always comes back."

The wagon wheel caught a root and jolted. Zeke steadied the reins.

"Always's a big word," Zeke chimed in.

Edwin didn't answer.

Marisol rested her forehead against the side rail, her skin pressed into rough wood. Her eyes stayed on the darkening forest, on the spaces between trunks where the last copper light dissolved into shadow. She hadn't spoken since they'd loaded up. Hadn't argued with Edwin, hadn't fussed over Rosa's blanket, hadn't asked for a story or a snack or any of the small comforts that usually filled a ride home.

She just watched.

Zeke tightened his grip on the reins. The leather creaked against his palms. Gin looked at Marisol and thought about Edwin's observation, about River's certainty, about the way those children moved in unison without a voice to guide them. She thought about the woman with the honey stick and the stillness in Rosa's face when she'd leaned against a stranger's arm.

She thought about the phrase 'supposed to'.

The road turned north, and the last of the light bled out behind the ridge. Rosa slept curled under the blanket with her thumb near her mouth. Edwin stared at the first stars punching through above the treeline. Marisol hadn't moved.

Something had begun to take root.

Chapter Twelve

What is Passed Down

Jo woke before the fire burned down to coals.

It wasn't pain that roused her. Not exactly. The ache in her hands and knees had become an old companion, predictable as weather. It was the quiet that woke her. A particular kind of quiet that only came in the minutes before the Lodge stirred, when the house seemed to breathe in and hold it.

She lay still a moment, listening.

Floorboards creaked overhead. Quinn, probably. The boy paced at odd hours, his footsteps uneven in a way that had nothing to do with balance. The low murmur of Grace's voice drifted down the hall, too soft to make out the words but steady, the kind of tone you used with a horse that spooked in the dark. Someone in the far room coughed. A kettle lid rattled faintly in the kitchen where Clare had likely risen before everyone else, because Clare always did, because Clare believed the world could be set right if the water was already hot when people came down the stairs. Jo laughed at how much Clare reminded her of her younger self.

Jo pushed herself upright and reached for her cane. The swollen knuckles of her right hand complained as they closed around the worn hickory grip. Odin lifted his head from the braided rug, thumped his tail once, and stood, stretching long before padding to her side. His nose found her knee. She rested her fingers against the warm crown of his skull.

"Another day," she murmured with a smile. "Come on boy, let's get crackin'."

The Lodge answered in layers. A door latch clicked softly on the second floor. Water ran somewhere through old pipes that Gus had patched three times and would patch again before the ground froze. A child laughed, cut short by a whisper, and then the scuffle of small feet retreating from wherever they'd been told not to go.

Jo eased herself up. The cane took the weight her knees refused. Odin pressed against her left leg, solid and warm, and they moved together down the stairs and through the great room where last night's fire had collapsed to a bed of orange and ash. She stopped at the hearth. The stones still held heat. She could feel it through the wool of her stockings, rising through the wide pine planks that Gus had sanded and sealed himself thirty-five years ago, back when this place was all rotten timber and raccoon nests and a dream she'd been foolish enough to speak out loud.

She'd been pregnant with Judith. Standing in the doorway of what would become this room, one hand on her belly and the other holding a lantern, telling Gus she could see it. The whole thing. A home big enough for all of them and whoever came after.

He'd looked at her like she'd lost her mind when she mentioned the real estate ad for the property. Then he saw it and picked up a hammer.

The kitchen glowed. Clare stood at the counter with her back to the doorway, sleeves rolled to the elbow, slicing yesterday's bread into thick pieces. A pot of water sat on the woodstove, not yet steaming. Two candles burned on the windowsill, their light catching the frost that feathered the glass.

Clare didn't turn around.

"Kettle's almost ready. Sit down, we will have tea."

Jo lowered herself into the chair at the head of the table. Odin circled once and dropped at her feet with a grunt. The candle flames bent sideways as Clare moved past them, setting a cup in front of Jo. Mint and chamomile. Jo wrapped both hands around the warmth and let it seep into the joints.

"You sleep?"

Clare's knife paused against the board. "Enough."

"That's not an answer."

"It's the only one I've got." Clare resumed cutting. The bread was dense, brown, and flecked with oat. "Leah had a nightmare. Took a while to settle her."

Jo sipped. The mint was sharp and clean, cutting through the fog of a restless night. Outside the window, the sky had begun to pale along the eastern ridge, a thin line of grey separating the mountain from the dark.

"Gin brought the kids home late yesterday," Clare said, still not turning. "Edwin was quiet at supper."

"I noticed."

"Marisol, too."

Jo set the cup down. The ceramic clicked against the table.

"What did Gin say? She loves all the kids, but those three have stolen her heart."

Clare turned then. Her face was composed, but her eyes held the same look Jo had seen on her own reflection more times than she could count. The look of a mother measuring a distance she couldn't close.

"Nothing yet. That's what worries me."

Clare reached for a second cup, but Jo waved her off. "I'll talk to Gin after breakfast. Let her come to it."

Clare nodded. She knew better than to push. They both did.

The kitchen filled, the way it always did. Not all at once, never a flood, but a steady current of bodies and voices drawn by the smell of bread warming on the stovetop and the promise of something hot to drink.

Leah appeared first from the hallway, hair still mussed from sleep, dark circles faint beneath her eyes. She didn't speak. She pulled a chair to the far end of the table, rolled her sleeves to her elbows, and dragged a shallow wooden bowl toward her. Dried beans and pebbles. She picked through them with the kind of focus that said she'd rather be doing this than thinking about whatever had chased her through her dreams. Her fingers moved without hesitation. Bean. Bean. Pebble. Bean. The rejected stones pinged against a tin cup at her elbow.

Gemma leaned against the counter near the window, a small stack of papers held close to her face in the thin morning light. She'd written them the night before. Jo could tell by the smudged pencil and the way the lines tilted downward at the edges, the handwriting of someone fighting sleep. Observations. Notes about a cough in one of the younger boys at the school that had hung on too long, the kind of cough that started dry and turned wet and kept a medic up at night running through every possibility that ended badly.

Gemma didn't look up. She chewed the inside of her cheek and turned a page.

Hunter stood near the back door, shoulders squared beneath a flannel shirt that had belonged to one of Jo's sons. He held his hands at his sides the way a man does when he's ready to move but hasn't been pointed in a direction yet. Old habit. Boot camp posture in a farmhouse kitchen.

"Morning, ma'am," he said when Jo caught his eye.

Jo snorted. "If you call me that again, I'll make you peel potatoes."

"Yes, Jo," he corrected, without missing a beat.

She liked him for that. The boy had manners deep enough to choke on, but he learned fast which ones to keep and which ones to drop. She caught the faintest shift in Gemma's posture at the sound of his voice. A straightening. Gemma's eyes stayed on her notes. The corner of her mouth didn't move. But something moved. Jo tucked that away and said nothing.

Grace wove between the stove and the table, distributing mugs with a quiet efficiency that reminded Jo of a nurse she'd once known. No wasted movement. No fuss. A cup appeared in front of Leah. Another at Gemma's elbow. Grace set one near Hunter's post by the door and didn't linger.

Quinn stood at the sink. Sleeves pushed past his elbows, the prosthetic arm braced against the basin's edge while his right hand worked a rag over last night's plates. Water sluiced across the ceramic and dripped from his wrist. The rhythm was deliberate. Still new enough to require thought, each motion a negotiation between memory and what remained. The stump sat in its fitted cuff, the leather dark with water spots. He didn't angle it away. Didn't flinch when Leah glanced up from her beans, and her gaze caught there for half a second before returning to her work.

He washed. Rinsed. Stacked. That was enough.

The back door banged open, and Rowan swept in with a wire basket of eggs balanced against her hip, fresh Spring air trailing her like a cape. Pine needles clung to her coat.

"Declan says the fence along the east pasture's sagging again." She set the basket on the counter with practiced care. "And Donovan swears it wasn't like that yesterday."

"It wasn't." Marcus filled the doorway behind her, arms crossed, steam curling past his jaw from his cup. "Wind picked up overnight."

Rowan lifted her chin. "Then we fix it. I'll go grab the fence stretcher."

She was through the door before anyone could answer.

Jo watched her boots disappear down the porch steps and felt something tighten behind her ribs. Not fear. Recognition. Rowan had always moved like the boys, fast and loose and looking for the next thing to climb or carry. Lately, she moved like something else entirely. Not softer. Not smaller. Just certain. The kind of certainty that doesn't ask permission or wait for a nod. It simply acts, and the world rearranges itself around it.

Outside, laughter rose. Deep and unrestrained. The kind that carried weight and weather in it, the kind that belonged to a man who'd never learned to keep his voice down and saw no reason to start.

"That'll be Zeke," Clare said, glancing toward the window.

As if summoned by name, Zeke's voice rolled through the yard like a stone tumbling downhill, gathering speed.

"I'm telling you, Gus, if I hadn't stepped in, that whole Market would've collapsed under its own confusion. Folks were wandering around like sheep without a shepherd."

The door swung open without ceremony, and Zeke strode in as if he owned the place, which in many ways he did. He'd been walking through that door since before most of the people in the room were born, and the threshold had long since stopped asking his permission. His hands had worked beside Gus's; a friendship, or more accurately, a brotherhood, had grown between the men as the Lodge grew around them. His hair had gone completely silver after Emma Jean died, and his coat bore more patches than original cloth, but his eyes were bright and mischievous as ever. He carried the cool breeze in with him, and something else. Energy. The restless, crackling kind that kept him moving when other men his age had slowed to a shuffle.

Behind him came Gus, slower, steady, amusement tucked into the corners of his mouth like a card he hadn't decided to play yet.

"You stepped in," Gus repeated dryly, removing his hat and hanging it on the peg. "Is that what you call cornering half the women at the cider table and telling them how you used to run things?"

Zeke grinned, all teeth and no shame. "They asked."

"They didn't," Gus said.

"They were thinking it."

Buck appeared in the doorway last, hat tipped back, wild, white beard catching the morning light. He ducked under the frame out of habit, not necessity, and let the door close behind him with a quiet click that stood in sharp contrast to Zeke's entrance. Zeke and Buck shared a cabin, with Zeke's old dog, Sandy.

"You two sound like hens arguing over who laid the egg." Buck griped as he walked in.

Zeke pointed at him. "Careful, mountain man. Those ladies at the school adore me."

"They adore the dog," Buck corrected, his voice flat as a creek stone. "You're just attached to the leash."

At the mention of Sampson, Rosa came barreling into the room from the hallway, Edwin close behind. Her braid had already come loose again, and her socks slid on the wood floor as she rounded the corner of the table.

"Is he here?" she demanded.

Zeke crouched, arms open, knees popping loud enough that Clare winced. "He'll be by this afternoon. Sampson's got his own admirers to visit first."

Rosa pressed into his side without hesitation, her small fingers gripping the patched lapel of his coat. He steadied her with one gnarled hand against her back.

Edwin slid to a stop, breathless. "You going to the school again this week?"

Zeke straightened, brushing flour from his coat that had transferred from Rosa's sleeve. "Well, somebody's gotta keep the peace. Can't let those young folks forget who trained Sampson proper."

"I trained Sampson," Gus said mildly. He poured himself coffee and leaned against the counter beside Jo, his hip brushing hers.

"You supervised once in a while," Zeke countered. "There's a difference. A foreman don't lay the brick."

"You didn't lay any brick either. You sat on a stump and told the dog to sit."

"And he sat. That's called results."

Laughter rippled through the room. Grace covered her mouth with the back of her hand. Quinn's shoulders shook once at the sink, and the plate in his grip clinked against the basin. Hunter looked at the floor, jaw tight with the effort of keeping straight-faced. Even Gemma set her notes down, her eyes crinkled at the corners..

Jo watched the children's faces. Rosa leaned into Zeke's side without hesitation, her fingers still curled in his coat and eyes sparkling. Edwin, Jake, and Max hung on every word, chins lifted, eyes tracking the volleys between the two men like a spectator at a match he wanted desperately to join. Even Marisol, standing just behind them in the doorway to the hall, allowed the corner of her mouth to lift. A small concession. Hard-won from a girl who rationed her smiles the way Jo rationed sugar.

They were memorizing this. It was seeping into their memories for later recall.

Not the facts. Not who trained the dog or who stepped in at the Market, or whether any of it was true. The cadence. The volume. The way Gus's voice dropped when he was winning, and Zeke's rose when he wasn't. The rhythm of two men who'd known each other long enough to sharpen their words without drawing blood. The way Gus and Zeke circled each other like old roosters but never truly struck.

Ty stepped in from the porch, wiping his hands on his jeans. Grease darkened the creases of his knuckles and a smear of axle black ran across his forearm where he'd rolled his sleeve. He didn't live at the Lodge, but he came often enough that the door never needed knocking. He'd spent the night helping Boone and Owen repair a broken axle on one of the wagons, and the work still clung to him like a second skin.

"Morning," he said, nodding to the older men.

Zeke clapped him on the shoulder hard enough to rock him forward half a step. "You hear about the Market chaos last Tuesday?"

Ty's mouth twitched. "Heard it went smooth as ever."

"Because of me," Zeke said.

"Because of the Rules," Ty corrected, though his tone held affection. He reached past Ellie for the bread basket, tore off an end piece, and ate it standing, the way his mother, Zara, would have scolded him back when scolding was still the worst thing that could happen in a kitchen.

Zeke wagged a finger. "Rules don't enforce themselves, son. Takes a presence. A certain... gravity."

"Gravity," Buck repeated from the corner, flat as a barn door. "That's what we're calling it now?"

Zeke ignored him with the practiced ease of a man who'd been ignoring Buck's sass for the past year.

Rosa tugged Zeke's sleeve. "Did Sampson really chase a chicken through the Market?"

"That part's true," Gus admitted.

"It was a rooster," Zeke clarified. "And Sampson was provoked. He's a good boy."

Hunter leaned against the wall near the pantry door, arms folded across his chest, watching the exchange with the quiet attention he gave most things. His eyes moved from face to face the way they moved across a treeline. Not searching for threat, not here, but reading the terrain. He caught Quinn's eye across the room and tilted his chin subtly toward Gus, who had lowered himself into a chair at the head of the table with more care than he used to. The motion was slower now. Deliberate. One hand braced against the table edge, the other pressed flat on his thigh as he settled his weight. It wasn't pain, exactly. It was an economy of movement. The kind of movement a man learned when his body started charging interest on every debt he'd ever asked of it.

Quinn noticed.

He set the plate he'd been drying on the rack without looking and crossed the room. His prosthetic caught the light from the window as he reached for the kettle on the stove, lifting it before Gus's hand left the table.

"Stay," Quinn said. Not loud. Not soft. Just a word with weight behind it.

Gus looked up, jaw already set, the retort halfway formed. Quinn knew the look. Everybody did. The look that said I've been pouring my own coffee since before your father was born. But Gus paused. His eyes moved from Quinn's face to the prosthetic gripping the kettle handle, steady and sure, then back again. He studied what he found there. Not challenge. Not pity.

Readiness.

Gus sat.

Quinn poured the faux-coffee. Dark, no sugar, the way Gus had taken it for forty years. He set the mug down, turned, and walked back to the sink without ceremony.

Nobody spoke about it. Clare busied herself with the bread. Grace's knitting needles resumed their rhythm. Gemma bent over her notes. Hunter looked at the floor, then out the window, arms still folded, something quiet and satisfied in the set of his mouth.

Jo felt it then. The shift she'd been waiting for and dreading in equal measure. It lived in the space between Quinn's hand and the kettle. In Ty's grease-blackened knuckles and the way he didn't ask permission to eat. In Rowan's certainty at breakfast, and Hunter's steady presence at the door, and the way Gemma no longer waited for her father to confirm a diagnosis before she acted on it.

The young ones were not asking anymore.

They were stepping up.

Into doorways. Into silences. Into the gaps the older bodies left as they narrowed and slowed. They filled the spaces with their own hands, their own judgment, their own quiet authority. The way water fills a channel cut by seasons of rain. Not rushing. Not forcing. Just moving where the ground allowed.

Gus wrapped both hands around his mug and drank. His eyes found Jo's across the room.

She held his gaze. Held it long and steady, the way she'd held everything that mattered in this life. Then she reached down and rested her swollen fingers in Odin's fur, and let the kitchen carry on without her saying a word.

The screen door clapped shut behind Buck as he stepped onto the porch, boot heels heavy on the boards. His voice carried back through the open window into the kitchen, aimed at nobody in particular and everybody at once.

"If you ask me, those Harbinger kids are too quiet."

Zeke settled into the rocker beside him, the old wood groaning under even his spare frame. "Quiet's not a crime."

"Neither's loud," Buck shot back. "But loud lets you hear yourself think."

Rosa had followed them out, bare feet on the cold planks, one hand still clutching the last corner of her bread. She stopped at the railing and frowned up at Buck with the serious weight only a five-year-old could muster.

"What's wrong with quiet?"

Buck crouched to her level. His knees popped. His eyes, usually hard as creek stones, went soft in a way that would have embarrassed him if anyone had mentioned it.

"Nothing, little bit. Long as it's your quiet and not someone else's."

Rosa chewed her bread and considered this. Edwin stood just inside the doorway, leaning against the frame with his arms crossed in a posture he'd borrowed from Hunter without realizing it. He turned Buck's words over, gaze flicking from Buck to Zeke to Gus, who had come to stand behind Jo's chair with his mug in both hands.

"What did you tell them last time?" Edwin asked Zeke suddenly. "About how the Market used to be?"

Zeke puffed up slightly, the way a banty rooster lifts its chest feathers before a crow. "Just told 'em how things were organized before. Who handled what. Where the good stalls were. Told 'em all about what rules we had too." He waved a gnarled hand. "Folks like hearing history."

"History...ancient history, it seems like." Gus echoed.

There was a sudden uncomfortableness, a tension that was noticed by all.

Ty's jaw stopped working on his bread. His eyes sharpened, darting between the old men. Hunter shifted his weight against the pantry wall, arms still folded, but his shoulders had squared in a way that had nothing to do with comfort.

Marisol stood near the window, holding a mug of warm water between both palms. She looked at Zeke a moment too long. Her dark eyes held something that hadn't been there a month ago. A kind of measuring. A weighing of words against intention that no nine-year-old should have needed to learn.

Jo tapped her cane lightly against the floor. One tap. Not sharp, not angry. Just enough to pull the room toward her like a compass needle finding north.

"History's worth knowing," she said evenly. Her fingers rested on Odin's broad head. "But so is knowing when to keep your stories close."

Zeke opened his mouth. His lips parted around the shape of something clever, something that would have turned the moment sideways with a laugh and a slap on the knee. Then he looked at Jo. Looked at the way her chin was set. At the stillness in her freckled face and arched brow, that had nothing still about it underneath.

He closed his mouth again. For once, he didn't have a joke ready.

Silence settled over the room. Not heavy. Not the kind that pressed down on chests and stole breath. Just aware. The kind of silence that happens when a family realizes, all at the same moment, that they've been thinking the same thing and nobody wanted to be the first to name it.

Grace broke it. She slid a plate of biscuits onto the table with both hands, the edges golden and cracked from the oven's uneven heat.

"Eat before they're gone."

The room filled again with motion. Chairs scraped across the floor. Mugs clinked against the table. Rowan shoved Donovan's shoulder and argued about which fence posts needed replacing first, and Donovan shoved back and said all of them. Gemma tapped Hunter's arm and asked him to fetch a jar from the high shelf in the pantry, and he went without a word. Clare leaned into the hallway and called for Leah to bring in the laundry before the clouds rolling in from the west made good on their threat.

Life resumed its noisy, overlapping rhythm. Hands reaching. Voices tangling. The ordinary machinery of a household grinding forward through another morning.

But Edwin stayed in the doorway a beat longer than the rest. His fingers drummed against his arm once, twice, then stopped. He watched the trail that led south from the Lodge, past the barn and the watchtower and down through the birch stand, toward the road that eventually, if you followed it far enough, wound its way to Little Bear Lake.

Jo stood at the head of the table and watched.

The kitchen had filled the way it always did after a meal that should have ended twenty minutes ago but hadn't, because nobody wanted to be the first to leave. Plates pushed aside, mugs refilled, elbows planted on the smooth table like claims staked in good earth. Odin had settled beneath her chair, his broad side warm against her ankle, his breathing slow and even.

Gus leaned back, one hand resting over the other on the table's worn wood. His white, close-cropped beard caught the light from the window, and the lines around his eyes deepened as Zeke launched into another story about the summer he and Gus had tried to dam the creek behind the Thompson place with nothing but fieldstone and sheer pigheadedness. Zeke gestured broadly, his gnarled fingers cutting shapes in the air like he was conducting an orchestra only he could hear. Buck shook his head from his seat by the stove but listened anyway, one boot crossed over the other, his coffee balanced on his knee.

The young adults moved around them. Not replacing. Supporting.

Grace cleared plates without interrupting the flow of conversation, stacking them in the crook of her arm with a quiet efficiency that had become second nature. Gemma leaned against the counter beside Hunter, her medical notes tucked under one arm, murmuring something about the Jenkins boy's follow-up that made Hunter nod and reach for his jacket. Donovan passed behind Gus's chair and dropped a hand on the old man's shoulder as he went, brief as a heartbeat, barely noticed by anyone except Jo.

Quinn took the kettle off the stove before it screamed. Poured hot water into Gus's mug again without asking. Set the kettle back and returned to the sink, his prosthetic hand gripping the iron handle with a steadiness that would have been unthinkable a mere six weeks ago. He didn't look up. Didn't need to.

Rowan appeared in the back doorway, mud on her boots and a fence post tally scratched on a scrap of paper. She handed it to Gus without waiting to be called on.

"South line needs four replacements before asap. I marked which ones."

Gus glanced at the paper, then at her. Nodded once.

Ty sat at the far end of the table, his plate clean, his hands wrapped around a mug of chicory that Clare had pressed on him. He had his own roof to sleep under. His own people at the school, but he came often. Every time Boone or Owen, or any of them, needed an/ extra set of hands in the shop, every time Gunny or Gus sent word, Ty showed up at the Lodge door before first light with grease already under his fingernails and no explanation offered.

Hunter stood near the pantry, arms folded, watching the older men the way a man watches a river he means to cross. Measuring. Not the men themselves but the distance between what they had been and what they were becoming. Between the strength that built this place and the strength that would be asked to hold it.

The children hovered close. Edwin still in the doorway. Merryn with crumbs on her chin and her eyes were wide and bright. Fiona at the window, her mug held in both hands, absorbing everything. Jake, Ian, and Max had wedged themselves onto the bench beside Zeke, mouths open, waiting for the part of the story where something caught fire or blew up.

Jo felt pride rise in her throat, sharp and steady as woodsmoke. It pressed against the backs of her eyes and sat in her chest like a coal that had been banked all morning and only now found air.

And beneath it, just barely, an edge of something else.

Her knuckles ached around the head of her cane. The kitchen was bright and loud and full, and every face in it was a face she loved, and the morning was ordinary, and ordinary was the thing she had fought hardest to give them.

Time did not ask permission.

It moved.

And someone would have to move with it.

Chapter Thirteen

What is Given Away

Edwin liked Market days because they made him feel older than he was.

Not because of the buying or selling. That part was fine, but it was adult fine, slow and careful and full of rules. Market days meant movement. Wagons creaking into place. People arriving with purpose. Conversations that didn't stop when he walked up. It was like he imagined a carnival would be.

He rode beside Gin this time, perched on the edge of the wagon seat, boots hooked on the rail. The horse snorted steam into the cold pre-dawn air, and the road stretched ahead in familiar bends. Edwin held his hands together so he wouldn't fidget.

Behind them, Fiona and Leah sat huddled together, voices low and quick, picking apart which classes they'd sit in on today. Fiona wanted the drawing hour Mary ran out of the art room. Leah wanted the plant medicine session Gemma had started two weeks back. They debated without heat, their breath rising in thin ribbons that dissolved against the gray sky. The children from the lodge and the school traveled between the two, now that spring had come, for classes and for extra labor as needed.

Marisol sat with her arms folded, Rosa leaning against her shoulder. Rosa hummed softly, a tune Edwin recognized now without thinking. He didn't know where she'd learned it. He only knew it showed up on Market days.

Gin didn't comment.

The wagon wheels found a rut and jolted them sideways. Edwin caught himself on the seat rail. Gin didn't flinch, just adjusted her grip on the reins and let the horse correct. Her rifle lay across her lap, barrel pointed left, stock braced against her thigh. She wore it the way other people wore shoes or pants. Like forgetting it would be the strange thing.

When they pulled through the school gates, Gin looped the reins and climbed down. She helped Rosa off the back, set her on the ground, and watched all five of them scatter toward the chalkboard and the first vendor tables before she turned toward her fence.

She leaned into it, one boot up on the lower rail, and let her gaze travel the perimeter. The south gate was manned. The supply sheds were locked. Three families had already set up near the old dugout, their tables heavy with root vegetables and bundles of dried herbs tied with kitchen string.

She had no idea how this had become her job. Post-apocalyptic babysitter. She shook her head at the way life unfolds. A few years ago, this would have been torture. Forced proximity to sticky fingers and runny noses, and the kind of questions that didn't have answers. Now she looked forward to it. Something about their noise felt like proof that the world still had a pulse and she still had a heart.

She wouldn't have admitted that out loud for all the ammunition left on the eastern seaboard.

Edwin appeared at her elbow. He had a way of materializing, that kid. Like a cat who'd heard a can opener three rooms away.

"You know what Zeke says?" Edwin said, because silence felt like a missed opportunity.

Gin glanced at him. "What does Zeke say?"

Edwin smiled. He liked it when people asked him questions. "He says the Market only works if everyone knows who's good at what. Otherwise, it's just noise."

"Hm," Gin said, noncommittal.

"He used to run it. Before." Edwin puffed up a little. "Everybody listens to him."

"Everybody listens to Zeke because Zeke doesn't stop talking until they do."

Edwin considered this. His brow furrowed, and for a moment, he looked every bit of his eleven years, caught between wanting to defend Zeke and suspecting Gin had a point.

"He knows a lot, though."

"That he does."

"About people. About what they need."

Gin looked down at him. The boy's face was open and serious, his dark eyes scanning the Market grounds the way she scanned a fence line. Looking for gaps. Looking for patterns.

"Yeah," she said, quieter. "He does know that."

Behind them, Rosa's humming floated up from somewhere near the chalkboard, that same melody threading through the morning noise. Marisol's fingers tightened slightly in Rosa's sleeve.

The schoolyard was already alive with noise. Children streamed in from every direction, dropping out of wagon beds, sprinting from nearby houses with chores left half-done, eyes pulling toward the other kids, toward the new soup stand trading bowls for bullets, and toward whatever the market might offer up today.

The Harbinger children were there... again.

They didn't rush forward. They never did. They waited near the tree line, baskets set neatly at their feet. When Edwin caught their eye, one of the boys nodded, like they'd been expecting him.

"Hey," Edwin said, jogging over. "Market day."

"Yes," the boy replied. "We heard."

That felt nice. Being heard.

They shared food the way they always did, quietly, carefully. Bread passed hand to hand. Apples cut cleanly. Rosa was there too, sitting on the ground with Merryn and Elin, arranging three small dolls between them. Merryn laid out squares of cloth for doll blankets. Elin whispered something that made Rosa giggle, a rare sound that turned heads.

"She's not supposed to get honey today," Marisol said softly, intercepting a stick before it reached Rosa.

The Harbinger girl inclined her head. "Of course."

No argument. No disappointment.

Edwin watched that, then shrugged it off. He had other things to say.

"Zeke trained Sampson," he told the group, apropos of nothing. "The dog. He says you can't train a dog unless you let him think it was his idea."

"That makes sense," one of the Harbinger girls said. "People are like that, too."

Edwin laughed. "Yeah. Zeke says that all the time."

"What else does Zeke say?" the River asked, voice mild.

Edwin leaned back on his hands, warming to the attention. "He says if you want to know how things really work, you watch who people go to when something breaks. Not who's loudest. Who they trust."

"That's wise," Wren said, tucking her dark braid back over her shoulder. She said it the way she said everything. Level. Measured. Like she was filing it away in a drawer she'd open later when she needed it. Edwin didn't notice that part. He noticed the way she looked right at him when she spoke, and how that made him feel like his words carried weight.

"Zeke built a whole farm," Edwin continued, pulling one knee up. "Him and Emma. Before the blackout, before any of this. He says the land tells you what it wants to grow if you shut up long enough to listen."

The older boy, the one they called River, tilted his head. "Does he grow food for your family?"

"For everybody. He runs a table at the Market sometimes. Potatoes, squash, whatever's in season." Edwin paused. "He gave us seed potatoes for the Lodge's first spring. Didn't ask for anything back."

River's expression didn't change, but his eyes moved, just slightly, toward the girl beside him. She gave the smallest nod. Edwin missed it entirely. He was watching Rosa and Merryn stack their dolls into a tiny tower that kept toppling sideways.

"Your family sounds strong," River said.

"They are." Edwin picked at a blade of grass. "Gus and Jo built the Lodge years ago. They are awesome. Marcus, Franklin, Cole, and Gunny handle security. Gemma and Tobias are our doctors, kind of. Everybody does something."

"Everyone has a role," the girl echoed. "That's how it should be."

Marisol, sitting three feet away, looked up from the apple slice in her hand. She chewed slowly, watching Wren's face. Something in the phrasing snagged her, a thread she couldn't name. Not wrong, exactly. Just too smooth. Like a stone worn down by a river until all its edges were gone.

She didn't say anything.

"What about you?" Edwin asked River. "What's your role?"

River smiled. It was a careful smile, the kind that showed teeth but started behind the eyes. "I listen," he said. "I learn what people need."

"Like Zeke."

"Something like that."

Rosa squealed as the doll tower finally held, three figures balanced on top of each other, leaning but standing. Elin clapped her hands, and the sound scattered a pair of sparrows from the low branches overhead. Merryn giggled as the tower tipped precariously.

Gin, forty yards away at the south gate, heard the squeal and looked over. She found Edwin cross-legged on the ground, surrounded. Talking with his hands. Giving away stories like they were free.

She shifted the rifle on her hip and resumed her watch.

Marisol looked up sharply.

Something had shifted in the way River repeated the word *role*, the way the girl beside him leaned forward half an inch. Marisol couldn't have explained it if someone asked. It was the feeling she got when Odin acted before Gran passed out, or the way Fegus hid before anybody else heard thunder. A feeling in her chest, tight and wordless.

But Edwin was already talking again.

"Zeke's kind of like the mayor," Edwin added, because that sounded impressive. "At least at the school. All the ladies like him. He's funny."

"Important," River said, tasting the word. He rolled it slowly, like he was turning a coin between his fingers, checking both sides before deciding whether to spend it.

Edwin nodded eagerly. "Yeah. Important. Almost as important as Gran or Pop."

The Harbinger children exchanged glances so brief Edwin barely registered them. Wren's hand moved to her knee. Thorn's chin dipped a fraction. The younger boy, River, beside them went still the way a rabbit goes still when a hawk's shadow crosses the grass. Then it passed, and they were just kids again, sitting on the cold ground with apple cores and bread crusts between them.

"So he helps keep things steady," Wren said. Her voice carried the same polished quality Marisol had noticed before. Not warm, exactly. Not cold either. Just smooth. Too smooth for a girl who couldn't have been older than twelve or thirteen.

"I guess," Edwin replied. "If people listen."

He said it offhandedly, already glancing back toward the Market tables where vendors hollered prices and a man with a gray ponytail argued over the weight of a smoked ham hock. Edwin liked the noise, the life of Market days. He liked being part of something that mattered. And he liked that these kids seemed to think he mattered, too.

Marisol set her apple slice down on her knee. She wasn't hungry anymore.

Nearby, Rita waved Zeke over, her hands full of ledgers and a look on her face that meant she'd already decided he was the solution to her problem.

"Zeke!" she called. "Can I steal you for a minute?"

He came willingly, as he always did, hat tipped back, grin ready. "For you Miss Rita? Always."

Rita thrust a ledger at his chest and pointed toward the row of vendor tables. Zeke caught it one-handed without looking, already nodding at whatever she was saying. He had that way about him, the kind of ease that made people hand him their burdens without thinking twice.

Zara joined them, her stride purposeful, arms folded. Then Jillian, another baby on her hip, brow furrowed in concentration over something she was working through in her head. Jillian was forever comforting a baby or two. Margaret drifted closer from the direction of the gate, adding her weight to the small knot of women gathered around the wiry old farmer like iron filings drawn to a magnet.

Edwin watched with pride. *See?* He wanted to say. *That's what I mean.*

He turned back to River and Wren, and the expression on his face was open, unguarded. Bright as a window with the curtain pulled back.

"That's Zeke," he said, pointing. "Right there."

River followed the line of Edwin's finger. His gaze settled on the old man and didn't waver. He watched the way Zeke held the ledger. The way Rita leaned in. The way Margaret angled her body, rifle slung casually across her back, positioned between Zeke and the open gate without seeming to think about it.

"He looks like someone people count on," River said quietly.

"Everybody counts on Zeke," Edwin confirmed.

Marisol pulled her knees to her chest. She watched River watching Zeke, and the tight feeling in her chest wound another turn. She opened her mouth, then closed it. Rosa laughed beside her, still playing with Merryn, still stacking dolls.

Gin's hand settled on the stock of her rifle across the yard. She hadn't moved from the gate, but her weight had shifted forward onto the balls of her feet.

From the edge of the group, Buck stood with his arms crossed, his weight settled back on his heels like a man watching weather roll in. He didn't speak. Didn't need to. His eyes tracked the conversation the way they tracked game in the brush, patient and unhurried, cataloging the small movements others missed. The tilt of River's head. The way Wren's fingers had gone still against her knee.

Ty came from the wagon area, hauling a crate of tallow candles Boone had sent for trade. He paused mid-step between the soap vendor and the wool table, the crate balanced against his hip. His eyes narrowed, just slightly, as he watched Edwin gesture toward Zeke. Something about the Harbinger boy's posture didn't sit right. The kid was listening the way Ty listened when his mother briefed the Stewards. Not like a child. Like someone taking notes.

Hunter's gaze flicked from Zeke to the Harbinger children and back again, his jaw setting. He stood near the south gate with one boot propped on a fence post, close enough to hear the laughter but far enough to see the whole field. His hand didn't move to his sidearm. It didn't have to. The readiness lived in his shoulders, in the line of his back. Three sets of adult eyes, trained on the same cluster of children, and not one of them spoke a word.

No one said anything.

The Market bell rang once, an hour later, a minor dispute between two women over a bag of salt was already resolved by the time Rita crossed the yard. Trades wound down. Vendors folded canvas over their tables.

Edwin stood near the chalkboard, helping Rosa gather her things, when he heard it.

A Harbinger boy, one of the younger ones whose name he hadn't caught, said to another child, "You watch who people go to when something breaks."

It was said casually. Easily. The way you'd repeat a line from a song you'd heard and liked.

It was said exactly the way Edwin had said it. His words. His cadence. Pulled from a conversation he'd had with River not two hours ago about why Zeke mattered, about how you could tell who held a place together by watching who people turned to when things went wrong.

Edwin's smile faltered. Just a little. He wasn't sure why.

Rosa's laughter cut through the moment, high and sharp as a bird call. She'd knocked one of the dolls over during a game with Merryn, and Merryn was protesting loudly, her small face crumpled with injustice. Rosa scooped the doll up, brushed dirt from its cloth dress, pressed it back into Merryn's hands with all the earnest apology a five-year-old could muster. Wide eyes. Gentle hands.

"You okay?" Edwin asked her.

Rosa nodded, her cheeks pink from the cold. "I don't want to leave yet."

Marisol stiffened beside him, her fingers curling around the hem of her jacket.

"We're not leaving yet," Edwin said quickly, because that felt like the right answer. Because Rosa's angry red face needed it to be the right answer.

The wagon ride home was quiet. The wheels found every rut in the road, and the sound filled the spaces where conversation should have been. Gin held the reins loosely, her rifle across her lap, her eyes on the tree line, as usual.

"Who were you talking to today?" she asked. Her voice carried no accusation. Just the question, clean and direct.

Edwin shrugged, suddenly unsure why the answer felt heavier than it should. "Just kids."

"And what did you tell them?"

He thought about that. About Zeke. About important people. About how good it had felt to be listened to, really listened to, by someone his own age who didn't interrupt or tease or look away.

"Just stories," he said.

Gin didn't reply right away. The wagon creaked. A crow lifted from a pine and banked west.

Behind them, Rosa had fallen asleep against Mary's shoulder, her face smooth and peaceful. Merryn curled up, snoring lightly in Clare's lap. Rosa's fingers twitched in her sleep, reaching, curling around empty air, searching for a small hand that wasn't there.

Marisol stared out at the road. Her heart hammered against her ribs, and she couldn't have said why. She only knew the feeling, the same one from before. Tight. Wordless. Like standing at the edge of something you couldn't see the bottom of and didn't understand.

Somewhere between the school and the Lodge, Edwin understood, dimly, the way you understand a bruise before it colors, that stories didn't always stay where you put them.

And once spoken, they didn't belong to you anymore.

Chapter Fourteen

When Someone Is Needed

The decision didn't arrive with ceremony.

It settled into place over cooling mugs and half-finished sentences, the way most necessary things did now. The kitchen smelled of chicory and woodsmoke, and the last of the morning light came through the window in pale, watery bars that didn't quite reach the table.

"We can't keep doing it like this," Rita said, fingers tapping once against her ledger. The leather cover was scarred from use, the pages inside a mess of tallies and guard rotations she'd rewritten three times this week. "Too many kids underfoot. Too many moving pieces."

"Not exactly unsafe," Zara added, carefully. She sat with one hand wrapped around a mug she hadn't drunk from. "Just... harder to manage."

Gin stood at the counter, arms crossed. She hadn't sat down. She hadn't needed to. Her jaw worked once, the way it did when she was sorting through what to say and what to hold back.

"Harder turns unsafe when people stop paying attention," she said. "And they already are."

The words landed like a stone dropped into still water. No one rushed to fill the silence that followed.

Gunny leaned back in his chair, the wood groaning under him. He rubbed one hand across his face and looked at Marcus, who sat with his arms on the table, fingers laced. Marcus's expression gave nothing away. It rarely did. But his thumbs pressed together, white at the nail.

Franklin glanced across the table at Cole. The brothers had a silent conversation, causing both to nod before looking back to Gunny and Marcus.

Jo lifted her eyes from her tea and cleared her throat. The room stilled. Not because Jo demanded it, but because she rarely interrupted. When she spoke during meetings like this, the words had weight behind them, earned through months of watching and listening while others talked themselves in circles.

"How tight?" she asked.

Gin didn't hesitate. She'd been turning this over since the ride home two days ago. Since Edwin's words had come back to her from a stranger's mouth.

"Younger kids, let's say eight and under, stay back unless there's a reason. No lingering after chores. School kids head home. Lodge kids ride out when business is done. I also think we should limit it to maybe three or four kids at a time, no matter what the age. Obviously, the young adults here are not included in the word 'kids'. "

Marcus frowned. "That's going to be noticed."

"Yes," Gin said. "That's the point."

Rita set her pencil down and looked at Zara. Something passed between them, quick and practiced. They'd had this conversation already, or one close enough to it.

"We're not shutting anything down," Zara said. "The Market works. People need it."

"Nobody said shut it down." Gin uncrossed her arms and placed both palms flat on the counter behind her. "I said tighten it. There's a difference."

"The kids won't understand the difference," Gunny said. His voice was low, almost gentle, which meant he was taking it seriously. "Edwin's going to ask why. Rosa's going to cry."

"Then we answer Edwin, and we let Rosa cry." Jo's thumb traced the rim of her mug. "Children don't need to understand every decision we make. They need to trust that we made it for the right reasons."

Gus had been quiet the whole time. He stood near the doorway with one shoulder against the frame, his big arms folded across his chest. He watched his wife's face the way he always did when the room got heavy, reading something the rest of them couldn't see.

"Gin," he said.

She looked at him.

"You're not just talking about the Market."

It wasn't a question.

Gin held his gaze for a beat. Two. Then she shook her head, just once.

"No, sir. I'm not."

The fire popped. Odin shifted at Jo's feet, his heavy head settling onto his paws with a sigh that filled the room like punctuation.

Rita picked up her pencil again and opened the ledger to a clean page.

"All right," she said. "Let's write it down."

Rosa had her boots on before Gin finished buckling the wagon traces.

She stood by the Lodge door, mittens clutched in both hands, eyes shining with that particular brightness that only Market day produced. Her braid was already done, a little crooked where she'd attempted it herself, and she'd tucked a sprig of dried lavender behind one ear. Something Elin had shown her, last time.

Gin saw her through the open barn doors and felt the weight of what was coming settle across her shoulders like a yoke.

Edwin was already in the wagon bed, arranging the trade crates with a focus that made him look older than his years. Marisol sat on the bench seat, quiet, watching the tree line the way she'd started doing lately. Neither of them had argued when Gin told them the new rules that morning. Edwin had gone still for a moment, processing. Marisol had simply nodded, as though she'd been expecting it.

Rosa hadn't been told yet.

Gin cinched the last trace and ran her hand along the horse's flank, steadying herself as much as the animal. Then she crossed the yard, boot heels crunching on frost-hardened ground, and knelt in front of the girl.

Rosa beamed up at her.

"Not today, little one," Gin said. Gentle as she could manage.

Rosa blinked. The lavender shifted behind her ear. "But...Why?"

"You're staying here. With Rowan."

Rosa's face tightened. The brightness didn't fade so much as fracture, confusion flashing fast into something closer to panic. Her fingers squeezed the mittens until her knuckles went pale inside them.

"I want to go."

"I know."

"I didn't do anything." Rosa's voice cracked down the center like green wood. "I was good."

Gin's chest ached. Her heart actually hurt. A deep, structural thing, the kind that didn't show on the surface. She kept her hands steady on Rosa's arms.

"This isn't about that. You were perfect. Every single time."

Rosa's chin buckled. Her lips pressed together hard, fighting it, and for one breath, Gin thought she might hold. Then the dam broke.

The scream ripped through the Lodge. Raw, startled, nothing held back. It punched through the walls and scattered the birds from the porch eaves. Rosa dropped to the floor, boots kicking against the planks, fists pounding, breath hitching in great shuddering gulps hard enough to scare even herself.

Rowan appeared in the hallway. Stopped. Her hand found the doorframe.

Gin gathered Rosa up, pulling the small thrashing body against her chest and locking both arms around her. Rosa fought. Elbowed. Kicked one boot into Gin's shin hard enough to bruise. Gin absorbed it all without flinching, chin tucked against the top of Rosa's head, holding through the storm the way a breakwater holds through a surge. She held her and made soft comforting sounds, tears welling in her own eyes.

Then it passed.

Rosa collapsed against her, sobbing so violently her whole body shook. The mittens lay on the floor where she'd flung them. The lavender sprig had fallen, crushed under someone's knee.

"I want to go," she gasped between sobs. "I want to go."

Gin didn't let go. She pressed her mouth against Rosa's hair and breathed words of understanding and comfort.

When the wagon finally rolled out twenty minutes later, Rosa was asleep in Rowan's lap on the great room couch, tear tracks still drying on blotched cheeks. One small fist clutched a fold of Rowan's shirt. Rowan stroked her hair with slow, careful passes, jaw set tight enough to etch glass.

"This isn't fair," Rowan muttered. Not to anyone. To the room. To the silence that Rosa's screaming had left behind.

Gin heard it through the open window as she climbed onto the wagon bench.

She picked up the reins. Looked straight ahead at the road winding south through bare maples.

She didn't disagree.

At the school, the absence arrived before the wagons did.

The morning had that flat, colorless quality that came with overcast skies and no wind. Heavy dew still clung to the grass in the shaded spots along the fence line, and the vendors were slow setting up their tables. The gates hadn't opened yet, but the children were already out, the way they always were on Market day, drawn to the yard by habit and hunger and something less definable.

Elin sat near the edge of the yard, two dolls laid out carefully in front of her on a square of folded cloth. One wore a scrap dress made from a feed sack. The other had a pine-needle skirt held together with thread so fine it was nearly invisible. Rosa had helped tie that thread last week, her small fingers surprisingly steady for the work.

Elin looked up every time footsteps crunched on gravel.

The first wagon through the gate carried the Pratt family and their jars of rendered tallow. Elin's gaze tracked it, found no one she recognized, and dropped back to the dolls. The second wagon brought firewood and a man with a banjo strapped across his back. The third carried Gin, Ellie, Edwin, and Marisol.

No Rosa.

Elin watched them climb down. Watched Edwin pull a crate from the bed and hand it to someone. Watched Marisol drift toward the chalkboard without her usual companion beside her.

Meg was crossing the yard with a stack of bowls when Elin caught her sleeve.

"Is Rosa coming?"

Meg stopped. She looked down at the girl's face, at the careful arrangement of dolls, at the empty space on the cloth where a third child should have been sitting.

"Not today."

Elin nodded. Slow, the way children do when they accept words without understanding them. She folded her hands in her lap and turned back toward the gate.

She waited.

The dolls stayed where they were.

Minutes passed. The Market sounds built around her. Tables filled. Voices carried. Someone laughed near the soup stand, and the banjo man plucked a few experimental notes that nobody paid attention to. Children ran past Elin in clusters, calling to each other, drawn into the current of the day.

Elin stayed on her cloth square. She smoothed the pine-needle skirt on the smaller doll. Straightened its arms. Laid it beside the other one so they were shoulder to shoulder, faces pointed toward the gate.

A Harbinger girl noticed.

She stood ten feet away, half hidden by the corner of the tool shed, her dark braids hanging past her shoulders. Wren. She held a cloth bundle against her chest the way she always did, contents unknown, edges folded neat. Her eyes moved from Elin to the dolls to the empty cloth to the gate and back again.

She said nothing.

She watched the way Elin's fingers kept returning to the smaller doll. Watched the girl's chin lift each time gravel shifted near the entrance. Watched the hope hold its shape despite having no reason to.

Then Wren turned and walked back toward the other Harbinger children gathered near the chalkboard. She leaned close to River. Spoke a single sentence, barely loud enough to move the air between them.

River glanced toward Elin. His expression didn't change. He looked at the dolls, at the empty space, at Marisol standing alone by the board with her arms crossed tight against her ribs.

He looked at Edwin, who was laughing about something with a vendor but kept glancing over his shoulder toward the spot where Rosa usually sat.

River tucked that observation away like a coin into a pocket.

Zeke arrived midmorning, as he always did, hat tipped back, grin ready. The hat was an old brown felt thing, stained dark along the band from years of sweat and rain, and he wore it like a man who'd forgotten it was there.

"Well now," he boomed, surveying the yard. "Where'd everybody hide the kids?"

Rita smiled without looking up from the ledger spread across her table near the gate. "Keeping them closer today. New plan."

"Plans," Zeke said, waving it off with a gnarled hand. "Always loved plans. Had one once for a root cellar that was gonna change my whole operation. Dug three feet and hit a boulder the size of Emma's cookstove."

Rita's pen kept moving. "And?"

"Built around it. Called it a feature." He winked at no one in particular and moved into the yard, his boots scuffing the packed dirt with their familiar loose shuffle.

He lingered anyway, scanning the tables, the flow of people between them. Things were running smoother than usual. Quieter. The fence posts held firm, the Stewards stood at their positions without fidgeting, and the vendor rows had a kind of order to them that hadn't been there three weeks ago. He could see the hand of the younger ones in it. Ty's logic. Jenny's spine.

"Need me anywhere?" he asked Zara as she passed with a clipboard tucked under her arm.

She shook her head. "We're good."

Jillian came through a moment later, a baby fussing against her shoulder, one hand patting its back while the other clutched a list. She thanked him absently for holding the gate wider. Margaret nodded from the far table, already deep in conversation with a man Zeke didn't recognize, her hands moving in that clipped, military way she had when she meant business.

Zeke stood there a beat longer than he meant to. The yard hummed around him. Nobody needed a hand. Nobody called his name or waved him over to settle a question about seed stock or well depth or which way to hang a smokehouse door.

"Well," he said lightly, forcing a laugh that landed on nothing. "Guess I'll try not to get in the way."

He drifted toward the west fence where Buck leaned against a post, whittling a piece of basswood into something that might have been a spoon. They had ridden to the school together that morning. Buck liked to join Zeke from time to time when the mood struck him.

Buck caught his eye from across the yard, brow creasing. The knife paused.

"You alright?" Buck called.

Zeke lifted a thumb. "Never better."

Buck studied him a half second longer, then went back to the wood.

But as the morning wore on, a prickle settled between Zeke's shoulders. Not fear. Awareness. The way you sometimes felt when a trail went quiet all at once, the birdsong cut out, and the air just held still, like the woods were deciding something.

A Harbinger boy watched him. Not openly, not rudely. Just steadily. The boy stood near the chalkboard with his arms loose at his sides. River. He held a piece of chalk in one hand but hadn't written anything. His face carried no particular expression, but his eyes tracked Zeke the way a dog tracks a rabbit through tall grass, patient and calibrated and utterly still.

Zeke slowed. He pretended to inspect a jar of honey on the nearest table, turning it in his fingers, holding it up to the flat light.

Buck came up beside him. His hand landed on a table post, casual as anything, and he leaned his weight into it.

"You feel that?" Zeke murmured, barely moving his lips.

Buck's gaze flicked once toward the chalkboard. Sharp. Quick enough that no one watching would have caught it. His jaw tightened a fraction beneath his white beard.

"I do."

Zeke set the honey jar down. He straightened his hat, tugged the brim low.

"Huh."

Rita waved from near the schoolhouse. "Zeke, can I grab you a minute? I need your eye on something."

"Sure thing," Zeke said automatically, a huge grin spreading across his face. He clapped Buck once on the shoulder and turned, already hitching up his belt and falling into step beside her. "What're we looking at? If it's plumbing, I'll warn you now, Emma says I'm banned from pipes after the incident of '09."

Rita snorted. "Smokehouse rack. One of the crossbars split under the weight of the last batch. Harlan jury-rigged it, but I don't trust it to hold through a full cure."

"Well, there's your problem right there. Harlan's a good man, but, unless it is a motorized vehicle, he thinks everything can be fixed with baling wire and optimism."

They rounded the corner of the schoolhouse, voices from the Market fading behind the brick. The smokehouse sat thirty yards out, squat and dark, its tin chimney cold. Rita pulled the door open, and the smell of old hickory rolled out, sweet and sharp.

Zeke ducked inside. He ran his hand along the split crossbar, fingers reading the grain the way a blind man reads a face. He clicked his tongue.

"Green wood. That's the whole issue. Whoever cut this didn't season it proper. You need something hard and dry. Oak or sugar maple, cured at least six months."

"Can you fix it?"

"Fix it?" He looked offended. "I can replace it. I have just the thing in my toolbag in the wagon. Piece of maple I've been hanging onto. Give me ten minutes."

He stepped back into the daylight, squinting, and headed toward the line of wagons parked along the east fence.

Halfway there, something tugged at him. A sense, sudden and cold, that he should stop. Turn around. Say something different. It sat in his chest like a swallowed stone, heavy and wrong.

He didn't.

He kept walking, boots scuffing the same loose shuffle, hat tipped the same way, and the yard swallowed him whole.

Rita appeared at Gin's post near the south gate a quarter hour later, scanning the crowd.

"You seen Zeke? He was supposed to come back with a piece of maple for the smokehouse rack."

Gin shifted her rifle to the other shoulder. "He followed you out to the smokehouse, didn't he?"

"He did. Said he had just the thing in his toolbag in the wagon. Left and didn't come back." Rita frowned. "I figured he got to chatting with someone and forgot."

Gin looked toward the wagons. Zeke's rig sat where it had been parked that morning, Flora, Buck's mule, dozing in her traces.

"I'll keep an eye out," Gin said.

By noon, no one had seen him.

Gin asked twice more. Buck asked three times. Ty and Jenny checked the wagons, the barn, and the latrine behind the school. Margaret walked the full perimeter of the fence and came back shaking her head.

By the time the bell rang to close the Market, Buck was scanning the yard, unease tightening his jaw. He stood near the gate with his hands at his sides and his whittling knife forgotten in his pocket.

"Zeke?" he called.

No answer. Just the scrape of tables being folded and the murmur of traders loading their goods.

People shrugged it off at first. Zeke talked. Zeke wandered. Zeke always turned up with a story about where he'd been and a grin that made you forget you'd worried.

But as wagons rolled out and shadows stretched long across the field, Buck stood beside Gin and said quietly, "This ain't right."

Gin's hand rested on the stock of her rifle. Her eyes moved across the empty yard, the trampled grass, the chalkboard where River had stood that morning with his piece of chalk and his patient, measuring stare.

"No," she said. "It ain't. I hate to just go, but we have to get these kids home."

She sat at the table long after the lamps were lit, replaying the day again and again. The honey jar. Buck's warning. River's eyes. Rita's wave. Zeke's grin as he walked away, easy as breathing.

She searched for the moment she could have chosen differently. The second where she might have called out, crossed the yard, put herself between Zeke and whatever pulled him past the edge of the fence and into the silence beyond it.

Somewhere between tightening the rules and letting the wrong man walk away alone, a line had been crossed.

And Zeke was gone.

Chapter Fifteen

What Has a Name

Marcus knew something was wrong before anyone said Zeke's name.

It was the way Gus sat at the table, too still, both hands wrapped around a mug he hadn't touched. He stared at the steam as if it might explain something if he watched long enough.

"He probably stayed over," Judith said, breaking the quiet. "Zeke's done that before."

"Yes," Mary agreed. "Plenty of times. Especially if he gets talking."

Someone chuckled softly, but it didn't land.

Gus's jaw worked. "He doesn't stay over without telling me."

The room stilled.

Jo moved to his side without comment, resting a hand on his shoulder. Gus didn't lean into it. Didn't pull away either. His eyes stayed fixed on the table, red-rimmed and furious in a way Marcus had only seen once before, after their parents died.

"He'd have come back," Gus went on, voice rough. "Or he'd have sent word."

Buck stood near the door, already half-ready, coat in his hand. "Man doesn't just wander off mid-task," he said. "Not Zeke."

Jo squeezed Gus's shoulder, firm. "We don't know that yet."

Gus finally looked up. "I do."

Marcus pulled a chair out and sat across from his brother. He kept his voice level, the way he'd kept it in a hundred briefings where the news was bad, and the margin for error was gone. "Walk me through it."

Gin stood against the kitchen doorframe, arms crossed, her face stripped of everything but hard facts. "Rita asked him to look at a busted smokehouse rack. He went inside, checked the rack, and said he had something in his wagon to replace it. Left. Never came back."

"His rig?"

"Still parked. Flora still in her traces."

Marcus let that settle. A man leaves his tools and his animal. Doesn't come back. Doesn't send word. That wasn't forgetfulness. That wasn't wandering.

"How long between when he left the smokehouse and when Rita noticed?"

"Fifteen minutes. Maybe twenty."

Franklin leaned against the counter, thick arms folded. "That's enough time. Somebody waiting, somebody who knew where he'd be walking alone."

"Or somebody who made sure he'd be walking alone," Gin said.

The words dropped into the room like a stone into still water. Nobody spoke for a long moment. Owen shifted his weight by the window. Judith pulled Luke tighter against her hip. Mary's hand found Franklin's arm. Boone and Tobias glanced at each other.

Gus set the mug down. Careful. Deliberate. The ceramic barely clicked against the wood, but Marcus watched his brother's knuckles go white around it before he let go.

"I want to ride out tonight."

"No." Marcus held his gaze. "Not in the dark. Not angry. Not without a plan."

"He's been my friend for over thirty years, Marcus."

"Which is exactly why you don't go stumbling down a trail at midnight where someone may be waiting for the next fool to walk out alone."

The silence between them had teeth. Gus's chest rose and fell. Jo's hand stayed on his shoulder, steady as a root. Her touch was the only thing that kept him in his seat.

Gunny sat forward then. He had followed the wagons up on horseback.

"We give him twenty-four hours," Gunny said, calm as ever, arms folded across his chest. "Zeke's capable. He's known to disappear into conversation. If he's not back by tomorrow morning, then we move."

Gus pushed back from the table. "Move where?"

"Carefully." Gunny's voice didn't waver. "With eyes open. I can have a couple of the Marines from the Inn ask around in the morning. Quietly. No noise."

The argument didn't sound like an argument.

It sounded like people circling the same truth and refusing to touch it.

"That's not enough." Gus's palm hit the table, rattling the mugs. Not a slam. Worse. Controlled. Like a man holding back the full force of what he wanted to do.

Buck stepped forward instantly, coat already half on. "Then we don't wait. We take the trails. I know where he'd go. Every shortcut, every deer path. If he's hurt, if he's lying in a ditch somewhere with a busted ankle...

I'll look for signs from the wagons out. Ground's been soft. If he walked, I'll find the track."

"And if he's not?" Gin hadn't moved from the doorframe, but her voice carried weight that stopped Buck mid-stride. "If somebody pulled him off that path on purpose, and they're sitting in the dark right now waiting to see who comes looking?" She looked from Buck to Gus, her expression stripped bare. "If we charge out blind, we lose more than one man."

Gus turned on her. "So we sit here. Do nothing?"

"We think."

"While he's out there."

"While we still can." Gin held his stare without flinching. She'd faced worse than an angry father, and Gus knew it, which was the only reason he didn't fire back.

The fire popped in the hearth. Odin lifted his head from Jo's feet, ears forward, reading the room the way he always did.

Jo raised her voice. Not loud, but sharp enough to cut through every thread of argument still hanging in the air. "Enough."

The room obeyed.

She didn't stand. Didn't need to. Her hand slid from Gus's shoulder and found his wrist instead, fingers wrapping around it, anchoring him to the chair, to her, to the part of himself that still listened.

She turned to face him, her expression gentler now, though her eyes held that fierce clarity that had guided this family through every storm Marcus could remember. "You don't lose him today by thinking," she said softly. "You lose him by doing something you can't take back."

Gus swallowed hard. His hands shook against the grain of the table. The tremor ran up through his forearms and into his shoulders, and Marcus watched his brother's whole frame vibrate with the effort of staying put. Decades of friendship sat in that chair. Years of shared fences and borrowed tools and bad jokes told over worse coffee. Gus wasn't a man who left people behind. It went against everything he was built from.

Buck glanced away, jaw clenched, his reflection ghosting in the dark window glass. His fingers worked the brim of his hat, turning it round and round.

Gunny nodded once. "Twenty-four hours," he said again. "Then we reassess."

The word hung there. Reassess. Clean and military and hollow as a spent casing.

No one liked it.

But no one overruled it.

Marcus watched the room settle into its uneasy truce. Franklin uncrossed his arms and put a hand on Mary's back. Boone stared at the floor. Owen pulled a chair out for Judith and took Luke so she could sit. Clare gathered mugs that didn't need gathering.

Gus didn't move. Jo kept her hand on his wrist.

Outside, the wind pressed against the Lodge walls, and somewhere in the dark, Flora stamped in her traces beside an empty wagon, waiting for a driver who may not come back to her.

The kids noticed the tension immediately.

They always did.

Not from the words. Words were easy to shape, and grown-ups had gotten better at shaping them since The Day. It was the spaces between the words that told the truth. The pauses before someone answered. The way a hand would reach for a mug that was already empty. The way laughter stopped one beat too soon, like a song cut short by a wrong note.

Edwin hovered near the doorway between the great room and the kitchen, one shoulder against the frame, fingers picking at a loose thread on his cuff. He'd been heading for the radio when the voices pulled him sideways. He didn't step in. Didn't step back. Just stood there, listening harder than he meant to, catching the shape of the conversation even when specific words dissolved into the low murmur adults used when they didn't want to be overheard.

He waited until Gin passed by, carrying an armful of firewood that she didn't need.

"When's Zeke coming back?"

He kept it light. Hopeful. Casual. The way he'd ask about the weather or supper.

Gin didn't break stride. "He'll turn up. Zeke always does."

Too quick. The words came out before she'd even looked at him. Like she'd rehearsed them. Like she'd already said them once to herself on the walk from the woodpile.

Edwin felt the answer land wrong in his chest, but he nodded anyway and drifted back toward the hall.

Rosa didn't ask.

She sat on the braided rug near the cold end of the hearth, her three cloth dolls arranged in a row beside her. She dressed one. Undressed it. Dressed it again in the same scrap of fabric. When the smallest doll tipped sideways and lay facedown against the rug, she didn't fix it. Her hand hovered, then pulled back. She stared at the fallen shape for a long moment, her dark eyes unblinking, before she pushed it gently aside with one finger and went still.

Marisol sat curled up with Sadie on the couch, reading, yet she watched everything.

She watched Buck leave through the back door without his hat. Watched Gus grip Jo's hand and then release it and grip it again. Watched the answers change depending on who asked. Clare's version was warm and complete. Gin's was short. Gus said nothing at all.

The adults smiled when they spoke and looked away when they finished.

Marisol sat, chest squeezing with a wordless need, and said nothing.

At the school, Rita and Margaret stood together near the gate, arms crossed against the cold that had settled in with the late afternoon. The road stretched empty in both directions. Rita's gaze tracked it south, then north, then south again. Margaret did the same, though neither acknowledged the pattern.

"I thought he would turn up by now," Margaret said. She kept her voice low, conversational. The kind of tone meant for discussing firewood rationing or what to eat for dinner.

Rita nodded. "I know."

Their eyes met. No panic lived there. Not yet. Something heavier, quieter. The kind of concern that didn't need words, because words would make it solid, would give it weight and shape and a name neither woman wanted to speak into the cold air. Margaret's jaw tightened. Rita shifted her rifle strap higher on her shoulder, a gesture so automatic it had become a kind of breathing.

A Harbinger woman passed along the inside of the fence, close enough that her plain wool skirt brushed the lower rail. She paused. Tilted her head.

"Perhaps he needed rest," she said gently, as if offering comfort to strangers grieving something small. Her face held the same patient softness all the Harbinger women wore, smooth as river stone.

Rita forced a smile. "Perhaps."

The woman dipped her chin and moved on, unhurried. Margaret watched her go. Rita watched the road.

It had been only a few hours since Gunny left to have his people start asking around, and Gus couldn't sit still.

He paced the porch, boots thudding against the boards, Buck a shadow beside him. The rhythm never varied. Eight steps east, turn, eight steps west, turn. The planks groaned under his weight in the same places they always had. Buck leaned against the post with his arms folded, matching Gus's silence with his own.

"Mid-task," Gus muttered. "He wouldn't leave like that. He was in the middle of helping."

Buck nodded. "Zeke finishes what he starts."

Gus stopped pacing. His hands gripped the rail, knuckles going white around the rough wood. He stared down the drive, past the watchtower, past the bend where the road curved through birch and hemlock before dropping toward the valley. The road gave back nothing. No creak of wagon wheels. No thin whistle carrying through the trees the way Zeke always announced himself, two notes high and one low, like a bird that never existed. Gus glanced across the meadow at the roses growing on Emma Jean's grave, and his heart clenched. Zeke old dog, Sandy, rarely left his cabin anymore, but she had come slowly up the path, and now lay at Gus's feet.

Gus said. "He once walked six miles on a broken ankle to return a borrowed axe head. Said he couldn't sleep knowing he had something that wasn't his."

Buck's mouth twitched beneath his beard. "Sounds right."

They stood there together, staring down the road as if willing Zeke to appear, laughing, arms wide, full of excuses. Some story about a lame horse or a wrong turn or an old woman who needed a shelf hung. Gus could hear it already, the way Zeke would wave off their worry, call them mother hens, spit tobacco juice into the dirt, and say something like *you boys act like I ain't been finding my way home since before your mamas had teeth.*

The road stayed empty.

Jo came out quietly and slipped her arm around Gus's waist. Odin padded behind her and sank onto the boards near Buck's boots. Gus didn't look at her. Didn't need to. He sagged into her then, the fight leaking out of him all at once. His shoulders dropped. The line of his jaw softened into something raw and open, and for a moment, he looked every one of his sixty-three years.

"I should've gone with him," he said, voice breaking.

"No," Jo said firmly. "You couldn't have known."

Gus shook his head. "I always know."

Jo pressed her forehead to his shoulder. Her fingers curled into the flannel at his back. "You know him," she said. "That doesn't mean you control the world."

The words steadied him. Just enough. He covered her hand with his own and held it there against his ribs, and they breathed together while the wind pulled the last warmth from the afternoon.

Buck said nothing. He reached down and scratched behind Sandy's ears, then straightened his hat and walked to the far end of the porch, giving them room without leaving.

As the morning dragged on, the Lodge felt off-balance. Too quiet in places that should've been loud. Too loud in places that should've been calm. Doors that usually banged shut were eased closed. Voices that usually carried dropped to murmurs behind walls. Grace moved through the kitchen without her usual bubbly efficiency, washing the same pot twice. Gemma organized her medical bag on the dining table, then packed it, then unpacked it again.

Rosa fell asleep in Gus's chair, dolls untouched beside her. One lay face-down on the armrest where it had slipped from her fingers. Edwin, Jake, Max, and Ian sat in the hayloft, uncharacteristically quiet. Their legs dangled over the edge. No one kicked. No one shoved. Edwin held a piece of hay between his teeth and stared at the barn wall like it held answers written in the grain of the wood.

Somewhere between reassurance and restraint, the truth stretched thin.

Zeke hadn't come home.

And everyone was pretending they didn't yet know what that meant.

Father Tom found Gus in the shed.

It wasn't locked. It never was. Gus believed locks were for people who wanted to pretend they could control outcomes. The door stood open to the pale morning, cool air drifting in around the stacked wood and the half-finished repair on the bench. A bridle hung from a nail, one cheekpiece still unbuckled where he'd stopped working on it two days ago.

Gus sat on a crate with his elbows on his knees, hands clasped so tight his knuckles had gone white.

Father Tom didn't speak at first.

He stood near the door, hat in his hands, waiting to be noticed. The shed smelled of pine shavings and linseed oil and the faint sourness of a man who hadn't changed his shirt since yesterday.

"You don't need to hover," Gus said eventually. His voice was flat. Controlled. "I know you're there."

Father Tom stepped in, set his hat on the edge of the worktable, and leaned against it. "I wasn't hovering."

Gus snorted once. It wasn't humor. "You always show up when someone's about to say something they don't want to hear themselves say."

"That's not why I came," Father Tom replied.

Gus looked up then, eyes bloodshot, jaw tight. The skin beneath them had gone bruised and hollow. "Then why?"

"Because you haven't slept," Father Tom said simply. "And because Jo asked me to check on you."

Gus laughed sharply. "Of course she did."

Silence settled again, thick and patient. A chickadee called somewhere beyond the shed door and received no answer.

"They're saying he stayed over," Gus said finally. "That he wandered. That he got distracted."

Father Tom nodded once. "I've heard."

"You believe any of that?"

"No."

Gus stood abruptly, pacing a short line between the bench and the wall. Three steps one way, three steps back. His boot caught a wood curl and sent it spinning across the floor. "Zeke doesn't leave mid-task. He doesn't forget to tell me where he's going. He doesn't disappear without a word."

Father Tom watched him move. "You've said that already."

"Because it's true," Gus snapped.

"I know," Father Tom said.

Gus stopped pacing. His shoulders sagged just slightly, the big frame folding inward like a barn losing its ridgepole. He braced one hand on the bench and stared at the bridle hanging from the nail. His thumb pressed hard into the wood grain.

"I want to go after them."

There it was.

"I want to walk straight into wherever they're hiding and end it, end them. I want it to be done. I want to make sure no one ever does this again."

Father Tom didn't flinch. He folded his arms and let the words hang between them, giving them weight, giving them room to exist without judgment.

"Almost forty years I've known that man," Gus continued, quieter now. "He helped me fix up this lodge. He treated me like a friend and brother. He sat with me once when Jo was very ill and almost died, and didn't say a single word for four hours. Just sat there." Gus's voice cracked on the last syllable. He swallowed it down. "And now some snake-oil prophet with a campfire and a God complex has him, and I'm supposed to sit here and wait?"

Father Tom let the quiet stretch. Then he uncrossed his arms and straightened.

"You're not wrong to feel what you feel."

Gus turned. His eyes were wet but fierce.

"But you walk in there alone, angry, with no plan and no sleep, and you don't come back either. Then Jo loses both of you."

Gus opened his mouth. Closed it.

"Zeke needs you sharp," Father Tom said. "Not righteous. Sharp."

Gus stared at the young priest for a long time. The chickadee called again, and this time another bird answered from deeper in the pines. Sandy appeared at the shed door, tail low, and pressed her graying muzzle into Gus's palm.

He sank back onto the crate. His hand moved over the dog's head, slow and absent.

"I don't know how to do nothing," he said.

"Then don't do 'nothing'. Plan. But plan with your family, not against them."

Father Tom settled back against the worktable. Sandy circled once and lay down across Gus's boots, her weight warm and deliberate.

"Wanting vengeance doesn't make you a bad man," he said quietly.

Gus's head snapped up. "It doesn't?"

"No." Father Tom's face held no performance, no pastoral polish. Just a young man who had seen enough in the last year to sand away everything that wasn't essential. "It makes you human."

Gus swallowed. His voice came rough, like something dragged over gravel. "But if I act on it?"

Father Tom met his gaze steadily. "Then you become someone else."

The words landed in the sawdust and oil-smell of the shed and stayed there, solid as river stone. Gus's hands trembled where they hung between his knees. He clenched them into fists, watched the tendons rise and fall beneath weathered skin.

"I don't know how to carry this."

"You're not supposed to carry it alone."

Gus scoffed. The sound scraped the walls. "Everyone's looking at me like I'm already supposed to know what comes next."

Father Tom nodded. "They trust you."

"That's the problem." The fierceness in it surprised even Gus. He stood again, paced two steps, stopped. Sandy lifted her head and watched him. "If I say it out loud. If I say what I think happened. I can't take it back."

"No," Father Tom agreed. "You can't."

They stood there. The quiet stretched between them like a wire drawn tight, broken only by the distant sounds of the Lodge beginning to wake. A screen door. A child's voice, thin and bright. The clang of the water pump handle, once, twice.

Father Tom spoke again, softer. "There's a difference between truth and timing."

Gus exhaled slowly. The breath left him smaller. "I don't want to lie."

"I know. And I'm not asking you to."

Gus leaned back against the wall. His eyes closed. The lids were thin and bruised, mapped with tiny veins. He looked every day of his sixty-three years and then some.

"I don't know if I can wait."

Father Tom stepped closer. Not touching the older man. But near enough to be felt, the way a wall of trees breaks the wind.

"Waiting isn't the same as denying."

Gus opened his eyes. They were clear now, wet but focused, the grief burned down to something harder underneath. "And if I'm right?"

Father Tom didn't answer immediately. He turned his hat in his hands, running his thumb along the brim where the felt had gone soft. When he spoke, his voice was steady as heartwood.

"Then saying it will matter. Not because it changes what happened. But because it changes what happens next."

Gus nodded once. He pressed the heel of his hand into his eyes, dragged it down his face. The stubble rasped against his palm.

"They took him because he mattered."

"Yes," Father Tom said.

"And if we become monsters to answer that..."

"Then they win," Father Tom finished quietly.

Gus laughed again, this time hollow, scraped clean of anything resembling humor. "Jo's going to say the same thing."

Father Tom allowed himself a small smile. "She usually does."

Gus straightened. Squared his shoulders. The motion was mechanical, a man assembling himself from parts that didn't quite fit together yet. "I'm not ready."

Father Tom picked up his hat. "That's all right."

He paused at the door. Light spilled across the threshold, catching dust motes and the silver in Sandy's muzzle.

"When you are," he said, "say it plainly. Not in anger. Not in fear. Just in truth."

Gus nodded.

Father Tom left without another word. His boots crunched across the frozen ground toward the Lodge, and then the sound faded, and there was only the shed and the cold and the dog breathing against Gus's ankles.

Gus remained there long after the morning had turned. His eyes rested on the far end of the bench where Zeke's tools still lay, exactly as they'd been left. A drawknife with a hickory handle worn smooth by decades of grip. A folding ruler, brass hinges green with age. A stub of a carpenter's pencil, sharpened with a pocketknife.

Outside, the Lodge hummed. Children called to each other across the yard. The pump handle clanged again. Somewhere, a horse nickered, and another answered.

Inside the shed, something waited. Held back by breath and will alone.

And soon, it would have a name.

Chapter Sixteen

No Sign

Gin was the first to hear it.

She'd been up since before light, moving through the Lodge with the restless energy of someone who didn't trust sleep anymore. The floorboards knew her weight by now, knew the pattern of her bare feet on cold pine. She'd checked the locks twice, counted heads once, and was standing at the kitchen counter with her hands wrapped around a mug gone tepid when the radio crackled from the shelf above the woodstove.

She turned the volume up slowly, as if sudden sound might break something already fragile.

"Lodge, this is Gunny."

His voice was steady. Deliberately so. The kind of steady that took effort, that a person built with their jaw muscles before they opened their mouth.

"We've had eyes out since yesterday morning. All night. Rotated teams. Covered the river trails, the old switchbacks, the spur roads. Checked every place a man might stop if he meant to rest, and every place he might stop if he didn't."

Gin closed her eyes. Her fingers tightened around the mug. The ceramic was cold now, slick with condensation.

"Yaz and Riley came in late yesterday from the settlement run. Yaz took the lead on tracking. If there was a turn-off, a hesitation, a doubled-back step, he would've seen it."

A pause. Just long enough to register. Just long enough for the kitchen to feel like it had lost all its air.

"No sign past where Zeke left his wagon."

The words settled into the room like dust on a coffin lid.

"He walked away clean," Gunny continued. "No struggle. No drag. No broken ground. Nothing after that."

He didn't say what that meant.

He didn't have to.

"We'll keep people out. Another sweep after daylight. But I wanted you to know, this wasn't missed. Everyone who could help did."

Gin reached for the table to steady herself. Her palm landed flat against the grain, fingers splayed white.

"Gunny out."

The radio clicked dead.

The kitchen held its breath. Somewhere down the hall, a child coughed in sleep and turned over. The woodstove ticked as the last log collapsed into coals.

Gin stood there. Mug in one hand. Table under the other. The space between her ribs felt hollowed out, scraped clean like the inside of a gourd.

She didn't move to wake Gus. Not yet. She gave herself ten seconds. Counted them off against her heartbeat. Let the knowledge settle into bone and muscle where it would have to live now.

Then she set the mug down, wiped her eyes with the back of her wrist, and walked toward the hall.

Gin waited until the last plate was cleared and the last mug set down. She'd watched them eat in near silence, forks scraping, eyes averted, the whole room moving through the motions of breakfast like people walking through fog. Rosa had asked for more bread. Nobody else asked for anything.

When Grace lifted the final bowl from the table and carried it to the basin, Gin spoke.

She kept her voice even. Reported what Gunny had said the way she'd been trained to deliver field assessments. Facts first. Terrain covered. Teams deployed. Duration. Findings.

No sign past where Zeke left his wagon. No struggle. No drag marks. No broken ground. Yaz had led the tracking effort himself and came back empty.

She finished. Set her hands flat on the table.

For a long moment, no one spoke.

Buck stood near the window, staring out at the pale morning like he expected Zeke to come walking up the road, hat tipped back, full of excuses. Clare sat with her hands folded tight in her lap, eyes flicking instinctively toward the kids clustered near the far wall. Rowan leaned against a post, arms crossed, jaw set hard, but her large eyes sad.

Someone exhaled shakily. Relief, of a sort, passed through the room. Not because the news was good, but because it was thorough.

They hadn't failed him.

They'd looked.

Gus sat at the table, unmoving.

Jo watched him closely. She hadn't left his side since he came back from the shed. She knew this posture. Had seen it once before, years ago, when grief stopped being loud and started becoming solid. His hands rested on the wood, fingers spread, as though the grain of the table was the only thing keeping him anchored to the floor.

"Yaz is the best tracker we've got," Buck said quietly. "If he couldn't find a trail..."

He let the sentence hang.

Gus nodded once.

Not agreement. Acceptance.

He stood slowly, the scrape of his chair loud in the hush. Every movement felt deliberate now, as if the world had narrowed to a single careful path. His shoulders filled the space between the window and the hearth, but something in the set of them looked different. Heavier. Not bowed, not broken. Compressed.

"The search mattered," Gus said.

Heads turned toward him.

"It matters that we looked. That we didn't leave him out there alone."

His voice was calm. Too calm. Jo felt her chest tighten. She pressed her knuckles into Odin's scruff beneath the table, and the dog leaned into her leg.

"But men don't just disappear after walking to their wagon."

Silence deepened.

"They don't vanish without a sign. Not like that. Not Zeke."

He swallowed once. His eyes moved from face to face. Not accusing, not asking. Just making sure they were all with him, listening.

"He was taken," Gus said.

No one argued.

"He didn't wander."

No one corrected him.

"He didn't stay over."

The children were very still now. Even the teens who'd been trying not to listen had stopped pretending. Edwin's hand rested on Marisol's shoulder. Lily's fingers gripped the edge of her chair.

Gus drew in a breath. Held it. Let it out slowly.

"Zeke is dead."

The words hit the room like a stone dropped into still water.

Clare's hands came apart and pressed flat against her thighs. Buck's jaw worked once, twice, then locked. Rowan's arms tightened across her chest, and she looked at the floor.

Jo didn't flinch. She kept her eyes on her husband. Watched the cost of those three words move through him like a tremor through bedrock. Invisible to anyone who wasn't looking.

She was looking.

She reached for his hand. His fingers were cold. Rigid. For a breath, she thought he might pull away, might retreat into that shed inside himself where no one could follow. But his thumb found the back of her knuckles, and he held on.

This time... Gus took it.

No one cried out. No one protested. No one asked how he could be sure.

Boone bowed his head. His shoulders curved inward, and Beth's hand found the small of his back without a word. She didn't rub circles or squeeze. Just placed her palm there and left it, the way you brace a fence post before the wind hits.

Gin closed her eyes. Her fingers curled at her sides, then slowly opened. She breathed through her nose, long and measured, the way she'd breathed through firefights and field hospitals and every ugly thing the Corps had asked of her. When she opened her eyes again, they were dry and hard and older than they'd been ten seconds ago. She slid her eyes over and looked at Edwin and Marisol, his small hand on her shoulder and despair on their young faces, and her heart broke again.

Beth looked at the kids. The older ones. Edwin standing pale beside Marisol. Lily gripping her chair so hard the wood creaked. Rosa somewhere in the library with the littles, blissfully unaware, building something out of blocks or buttons or whatever small bright thing she'd found to fill her morning. Beth's throat ached. Instinct sharp and immediate, she was already counting the cost of this truth against every small face in this house. Already grateful the littles were two rooms away, still wrapped in the ordinary noise of play.

Quinn stood near the counter, dish towel forgotten over one shoulder, prosthetic hand resting on the counter's edge. Grace moved closer without touching, her presence enough.

Hunter leaned against the doorframe near Gemma's chair, arms loose at his sides, watching Gus with an expression that belonged to a man twice his age. He said nothing. Didn't need to.

Father Tom, seated near the hearth, folded his hands and bowed his head. His lips moved without sound.

In the quiet that followed, something shifted. Not into panic. Not into rage. The room didn't crack open or catch fire. It settled. The way a house settles after a heavy snow loads the roof and the timbers take the weight and hold.

Gravity.

That was the word for it.

The air itself felt heavier, pressing down on collarbones and the backs of hands and the space between heartbeats.

This was no longer waiting. The watches, the searches, the careful phrases, the hope dressed up in caution. All of it fell away like bark peeling from a dead birch.

This was mourning.

Somewhere outside, a jay called. A horse stamped in the barn. Wind moved through the pines along the south ridge with a sound like breathing. Life, infuriating and stubborn, went on. The woodpile still needed splitting. The greenhouse still needed tending. Bread still needed baking. The world had not paused for Zeke, and it would not pause for them.

Even if they were not ready.

Gus looked down at Jo's hand in his. At her swollen knuckles wrapped around his thick fingers. He didn't speak again. Didn't need to. The truth stood among them now, unavoidably present, filling every corner and shadow of the room like woodsmoke with no draft to carry it out.

And from this moment on, nothing they chose would be accidental.

Chapter Seventeen

First Words

By midday, the Lodge had settled into a careful quiet.

Not the peaceful kind. The kind where people chose their words twice before speaking and still got them wrong. The kind where doors closed softly and laughter, when it happened at all, sounded startled, as if it had escaped by accident.

Clare moved through it all with a basket on her hip, collecting what didn't belong where it had been left. A scarf draped over a chair back. A mug cooling on the windowsill, untouched, a skin forming on the surface. Zeke's gloves, still on the hook by the door, fingers bent as if waiting to be filled.

No one had moved them.

She paused there longer than she meant to. The leather was cracked at the knuckles, darkened by years of oil and soil and grip. She could smell them from where she stood. Lanolin. Pine sap. That particular sourness of sweat worked into something so many times it became part of the thing itself. She shifted the basket higher on her hip and walked on.

Outside, the teens worked harder than usual. Wood was stacked too neatly, the rows so precise they looked architectural. Tools and stalls were cleaned and cleaned again. Quinn repaired a hinge on the chicken coop door that hadn't needed fixing, his prosthetic gripping the screwdriver with that deliberate focus he brought to every task now, as if care alone could keep the world from taking anything else. Rowan stayed close to the house, dragging brush from the south clearing and piling it near the fire pit with more force than necessary. Her jaw was set. Her eyes sharp. When Jake asked if she wanted help, she bit out a "no" that left him blinking, and then a beat later, softer: "Sorry. No, thank you."

The children felt it too.

Edwin followed Clare once through the great room, pretending to look for a book. Then twice through the kitchen, pretending to look for an apple. He stopped himself the third time at the library doorway, color rising in his cheeks, embarrassed by his own need. He didn't ask questions. He didn't joke. He watched adults' faces the way a dog watches a hand it isn't sure will strike or reach, searching for permission to breathe.

Clare handed him the apple without comment. He took it and sat in the corner near the cold hearth, turning it in his hands but not biting.

Marisol sat on the front steps with Rosa tucked against her side, one thin arm wrapped around her sister as if anchoring her against some current only she could feel. Rosa played with a piece of twine, winding it around her fingers, unwinding it again. Her lips moved, but no sound came. She didn't sing. The absence of that small, constant humming left a shape in the air where something warm used to be.

Clare set the basket down by the kitchen table and stood at the window. From here, she could see Marisol's narrow back, Rosa's dark head against her ribs, the twine going round and round. Beyond them, the yard. Beyond that, the tree line. Beyond that, the trail that led south to the road, and the road that led to town, and the market, and the place where a man had walked away from his wagon and simply never came back.

She pressed her fingertips to the glass. It was a chilly morning for May. The kind that crept into houses and made you shiver unexpectedly.

Leah appeared at the kitchen doorway, holding a slate and a nub of chalk.

"Mom? Should I still do my lesson?"

Clare looked at her daughter. Fourteen and already learning to read a room faster than any book.

"Yes, sweetheart. Go ahead, if you'd like."

Leah hesitated. "Is Pop going to be okay?"

Clare's hand came away from the window. She wiped the condensation on her skirt.

"Pop's going to be Pop. We give him room, and we give him time. He has a big heart, and it is broken right now."

Leah nodded once and disappeared back down the hall, chalk tapping against the slate like a second heartbeat.

Clare picked up the basket again. There was still the scarf. Still the mug. Still the rest of the house to move through, collecting the small evidence of people too shaken to put things where they belonged.

She always noticed.

That was the thing about Clare. She noticed everything. The cost was that she carried it.

Clare set the basket on the ground beside the shed wall. She pressed her back against the rough-hewn boards and went still, one hand flat against the wood. The voices were close. Three feet, maybe four, just around the corner where the shed met the woodline.

Kosinski stood with Franklin and Cole, the three of them close enough that their shoulders nearly touched. Old habits. Old lines. She could picture them without looking. The way military men stood when they talked about things that mattered. Feet planted, weight centered. Bodies already braced for what came next.

"We can't pretend this isn't what it looks like." Kosinski's voice was flat, practiced. "This wasn't random. This was removal."

Franklin nodded once. "Agreed."

Cole shifted his weight. "Still no proof."

Kosinski snorted quietly. "Proof's a luxury now. Pattern's enough."

Clare felt her stomach tighten. She held her breath and listened harder, though part of her wanted to walk away. The part of her that was still a teacher. The part that believed in process, in conversation, in sitting down at a table and talking things through until the hard edges wore smooth.

That part was getting smaller every day.

Franklin rubbed a hand over his jaw. "If it was a grab, they didn't do it sloppily. No tracks. No blood. No witnesses. That's not a crime of opportunity."

"No," Kosinski agreed. "Which means it was deliberate."

"And if it was deliberate," Cole said slowly, "it'll happen again."

There it was.

The first words of violence didn't sound violent at all.

They sounded reasonable.

Kosinski's gaze lifted, scanning the tree line out of instinct. Clare could hear the slight creak of his jacket as he turned. "We wait, we risk another one. That's just math."

Franklin exhaled through his nose. "You're saying preemptive."

"I'm saying preventative." Kosinski corrected. "There's a difference."

A long silence. Wind moved through the tops of the hemlocks and carried the smell of rain. Somewhere far off, a crow called.

Cole spoke first. "Dad won't go for it."

"Dad's compromised," Franklin said. The words were quiet. Not cruel. Just honest, and that was worse. "He loved Zeke like an older brother. He's grieving. He's not going to think straight about this for a while."

"So what?" Cole's voice took an edge. "We go around him?"

"We go to him with a plan." Kosinski folded his arms. "Not a feeling. Not a guess. A plan with contingencies, actionable steps, and a clear objective. He's not a fool. Give him something solid, and he'll listen."

Franklin cut in. "And if he doesn't?"

The silence that followed was a different kind. Heavier. Clare pressed her shoulder blades into the shed wall and felt the grain bite through her shirt.

"Then we have a harder conversation," Kosinski said.

Cole turned away. She heard his boots grind against gravel. "I'm the law here. Whatever's left of it. If we move on that camp, it goes through me."

"Fine." Kosinski's voice held no argument. "Then start thinking like a sheriff and not a son and friend."

Clare closed her eyes. The wind shifted and she smelled woodsmoke from the chimney, bread from the kitchen, the green dampness of the forest floor waking into spring. Normal smells. Safe smells. They didn't match what she'd just heard.

Clare stepped out from behind the shed before the words could settle deeper.

“There is a difference between preemptive and prevention,” she said evenly. “And you’re standing right on the line between them.”

All three men turned.

Kosinski straightened. “Didn’t mean for you to hear that.”

“I know,” Clare replied. “That’s why I am here.”

Franklin glanced toward the Lodge. “We’re not talking about anything yet. Just... acknowledging reality.”

“So am I,” Clare said. “And the reality is that the kids are watching who says what first.”

Cole frowned. “They shouldn’t be.”

“They are,” Clare said gently. “Whether we want them to be or not.”

Kosinski’s jaw tightened. “You think waiting makes us safer?”

“I think choosing violence first teaches them something we can’t undo,” Clare answered.

Franklin looked away.

None of them argued.

Clare walked off toward the house, her steps getting quicker as she neared the porch.

Inside, Clare set the basket on the table and stood with both hands on the wood. Her wedding ring clicked against the grain.

The house settled around Jo the way old timber does in cold weather. Small groans and shifts, the language of a structure bearing weight it never asked to carry. She snorted to herself quietly as she thought. "Nobody asked me either, house. I know how you feel."

She sat at the long table with her hands folded over each other, her right hand resting against the left. Odin lay beneath the table with his broad head across her foot. She could feel his ribs expand and contract. Steady. Faithful. The one creature in the house that never needed her to explain a thing.

She hadn't spoken much since morning. Hadn't needed to. People came through the kitchen the way water finds a low point. They poured coffee, checked the stove, and lingered near the counter longer than the task required. They looked at her without looking at her. She felt their eyes the way she felt weather moving in, a pressure change behind the bones.

Gus sat in the chair beside her. Not leaning back. Not leaning forward. Just there. His hands lay flat on his thighs, big scarred hands that had built half the buildings on this mountain. He stared at the wall above the sink, where a calendar still hung from a world that no longer existed. They hadn't turned the page in fourteen months.

Buck stood near the door with his arms crossed over his chest, weight rocking heel to toe. He reminded Jo of a dog that smelled something wrong but couldn't find the source. His jaw worked beneath his beard.

"They're talking out there," Buck muttered.

Jo nodded. "I know."

Gus said nothing.

Buck shifted again, leather creaking. He looked at Jo, then at Gus, then back to the door. His mouth opened and closed. Whatever he meant to say, he swallowed it and stayed where he was.

Father Tom passed through the room from the hallway. He moved the way he always moved, unhurried, present, quiet, his footsteps soft on the worn pine boards. He stopped behind Jo's chair and set his hand on her shoulder. Warm. Firm. No words. Just the weight of a man who understood that silence could hold more than speech. Then he moved on, checking the latch on the pantry door, straightening the bench by the wall, pulling a crooked candle upright in its holder. Making himself useful in the smallest ways, which were sometimes felt like the only ways left.

Jo watched him go. Gus stared.

Outside, boots crossed the porch. Through the window, Jo saw Gin standing at the Market board they'd hung from two nails on the post. The board was rough pine, sanded once and never painted. Names and rules written in charcoal pencil that smudged in the rain.

Gin didn't announce what she was doing. She didn't turn to ask permission.

She pulled two names from the roster, erased them clean with the heel of her hand. Then she picked up the pencil stub from the nail and wrote three new lines beneath the remaining names. Steady block letters, the kind a Marine leaves on a duty board.

No unsupervised gathering.

No shared food beyond assigned stalls.

No lingering after trade.

Jo read the words through the glass. She felt Gus shift beside her. Felt him see it too.

Mary appeared at the bottom of the porch steps, a folded shirt pressed to her chest. She read the board, then looked at Gin. Gin didn't look back. She hung the pencil on its nail and walked off toward the barn.

Mary's eyes found Jo through the window. A question in them. Jo held her gaze until Mary looked away.

Across the yard, Marcus stood near the woodshed with his hands in his jacket pockets. He watched Gin's retreating back. Then his eyes lifted and found Jo's through the same kitchen window.

No words passed between them.

But understanding did. Clear as a signal fire on a dark ridge.

Something was changing. Jo could feel it in the way people moved, the way they didn't quite finish their sentences. The way conversations stopped when children entered rooms.

She unfolded her hands and placed them flat on the table and took a slow, deep breath.

Odin pressed harder against her foot.

The light bled out of the sky in thin ribbons of copper and ash. Clare walked the fence line without purpose, boots scuffing the frozen mud, her hands deep in her coat pockets. She'd checked on Leah twice since lunch. Found her both times in the same spot on the library floor, cross-legged with a book open in her lap that she wasn't reading.

She spotted Gemma at the far corner of the pasture, where the split-rail met the tree line. Gemma stood with one boot on the lowest rail, her auburn braid over one shoulder, face turned toward the hills. The last of the day pooled orange along the ridgeline like something spilling.

Clare stopped beside her. Waited.

"They're scared," Gemma said quietly, without turning.

"Yes," Clare replied.

"And angry."

"Yes. Very."

Gemma's mouth pressed into a thin line. She pulled her boot off the rail and stood square, arms folded.

"That makes people sloppy."

Clare studied her daughter. Not the way she'd studied her at fourteen, checking for signs of mischief or fatigue. She studied her the way one studies a person who has crossed into territory you recognize but never wanted them to find. The steadiness in Gemma's jaw. The clarity in her eyes, hard-bought and still sharpening. The weight she carried across those young shoulders without anyone strapping it there.

"It does," she said.

Gemma nodded once. A single dip of her chin, deliberate, final. "Then someone's going to have to make them chill out a bit."

Clare felt a chill settle across the back of her neck that had nothing to do with the evening air. She opened her mouth, but what came out wasn't an argument or reassurance. What came out was silence, because Gemma hadn't asked a question.

They stood together until the hills went dark.

Supper was venison hash and the last of the stored carrots. Ellie served it without fanfare. Plates went around the long table, and the scrape of forks was louder than the conversation. Quinn ate with his prosthetic braced against the table edge, methodical, eyes down. Hunter sat beside Gemma and didn't speak. Fiona pushed her food into a ridge along the rim of her plate. Edwin stared at his hands.

Most of the plates came back with food still on them.

Jo sat at her usual place through all of it. She ate what was in front of her because that was what you did. She listened to the quiet and the not-quiet. The chair legs shifting. Buck's boot tapping once, then stopping. Gus's breathing beside her, shallow and measured, the way a man breathes when he's holding everything behind his teeth.

When the last fork went still, Jo rose.

Not to speak. Not yet.

She braced one hand on the table and the other on her cane and stood the way the house itself stood, square on its bones, bearing what it bore.

She looked around.

Rowan's red-rimmed eyes. Boone's hands knotted together in his lap. Franklin's fidgeting. Cole's blank stare. Judith's soft, sad sigh. Clare's careful stillness and the way her gaze kept drifting toward the children's end of the table. Marcus, with his jaw set like granite. Gin's empty chair.

She saw the grief mapped across every face. She saw the anger tightening their shoulders, pulling them inward, coiling. And she saw the fear. It crept in around the edges like frost on a window, quiet at first and then everywhere.

She understood, with a clarity that hurt, that this silence would not hold.

Soon, someone would demand action. A name for the thing that took Zeke. A direction to ride. A throat to grab.

Soon, restraint would feel like weakness. Like cowardice. Like betrayal of a man who deserved better.

And when that moment came, the children would be there to see and experience it. To forever be changed by it.

Rosa with her bread-crust ridge. Edwin, with his restless hands. Marisol, watching everything from her corner seat. Leah, pretending to read. Jake and Max, trading glances they thought no one caught.

Watching.

Learning.

Waiting to see who the people they loved became.

Chapter Eighteen

The Line

They didn't call it a meeting.

People just stopped what they were doing and drifted toward the great room as if pulled by the same low current. No one brought food. No one sat comfortably. Chairs scraped. Boone stood instead of sitting, then sat anyway, elbows on his knees. Beth settled beside him without a word.

Clare took a place near the wall, where she could see everyone without being seen too much herself. She watched the teens first. Always did. Rowan leaned against a beam, arms crossed tight, the collar of her flannel turned up like armor. Quinn hovered near the back, jaw set, prosthetic resting against his thigh. Hunter stood close enough to Jo that it looked accidental, but wasn't. Gemma sat on the edge of a bench, spine straight, eyes alert, saying nothing.

The kids knew something was coming.

Father Tom had settled into a chair near the hearth, Bible resting on one knee, hands folded over it. He watched the room fill with the patience of a man who had sat through worse vigils and knew what a room sounded like before it broke open.

Gus stood by the window. Not facing anyone. His hands hung at his sides, and his shoulders carried the particular rigidity of a man who had already made his decision and was waiting to see if anyone else would say it first.

Jo sat in her chair at the head of the table, cane propped beside her. Odin lay pressed against her leg, chin on his paws, eyes tracking every person who entered. Her face gave nothing away. The lamplight caught the white streaks in her braid and the swollen knuckles wrapped around her mug of gone-cold tea.

Buck stood near the center of the room, hat in his hands. He kept turning it over, fingers worrying the brim, as he paced in circles. He hadn't spoken much since Gus said the word. The skin around his eyes looked older than it had a week ago, weathered into something beyond tired. When he finally spoke, the room went still in a way that had nothing to do with respect and everything to do with recognition.

"I'll say it." His voice was rough, unpolished, like a file drawn across green wood. "Because everyone else keeps circling it."

No one interrupted him.

"They didn't take Zeke by accident." He set the hat against his leg. "They didn't scare him off. They didn't wait for weather or bad luck to do the job for them."

He looked at Gus then. Not accusing. Just honest. The way one old man looks at another when the pretending is over.

"They removed him. For just being him, I think."

A murmur rippled through the room. Agreement, fear, something else that sounded like relief at having the shape of it named. Marcus shifted in his seat. Gin, standing in the doorway with her arms folded, didn't move at all.

Buck straightened. "And people who do that don't stop unless they're stopped."

Silence pressed in. The fire popped once, and no one flinched, which told Clare more about the mood in that room than any words could have. They were past flinching.

"We can pretend this is about patience," Buck went on. "About being better than them. About waiting it out."

He shook his head once, slowly. "That's not what this is."

He lifted his gaze and met eyes one by one. Boone. Marcus. Gin. Gus. Then Jo, last, and held there the longest.

"They need to die."

The words landed hard. Final. Unavoidable. They filled every corner of the room and settled into the walls like smoke, the kind you couldn't air out.

Someone sucked in a breath. Rowan's head snapped up. Quinn's hand clenched at his side, the prosthetic creaking faintly against his leg. Hunter went very still, the kind of still that only a man trained to be still could manage.

Clare felt her heart pound, sharp and loud in her ears. She pressed her shoulders into the wall behind her and kept her face level.

Buck didn't raise his voice. Didn't posture. He stood in the center of the room, the way a fence post stands in a field, plain and immovable and not asking permission.

"I'm not talking about revenge. I'm talking about prevention. You cut the head off, the body stops moving."

"That's not how belief works," Clare said quietly.

Buck turned to her. His eyes were red-rimmed but clear. "Belief doesn't kill men. People do."

Kosinski nodded once, slowly, from his place near the doorway where he'd been leaning with his arms crossed. "He's not wrong about the threat."

Jo hadn't moved. She watched Buck with an expression Clare couldn't read. Grief layered over something harder, something mineral and deep, like bedrock showing through after a landslide.

Gus spoke then.

"Don't put his name on it."

Every head turned.

Gus stood at the window, hands flat on the table now, fingers spread wide against the scarred wood. His face was gray with exhaustion, his eyes sunk deep into hollows that hadn't been there two weeks ago, but his voice was steady. The voice of a man who had been turning a thing over in the dark for days and finally set it down where he could see it.

"If you're going to say that," he continued, nodding once toward Buck, "say it clean. Don't dress it up like you're doing Zeke a favor."

Buck's jaw tightened. The hat in his hand went still. "I didn't mean—"

"I know what you meant." Gus didn't blink. "And I'm telling you. If you go down that road, don't carry him with you. Don't say it's for him. He doesn't get to choose that. You shouldn't think you can choose for him either."

The room held its breath. The fire ticked behind the grate. Odin's ear flicked once, and Jo's hand found the dog's head without looking.

"If you act," Gus went on, quieter now, the words stripped bare, "you act knowing exactly what it costs. Lives you didn't plan to take. Kids who don't understand why their world just burned down." He paused. Let that one land. "And you carry that forever."

No one argued. Beth's hand found Boone's sleeve. Gemma stared at the floor between her boots. Father Tom's fingers tightened on the Bible, but he held his silence, giving the room what it needed, which was not scripture but space.

Kosinski rubbed his hands together slowly, the dry sound of calloused skin filling the gap. "If we don't act," he said, "and someone else disappears—"

"That blood's on us," Franklin finished.

He stood near the back, arms folded, grease still under his fingernails from the morning's work. His voice carried the flat certainty of a man who had weighed operational costs before, in places far less forgiving than this room.

There it was. The other truth. Ugly and sharp and just plausible enough to hurt.

Clare looked at Gus's hands, still pressed flat against the table. At Jo's face, unreadable as stone. At Buck, who had the decency to look like a man who wished he hadn't been the one to say it but would say it again if he had to.

The two truths sat side by side in the middle of the room, and neither one flinched.

Clare watched Jo then.

Jo's shoulders were squared, but her hands trembled faintly in her lap. She was holding something back. Clare could feel it like pressure in her own chest, a tightness behind her ribs that had nothing to do with breathing.

Around them, the Lodge fractured. Not loudly, not cleanly. Just enough.

Rowan shifted closer to Buck, drawn to certainty the way cold hands reach for a flame. Gin looked torn, her eyes flicking between Buck and Gus, jaw working on words she did not yet have. Hunter took a half step closer to Jo without realizing he'd moved, his body answering something his mind hadn't named. Gemma leaned forward, elbows on her knees, listening harder than anyone in the room, her fingers laced tight, knuckles white.

Quinn stood near the back wall with Grace beside him. His prosthetic hand rested flat against his thigh. He didn't move toward either side. He just watched, the way a person watches weather roll in off a ridge when there's no shelter left to reach.

Father Tom sat, hands folded, face grave. The firelight caught the hollows under his cheekbones and made him look older than his years.

"There are sins we commit," he said softly, "and sins we allow."

He said nothing else.

The silence that followed was heavier than before. It pressed against the walls, the beams, the people inside them. Clare could hear the fire settle, a log shifting on the grate. She could hear Odin's breathing, slow and steady as a metronome.

She looked at Edwin. He sat on the floor near the hearth, knees drawn to his chest, watching the adults with eyes that missed nothing and understood too much. Beside him, Marisol had her arm around Rosa, whose face was blank in a way that no five-year-old's face should ever be. Lily and Fiona held hands, and Max and Jake held little Lucy on the cushion between them.

Clare knew, in that moment, that silence was no longer neutral. It had weight. Direction. Every second it lasted, it pulled them closer to Buck's truth and further from Gus's caution, because anger moves and grief sits still, and the room was tired of sitting.

She looked at Jo and saw the same realization land there. Saw it in the way Jo's fingers stopped trembling and went rigid instead, pressing down into her own thighs like she was holding herself to the chair.

If Jo didn't speak soon, clearly, publicly, someone else would act. Kosinski was already half-decided. Franklin had the operational mind to plan it. Buck had the conviction to lead it. And the younger ones, Rowan, Quinn, even Hunter, may follow because following felt better than waiting, and waiting felt like dying by inches.

And once that happened, there would be no daylight bright enough to undo it.

Jo shifted in her chair.

The polished wood of her cane caught the firelight as she gripped it, and Odin pressed against her leg, solid as a cornerstone. Her auburn braid hung over one shoulder, the white streaks catching orange from the hearth. Her knuckles wrapped around the cane's handle until the skin went tight.

She cleared her throat and leaned forward.

Everyone felt it. The shift from argument to reckoning, from possibility to decision. Buck went quiet. Gus lifted his head. Kosinski uncrossed his arms. Father Tom's hands unfolded and fell to his sides.

The kids leaned forward without knowing why. Edwin's chin came up off his knees. Marisol's arm tightened around Rosa. Leah closed the book she hadn't been reading. Declan and Donovan sat together near Ellie, eyes wide in stunned silence. Ian had curled into his Mother's lap, and Beth rubbed his small back.

Jo sat there, at the head of the table where she had fed them and taught them and held them together with bread and bluntness and the stubborn refusal to let the dark win.

The future, impatient and watching, waited for the next words.

Chapter Nineteen

Daylight

No one spoke after Buck finished.

The silence didn't feel respectful. It felt unfinished.

People shifted. A chair scraped. Boone cleared his throat and stopped, his hand finding Beth's knee instead. The room wanted something. Permission, maybe. Or direction.

Jo stayed seated.

That, more than anything, unsettled them. Jo always rose when she had something to say. She planted her cane and stood and faced whatever needed facing. But now she sat with her hands flat on the table, fingers spread wide, and Odin's chin heavy on her foot.

Kosinski broke first. "He's not wrong." He said it carefully, the way a man handles a loaded weapon he didn't build. "If they did this once, they can do it again."

Franklin nodded from the far wall where he leaned with his arms crossed, boot flat against the baseboard. "And next time it might not be someone who can disappear quietly."

A murmur followed. Agreement edged with fear. Clare watched it move through the room like wind through tall grass, bending people in the same direction without any of them choosing to lean.

Buck didn't repeat himself. He didn't have to. His point had already taken root. He stood near the hearth with his arms at his sides and let the quiet do its work, and Clare hated him a little for knowing exactly how effective that was.

Gus stared at the table, jaw clenched. He hadn't moved since he spoke. It was as if motion itself might fracture something he was holding together by force alone. His big hands lay curled on the wood, not fists but close. Jo's fingers were six inches from his, and neither of them reached.

"They're testing us," Morales said from beside the doorframe. "Seeing what we'll tolerate."

"That's how this starts." Hunter's voice came low and flat from where he stood near Jo's chair. "You wait too long, and suddenly you're reacting instead of deciding."

Edwin's head turned at that. Clare saw the boy's lips part, then close. He pulled his knees tighter.

Jo lifted her head then.

Not fast. Not sharply.

Just enough.

The firelight caught the spray of freckles across her nose and the deep lines that framed her mouth, and her eyes moved across the room without hurry, settling on each face the way a woman counts her children before locking the door at night.

"This is where you're wrong," she said.

The room stilled.

"You think this started when Zeke didn't come home."

Jo stood. Slow. The cane found the floor and held, and she rose around it like something rooted. Odin shifted but didn't follow. He knew the difference between Jo moving and Jo rising.

"It started when people confused calm with harmlessness."

She looked at Buck. Not accusing. Not softening. Her eyes held his the way a woman holds a lantern in a doorway, illuminating without flinching from what the light reveals.

"They didn't take him because they thought we were weak."

She let that land.

"They took him because they thought we'd make this easy for them."

A few people frowned. Morales uncrossed his arms. Franklin's boot came off the wall.

"They want us to prove their story," Jo went on. Her voice carried the same weight it always did, low and textured and seasoned by decades of speaking only when she meant it. "They want us loud. Violent. Simple. They want to point at us and tell those people around their fire that the world out here is exactly as broken as he promised. That only he can keep them safe."

She shook her head once. "I won't give them that."

Someone near the back muttered. Sounded like Cole, maybe Harlan. "So we just do nothing?"

Jo's gaze snapped there like a rifle bolt.

"No."

The word cracked against the walls. Odin's ears flattened and rose.

Her voice hardened. Not louder. Harder. The difference between volume and authority was something Jo had never confused.

"We do the harder thing."

She turned, deliberately, her body opening toward the far side of the room where the kids sat. Edwin, with his knees pulled up. Marisol, with her hands in her lap. Rosa pressed against Gin's side, fingers curled in the hem of Gin's shirt. Leah, beside Clare, her book closed on her thumb.

Jo looked at them. Every one of them.

"This is not a battlefield problem."

She paused.

"This is a problem of ideology."

The words settled differently this time. Less like a speech. More like a diagnosis. Something clinical and careful, the kind of truth that arrives without comfort but brings its own strange relief because at least now you know where the sickness lives.

"They didn't need guns," Jo continued. "They needed time. Access. Quiet."

Her gaze moved to Gin. Held there.

"They needed children watching adults accept things that didn't sit right."

The room breathed in and didn't breathe out. Gin's face went still as pond water, and her hand moved to Rosa's shoulder.

A flicker passed across Clare's face. Something that had been building for days, maybe weeks, surfacing now in the tightening around her mouth and the way her chin lifted half an inch.

Jo saw it. She nodded once. Small. An unspoken handoff, mother to daughter, seamless as passing a dish across a familiar table.

Clare stepped forward. She didn't move to the center of the room. She didn't need to. She spoke from where she stood, beside Leah, one hand resting on the back of her daughter's chair.

"If we remove the leaders violently," she said, her voice steady but tight, like a wire under load, "we don't end this. We give it a legend." She paused.

Her eyes traveled the room, settling on each face the way her mother's had, though Clare's gaze carried something different. Younger. Sharper. The look of a woman who had spent her life in classrooms watching how stories took hold of minds.

"Every movement that dies by the sword becomes a martyrdom. Every dead prophet becomes proof of persecution." She let that sit. "Those people at Little Bear Lake already believe the world wants to destroy them. We show up with rifles and confirm every single thing that man has whispered in their ears for months."

She looked at Buck. At Kosinski. At her father.

"We manufacture the next cult," she finished. The word hung in the air, dark and precise.

The room absorbed that slowly. No one rushed to argue it. The fire popped and sent a scatter of sparks against the screen, and somewhere outside a barn owl called once and fell silent.

Jo picked up again. "They have children."

Not louder. Not softer. Just unavoidable.

"Children who depend on them. "

She let the silence do its work. Let it press against the walls and settle into laps and find the places where conviction lived next to doubt.

"You take the adults they love away with blood and fire, and you don't free those kids."

Her knuckles whitened on the cane. Odin shifted against her leg, solid and warm.

"You orphan them into a story that will eat them alive."

Buck's shoulders sagged. Not in defeat. In understanding. The kind that costs something to arrive at, the kind that pulls the ground out from under the simple answer and leaves a man standing on nothing but the truth. His jaw worked once, twice. He looked at the floor, then at Gus, then back at Jo.

"We don't get to decide violence is clean just because we're hurting," Jo said.

She paused. Her eyes moved across the room, touching every face, resting nowhere long enough to accuse but long enough to be felt.

"And we don't get to call it justice because we're afraid."

The room breathed. One collective exhale, ragged and slow, like a chest releasing a weight it hadn't known it carried.

From the bench near the wall, Gemma spoke. Not loud. Not hesitant.

"If we do this wrong," she said, "we teach them that safety belongs to whoever scares people best. I don't think any child should have to learn that lesson. Do you?"

No one moved. The fire popped. A log settled and sent a thin ribbon of sparks up the chimney.

Jo looked at her. Something passed between them, grandmother to granddaughter, a current that needed no translation. Jo's eyes shone, but not with pride. Recognition. The particular ache of watching someone you raised arrive at a truth you wish they'd never needed.

"Yes," she said quietly. "That's exactly it."

Hunter's hand found the back of the chair beside Gemma. He didn't touch her. Didn't need to. The proximity said enough. Across the room, Tobias watched his daughter with an expression that belonged to a man seeing the last of something familiar replaced by the first of something harder and more mature.

Jo turned back to the room. She planted the cane and let the weight settle through it, through her arm, through the floorboards that had held this family for decades.

"We shine a light. No secrets. No soft lies. No quiet allowances. We cut access. We tell the truth."

Gus uncrossed his arms. Not agreement, not yet. Acceptance that the shape of the fight had changed in his wife's hands, and he was going to let it. It had happened many times before.

After a beat, Jo said, "And we let what can't survive daylight burn itself out."

Her hand tightened on the cane. Odin pressed harder into her calf, reading the tremor she wouldn't let reach her voice.

"This will cost us. And it will mean living with fear and grief instead of pretending we've solved it."

Father Tom bowed his head. Not in prayer. In the simple act of listening to something he truly believed.

Buck stood with his arms at his sides, palms open, as though he'd been holding something heavy and had only just set it down. The anger still lived in his face. It hadn't gone anywhere. But it shared the space now with something older, something closer to sorrow, and the combination made him look like a man who had finally stopped running from both.

Jo met his eyes one last time. "But we will not become the thing our children are afraid of."

No one cheered.

No one clapped.

That was how Clare knew it had landed. She pressed her back against the wall and felt the log through her shirt and thought about Leah sitting with a book she wasn't reading, and Gemma on that bench with a certainty no eighteen-year-old should need.

The meeting didn't end cleanly. People drifted out in twos and threes, arguments unfinished, choices heavy on their shoulders like wet wool. Kosinski paused at the doorway and looked back at Jo, but said nothing. Franklin followed him. Beth squeezed Boone's arm, and they walked out together, steps matched. Outside, the sun slid lower, pale and unforgiving, throwing long shadows across the yard where Quinn stood with his prosthetic hand resting on the porch rail, watching faces for answers no one was giving.

Gemma stayed seated, watching the door. Her hands lay still in her lap. Hunter lowered himself onto the bench beside her, and neither of them spoke. He looked at her profile, and his heart stuttered, so he looked away quickly.

Marisol watched the adults. Her dark eyes tracked each departure, each whispered exchange, each look that passed over her head. She sat cross-legged on the floor near the hearth with Rosa's sleeping weight leaning into her shoulder, and she catalogued everything with the patience of a child who had learned that knowing what the grown-ups wouldn't say was the only kind of armor she could carry.

And Jo remained standing long after the room emptied, the fire burned low, and the windows turned to squares of copper light. Odin hadn't moved from her side. Gus hadn't either. He sat in his chair with his big hands on his knees and watched her the way he always did when she'd spent herself down to the last reserve, ready to catch whatever she'd let him carry.

She didn't sit. Not yet.

Restraint, once chosen, would now demand to be proven every single day.

Chapter Twenty

The Cost of Restraint

The morning after Jo spoke, nothing looked different.

That was the problem.

The Lodge woke the way it always did. Boots on the floor, kettles heating, animals needing care, whether men lived or died. Smoke lifted straight from the chimneys, pale against the cold sky. Someone laughed near the barn and immediately looked around, embarrassed by it.

Restraint had not made the world gentler.

It had made it sharper.

Clare stood at the edge of the yard with Gin, watching the children move through their chores with an intensity that bordered on overcorrection. Edwin and Jake split kindling too carefully, each stroke measured, the hatchet rising and falling with a deliberateness that had nothing to do with wood. Leah read while walking and nearly collided with a post. Rosa refused to let go of Marisol's sleeve.

"They heard everything," Gin said quietly.

Clare nodded. "Yes. As they should."

"They understood more than we think." Gin shifted her rifle to the other shoulder and squinted toward the treeline out of habit. "It is a lot for them, I think."

Clare didn't answer right away. She was watching Gemma, who stood with Hunter near the fence line. They weren't touching. They didn't need to. Their shoulders angled toward one another in a way that suggested shared gravity, maybe even attraction. Hunter said something low, and Gemma tilted her head, not quite a smile but close. The medical bag sat at her feet, packed and buckled, ready for rounds she hadn't left for yet.

"They always do, and yes, it is a lot," Clare said at last. "This is how they learn. They need to see that choices are always available, even when our emotions make us think otherwise. They need to know that we struggle, get angry, get scared."

Gin watched Edwin set another piece of kindling on the stump. The boy squared it with both hands before stepping back, checking his footing, lifting the hatchet with the same controlled precision he brought to the radio dials.

"That one hasn't asked about Market since yesterday."

"He won't," Clare said. "Not directly. He'll find a side door into it. He always does."

A screen door banged behind them. Quinn crossed the yard with a bucket in the prosthetic grip and a second hanging from his right hand. Grace followed three steps back, carrying a crate. Quinn's stride had changed in the weeks since Boone fitted the device. Less guarded. Still careful, but the carefulness now served function rather than fear.

Rosa's fingers tightened on Marisol's sleeve as Quinn passed. The metal glinted in the early light, and Rosa tracked it with wide, unblinking eyes. Not afraid. Fascinated. Marisol tugged her gently forward, resuming their path toward the chicken coop without a word.

Gin exhaled through her nose. "I keep waiting for one of them to crack. Throw something. Scream."

"Rosa already did," Clare reminded her. "In your arms, on the porch."

Gin's jaw worked. She remembered. The raw, animal sound of a five-year-old whose world had contracted to a single point of loss she couldn't name. Gin had held her until the shaking stopped, and the silence that replaced it felt worse.

"I meant the older ones."

Clare turned to look at her fully. Gin's face was drawn tight, the skin beneath her eyes bruised with sleeplessness. She wore the rifle the way other women wore shawls, draped and familiar, part of the body's architecture. But her hands weren't still. Her thumb traced the strap's edge in a repetitive loop that betrayed the rest of her composure.

"Give them time," Clare said. "They're doing what we taught them. Processing. Watching. Deciding who they want to be on the other side of this."

"And if they decide wrong?"

Clare looked back at the yard. Edwin set another piece on the stump. The hatchet rose. Fell. Clean split. He gathered both halves without rushing and stacked them on the pile with edges aligned.

"Then we'll be here for that too. That is also a form of learning."

Down the road, the Market came together again.

Not with fanfare. Not with protest. Just altered.

The tables went up in the same places. The same hands drove the same stakes into the same hard ground. George and Aeiden hauled water from the pump while Ty checked the gate hinges, oiling them with rendered fat that smelled of last week's deer. The vendors arrived in ones and twos, goods bundled in cloth and crates. A woman from the ridge set out jars of pickled ramps. A man from the south road laid three rabbit pelts across a plank.

Everything looked the same.

Nothing was.

Gin's new rules were posted clearly this time, written on a smooth plank of birch that had been sanded and nailed to the gatepost at eye level. No shared food between groups. No unsupervised children beyond the fence line. No lingering after trade concludes. The words were plain, the handwriting steady and deliberate, each letter formed with the care of someone who understood that ink on wood carried the weight of law now.

Rita noticed first. She stood at the south gate with her arms crossed and read the board without expression, then looked at Margaret beside her. Margaret's mouth formed a thin line. She gave one short nod.

Zara read the list twice from the doorway of the school. She folded her hands in front of her and said nothing. Her eyes moved across the yard where the vendors arranged their wares, measuring the distance between what was written and what it meant.

Temperance smiled when she arrived.

She came through the gate with two of the younger Harbinger children at her sides, each carrying a basket covered with a clean cloth. Her hair was braided and pinned. Her dress was patched but pressed. She moved through the entrance with the ease of someone who had never been refused anything.

It was the same smile as always. Soft, understanding, calm enough to feel like relief if you didn't look too closely. The kind of warmth that settled over a room like woodsmoke, pleasant until you realized your eyes were stinging.

"We were worried," she said to Rita, her voice pitched just right. Not too loud, not too soft. Concerned without presumption. "After yesterday."

Rita inclined her head. "We appreciate the concern."

Temperance's gaze flicked to the rules board and back again, curiosity carefully leashed behind those steady eyes. "Of course," she said. "Safety is everything."

She said it like an agreement.

She said it like a warning.

At the edge of the yard, a Harbinger woman knelt to speak to one of the school children. A boy no more than eight, boots too big for him, face solemn. His name was Peter. He belonged to the Dawson family, the ones who had come in from the south road six weeks ago with nothing but a tarp, a cookpot, and three children who flinched at loud noises.

Harry stood with his hands shoved deep into his coat pockets, shoulders drawn up around his ears. He had been watching the rules board with the kind of stillness that didn't belong on a child's face.

"You don't seem yourself today," the woman murmured.

Harry shrugged. His eyes stayed on the board. "They're... different."

"Yes," the woman said gently. "Change can feel frightening."

She didn't touch him. She didn't need to.

Her voice carried the same quality as Temperance's. That smooth, unhurried cadence that wrapped around a person like a quilt pulled up under the chin. She knelt at his level, hands resting on her own knees, face open and patient, and the space between them hummed with an intimacy that had been manufactured so carefully it was almost invisible.

Almost.

Marisol saw it.

She had been helping Jillian by watching Ming. They were counting acorns near the fence, the two of them crouched in the dirt with a pile of caps sorted between them. Ming had been talking about Elin's doll, and whether it had a name yet, her voice a soft, constant music, and Marisol had been half-listening, half-watching the yard the way Gin had taught her to watch. Not staring. Not searching. Just open. Like the way you looked at water to see what moved beneath the surface.

She didn't say anything.

She moved closer instead, placing herself between the boy and the woman without making it obvious. She picked up an acorn cap from the ground near Harry's foot, turned it over in her fingers, and stood there examining it as though it were the most interesting thing at the Market. Ming followed, wordless, hand in Marisol's, her small body pressed against Marisol's hip.

The woman looked up. Her smile widened to include them both. Warm. Practiced. The corners of her eyes creased in a way that looked real enough to fool most people.

"You're good sisters," she said.

Marisol's stomach tightened.

She did not correct her.

Ming was not her sister. Rosa was. They shared a room and a quilt and a family that had chosen them both, but the word *sister* in this woman's mouth felt like something borrowed without asking. Like the woman had reached into a drawer that wasn't hers and pulled out something precious and held it up to the light as though she had every right.

Harry looked at Marisol. His eyes were wide and wet at the edges, and she recognized that look. She had worn it herself once, in the early days, when every kind voice felt like a hand reaching through deep water. You grabbed at anything. You couldn't help it.

She dropped the acorn cap and took Harry's sleeve between her thumb and forefinger. A small thing. Barely a touch.

"Rita's got cider," Marisol said. "The warm kind."

Harry blinked. Looked at the woman. Looked back at Marisol.

"Okay," he said.

The three of them walked toward the school steps, Ming's hand still in Marisol's, Harry's too-big boots scuffing the packed dirt. Marisol did not look back at the woman. She felt the gaze between her shoulder blades like a palm held close to a flame. Present. Patient.

Waiting.

The shed smelled of pine sap and iron. Late afternoon light fell through the gaps in the wall boards in thin, dusty lines that striped the floor and the woodchips scattered across it.

Buck worked until his hands shook.

He split wood too fast, too hard, the axe biting deeper than necessary. Each strike sent a tremor up through his arthritic wrists and into his forearms, and the rounds fell apart like they'd been waiting for permission. He has been cutting wood for almost seventy years, and he knew better. He didn't stack them. He didn't pause to roll the next piece onto the stump with any care. He just grabbed, set, swung. Grabbed, set, swung. The rhythm was wrong. Too quick. The kind of pace that wears a man out in twenty minutes and leaves him standing in a pile of kindling with nothing solved and his palms blistered.

Franklin stood nearby, pretending to sort hardware. A coffee can of mismatched bolts sat on the workbench in front of him, and he moved them from one pile to another with no visible system. His eyes stayed on Buck. He didn't comment on the speed or the waste or the way the axe head buried itself two inches into the stump on every third swing, requiring Buck to wrench it free with a grunt that came from somewhere deeper than effort.

He waited a long time before he spoke.

"You still think she's wrong?"

Buck didn't look up. The axe rose and fell. A round of ash split clean down the center, and the halves tumbled off the stump in opposite directions.

"No."

Franklin set down a bolt. Picked up another one. Turned it between his fingers.

Buck drove the axe down again. The stump cracked beneath the force, and he had to shift the whole block to find a solid footing for the next piece. His breath came hard through his nose.

"That's the problem."

Franklin nodded once. Understanding without relief. He dropped the bolt back into the can and rested both hands flat on the bench.

The shed went quiet except for Buck's breathing.

"You know this means someone's going to test it," Franklin said.

"I know."

"And when they do?"

Buck rested his forehead against the handle of the axe. Closed his eyes. The wood grain pressed into the skin above his brows. Somewhere outside, a child laughed. A screen door banged shut. The world went on doing what the world did, heedless and ordinary.

"Then we see who we really are."

Inside the Lodge, Father Tom sat with Edwin at the long table. No book. No lesson. Just company.

The fire had burned low. Neither of them moved to feed it. Gray light from the window washed the room in the color of dishwater, and the only sound was the faint tick of the mantel clock that Boone had repaired last month with a gear salvaged from a wristwatch.

Edwin traced a groove in the wood with his finger. Back and forth, slow, like he was memorizing the shape of it.

"If Zeke were here," he said quietly, "he'd make a joke."

"Yes." Father Tom's voice carried no weight beyond the word. "He would."

Edwin swallowed. His finger stopped in the groove. "Would he be mad that we didn't..." He stopped.

Father Tom waited. His hands rested on the table, still as the room.

"...do something?" Edwin finished.

Father Tom folded his hands. "Zeke believed people should be able to look at themselves when the day was done."

Edwin thought about that. The clock ticked. Outside, someone crossed the yard, boots on gravel, heading nowhere in particular.

"Even if it hurts?"

"Especially then."

Edwin nodded slowly. He didn't smile.

But he breathed.

The wagon rattled over the frozen ruts, and Jo gripped the seat rail with one hand and her cane with the other. Gemma held the reins loose, letting the old draft horse pick his own path. He knew the road better than either of them by now.

"Eve's knee still bothering her?" Gemma asked without turning.

"She won't say so." Jo shifted the jar of salve in her coat pocket. Comfrey and beeswax and a little yarrow oil and a dash of cayenne, the last batch she'd put up before the cold settled in. "But I saw her limping Tuesday."

"Sounds like someone else I know."

Jo cut her eyes sideways. "Drive the wagon, girl."

Gemma smiled but said nothing more. The horse clopped on.

They reached the school grounds a little past noon. The Market was winding into its midday lull, vendors reorganizing their tables, a few traders lingering over barter negotiations that had stalled on principle. Gemma pulled up near the south entrance and set the brake.

Jo climbed down slowly, Odin dropping from the wagon bed behind her with a grunt. She found Eve near the livestock pen, elbows hooked over the top rail, watching two of the older boys attempt to convince a reluctant goat into a smaller enclosure.

"You're limping," Jo said by way of greeting.

Eve didn't look over. "And you're nosy."

Jo held out the jar. Eve glanced at it, then at Jo, then took it without ceremony and tucked it into her vest pocket.

"Rub it in before bed. Twice if it is damp or chilly out."

"Yes, ma'am." Eve's mouth twitched. "Anything else, Doctor Callahan?"

"Don't let those boys bribe that goat with grain. She'll hold out for better terms every time after."

Eve laughed. A real one, full in the chest. Jo let it settle around her like warmth, then squeezed Eve's arm once and walked on.

Gemma had already disappeared inside to find Doc. Jo knew she had questions about a cough that lingered in one of the Harris children, and she'd want to compare her notes against his. That would take a while. The two of them together over a medical problem were like dogs with a shared bone.

So Jo walked the perimeter alone.

Not because she had to.

Because she needed to feel the boundary under her feet.

The fence posts stood solid. Wire strung taut between. The gate hinges oiled, thanks to Ty she guessed. She let her cane tap against each post as she passed. Counting. Measuring. The rhythm of it steadied her pulse the way rosary beads steadied other women's prayers.

Gemma watched from the cafeteria window, a cup of chicory cooling in her hands. She'd spotted Jo through the glass and paused there. She knew sometimes you follow and sometimes you hold still. This was a holding-still moment.

Jo stopped at the far fence line, where the trees thickened and the path narrowed toward the trail that led north and then bent west toward Little Bear Lake. She stood there a long time. Cane planted. Shoulders square. Odin pressed against her left leg, ears forward, reading the woods the way she read people.

Wind moved through the bare hardwoods. A jay called once and quit. The forest breathed back at her, patient and indifferent, the way it always had. The way it would long after all of them were gone.

She knew what they'd chosen.

She knew what it would cost them.

Somewhere behind her, a voice carried from the Market yard. Calm. Reassuring. Pitched just loud enough to be overheard.

"Peace," Temperance was saying to a cluster of young mothers near the bread table. "Peace requires patience."

Jo closed her eyes.

Daylight had been chosen.

Now it had to be lived.

And already, quietly, the bill was coming due.

Chapter Twenty-One

The Door Left Open

Edwin liked being useful.

He didn't say that out loud. Not anymore. But he felt it settle into him when someone handed him a task and trusted him not to drop it. That morning it was simple: carry the updated Market list from the Lodge to the board near the school path. No urgency. No warning. Just routine.

Routine felt good.

He folded the paper carefully, tucked it into his jacket, and set off with a quick stride, boots thudding steady against the packed dirt. Adults were everywhere, but they were busy. Heads down, hands full, voices measured. No one watched him go.

That mattered more than he wanted it to.

The sky held that flat pewter color that meant snow was thinking about it but hadn't committed. Edwin kept his eyes on the trail. He passed the woodshed where Buck's axe had gone silent for the day, passed the place where the wagon tracks forked toward the school road. His breath came out in thin ribbons. He tucked his chin into his collar and kept walking.

Near the fence line, he slowed. Not because he meant to stop, but because someone was there who hadn't been before.

Temperance stood just beyond the boundary, hands clasped loosely, gaze lifted to the bare maples as if she were admiring them. She didn't turn when Edwin approached. She didn't call his name.

She waited.

Edwin hesitated, then cleared his throat.

"Morning."

Temperance smiled and turned, as if pleasantly surprised. "Good morning, Edwin."

He blinked. "You know my name?"

"Names matter." Her voice carried the same quiet warmth she used with the mothers at the bread table. "And you've been helping."

That pleased him more than it should have.

He shifted the paper in his pocket. "I'm just taking this to the board."

"Of course you are." Temperance tilted her head. "You're very observant. You notice when things change."

Edwin frowned slightly. "I do?"

She nodded. The wind caught a strand of her hair and she let it stay where it fell. "Not everyone does. Some people move through the world without really seeing it. That can be lonely. For children who do see."

Edwin thought of Zeke. Not the way the adults spoke about him now, careful and stiff, but the real Zeke. The one who noticed a crooked fence post before anyone else and fixed it without mentioning it. The one who could read a dog's mood from thirty yards. The one who'd look at Edwin sideways and say, *You caught that, did you?* like it was the highest compliment a person could pay.

His chest tightened.

"I don't mind seeing," Edwin said.

Temperance's smile warmed, just a fraction. "I didn't think you would."

She didn't step closer. Didn't reach for him. She stood exactly where she was, on her side of the fence, and let the silence between them breathe. It wasn't uncomfortable. That was the strange part. It felt like being listened to without having to say anything yet.

"The children talk about you," Temperance said after a moment. "River especially. He says you understand things the others don't."

Edwin's ears went hot. "River said that?"

"He did." She glanced toward the school, then back at him. "People like you hold communities together, Edwin. The ones who watch. The ones who remember. That's not a small thing."

He swallowed. The paper crinkled against his ribs where he'd pressed it flat.

"I should go put this up," he said.

"You should." Temperance stepped back, opening the space between them wider. "Thank you for stopping."

Edwin nodded once and walked on. His boots found their rhythm again on the hard ground, and by the time he reached the board and pinned the list with a bent nail, his pulse had steadied.

But he replayed her words the whole way.

People like you hold communities together.

He tucked the nail into his pocket, turned back toward the school, and didn't notice Gin watching him from the gate, coffee mug arrested halfway to her mouth, her knuckles white around the handle.

Edwin smoothed the last corner of the notice with his thumb, pressing it flat against the weathered board until the bent nail held firm. He stepped back, read it once, read it again, then nodded to himself. The handwriting was Jo's, precise and unapologetic, and it looked right up there against the grain. Official.

He turned toward the school steps and stopped.

Marisol sat on the bottom stair, knees together, hands folded in her lap the way she did when she was working something out. Fiona stood beside her, arms wrapped around a short stack of books she'd borrowed from the school library. The spines were cracked and soft. One had a water stain blooming across the cover like a bruise.

"You took longer," Marisol said quietly.

Edwin shrugged. "I talked to someone."

Marisol's eyes sharpened. Not angry. Not scared. Something in between, something that had been living behind her face for weeks now, since the first time the Harbinger children had shared bread without being asked.

"Who."

He hesitated. Glanced at Fiona, who hugged the books tighter against her chest. Then he leaned closer, dropping his voice below the wind.

"Temperance."

Fiona frowned. A line appeared between her brows, quick and deep. "Was she nice?"

Edwin thought about the way Temperance had said his name. Not the way adults usually said it, tagged onto the end of an instruction or a correction, but like it was a word worth holding. The way she'd noticed him. The way it had felt like being seen without being pulled anywhere. Like standing in warm light that asked nothing of you.

"She's... calm," he said.

Marisol's mouth tightened. Her hands stayed folded but her thumbs pressed hard against each other.

"What did she say?"

"That I notice things." Edwin picked at a splinter on the board's frame. "That it can be lonely."

The wind rattled the notice against its nail. Fiona looked at Marisol. Marisol didn't look back. She was watching Edwin's face the way Gin watched the treeline, searching for the thing that hadn't shown itself yet.

"Did you tell anyone?" Marisol asked.

Edwin's jaw set. "I didn't do anything wrong."

"I know," Marisol said quickly. Too quickly. She caught herself, drew a breath, lowered her voice until it barely cleared the space between them. "I just... sometimes people say true things so you'll trust them."

Edwin bristled. His shoulders pulled up and his chin lifted, and for a second he looked exactly like Gus squaring off against a fence post that refused to sit plumb.

"She didn't ask me for anything."

Marisol nodded. "I know."

They stood there, the three of them, the weight of unsaid things pressing in. Fiona shifted the books to her hip and stared at the ground.

Edwin opened his mouth, closed it. Opened it again.

"She just... listened."

Marisol said nothing. Her thumbs had gone still. Somewhere behind them a door banged and voices spilled from the cafeteria, bright and careless, belonging to people who hadn't been standing at this particular fence line on this particular morning.

Fiona touched Marisol's sleeve. "We should get back. Gin said before lunch."

Marisol stood, brushed off her pants, and picked up the canvas bag at her feet. She looked at Edwin one more time. Not with accusation. With something older than nine years should have put there.

"Okay," she said softly.

The three of them walked toward the gate where the wagon waited, boots falling into an uneven rhythm on the hard ground. None of them spoke. Edwin kept his hands in his pockets, fingers curled around the bent nail he'd pocketed without thinking, and the words Temperance had given him sat warm against his ribs like a stone pulled from the fire.

Father Tom stood at the kitchen window, drying a bowl with a cloth that had seen better days. The linen was soft from use, almost translucent at the corners, and he folded it over the rim with the same deliberate care he gave to everything.

Edwin crossed the yard with two buckets hanging from the yoke Boone had built for him, the one sized down from Quinn's rig. The boy had the rhythm of it now. Knees bent, shoulders square, steps measured so the water didn't slop over the edges. He'd watched Quinn do it enough times to learn the gait, and he'd made it his own without being asked.

Father Tom watched the boy set the buckets down at the base of the porch steps and roll his shoulders. Edwin straightened, pushed the hair from his forehead with the back of his wrist, and looked toward the road.

Just once.

A quick turn of the head, there and gone, the way a bird checks the sky before settling back to the ground. Then Edwin picked up the buckets again and carried them up the steps, spine straight, jaw set with that particular brand of determination that lived in every Callahan by blood or by proximity.

Father Tom opened his mouth.

Closed it.

He set the bowl on the shelf and reached for the next one. His hands moved but his thoughts had stalled, caught on something he couldn't name. Nothing was wrong. The boy had done his chores. The boy had come back from the Market on time, eaten his supper, helped Grace stack the clean plates without being told. He'd been quiet, but Edwin was often quiet when he was thinking, and the boy was always thinking.

Father Tom dried the second bowl and placed it beside the first. He folded the cloth into a neat square and hung it over the edge of the basin.

Nothing was wrong.

He said it again to himself, silently, the way he'd once repeated liturgy until the words became breath. Nothing was wrong. And yet his hands wouldn't quite settle, and he didn't know why.

The Lodge ticked and creaked its way toward sleep. Floorboards contracted, and rafters settled, in the chill of the night. Somewhere down the hall, Grace's knitting needles clicked three more times and stopped. A log shifted in the great room hearth and sent a scatter of sparks up the flue.

Edwin lay on his back in the bunk he shared with Jake, quilt pulled to his chest, eyes open. The ceiling beams were massive, hand-hewn, dark with age and smoke. He'd counted the knots in the wood above him so many times he could find them with his eyes closed. Seven on the left beam. Four on the right. One that looked like a cat's face if he squinted.

He wasn't squinting tonight.

Temperance's voice played through his memory, low and unhurried. *You're the kind who sees.* The way she'd said it, like it was rare. Like it cost something.

Then Marisol's voice, smaller, careful. *Sometimes people say true things so you'll trust them.*

He held the two thoughts side by side. Turned them over the way his fingers turned the bent nail still sitting in his pocket on the chair beside the bunk. Both things could be real. Both things could be true at the same time. That was the part nobody told you about growing up. Not that the world got harder, but that it got wider, and the extra room ached.

Seeing things didn't make him bad.

Wanting to matter didn't make him wrong.

He pulled the quilt higher and listened to Jake's breathing, slow and even on the bunk below. He wouldn't mention the conversation to anyone. Not because it felt like a secret. It didn't. It just didn't seem heavy enough to hand to Gin or Jo or Gus when they were already carrying so much.

He closed his eyes.

Outside, wind moved through the hemlocks the way it always had, that low constant murmur that sounded like the woods talking to themselves about things that happened long before anyone built a lodge here and would keep happening long after.

Inside, a boy made room for a new thought, and the small quiet space it opened behind his ribs felt almost good. Almost bright.

He didn't yet know that space, once made, never truly closes again.

For a while, it worked.

That was the dangerous part.

The Market ran without incident. The rules held. No shared food. No drifting clusters. No quiet corners where influence could hide. Trade happened quickly and cleanly, voices polite, eyes cautious. People came, did their business, and left.

From the outside, it looked like control.

Gin watched the board like a hawk, making small adjustments no one noticed unless they were looking for them. A vendor moved six inches past his boundary line, and by the next morning, the chalk mark had shifted to remind him. A woman lingered near the children's area without purpose, and Gin materialized at the fence post with her arms folded and said nothing at all, which said everything. Clare and Mary tracked who stood where, who lingered, who didn't. Father Tom came down once a week as usual, made himself visible without being intrusive. A presence, not a pillar. Jo visited the Market a few times a week now, leaning on her cane and scratching Odin's ears while her gaze swept the yard with the quiet patience of a woman who had raised five children and buried none of the lies they thought they'd gotten away with.

They were close.

That was the lie restraint tells you when it's doing its job.

The children felt the difference first.

Not fear. Structure.

They were kept closer now. Watched more carefully. Corrected more gently, as though volume itself had become suspect. Adults smiled with their eyes instead of their mouths. Conversations stopped when kids entered rooms, then resumed with softer words that carried less meaning. The air in the Lodge had changed the way pressure drops before a storm, not with any single sign but with the accumulation of small ones.

Edwin noticed all of it.

He didn't resent it. He understood why. Zeke was gone, and gone meant something no one wanted to say out loud around the younger ones, and the rules at the Market had teeth now that weren't there before. He'd watched Gin erase and redraw the chalk lines on the board three times in a single morning. He'd seen the way Clare positioned herself between the fence and the children's area without ever appearing to do it on purpose. He understood the machinery of protection because he'd grown up inside it, first in a world that made sense and then in one that didn't.

But understanding didn't stop the feeling that he was being moved around a board without being told the rules of the game.

He still ran errands. Still helped with setup and cleanup. Still did everything asked of him and a little more, because that was who he was, and because being useful was the only currency that bought you information in a house full of cautious adults. No one told him not to talk to anyone. They just didn't ask who he talked to anymore.

That felt different.

Marisol stayed close to Rosa, closer than before. She held Rosa's hand on the way to the outhouse. She braided Rosa's hair tighter in the mornings, as if neatness were armor. She watched the Harbinger children with a sharper eye now, listening for phrases that felt too smooth, too certain. She noticed how often the word peace came up. How it landed at the end of sentences like a period instead of a beginning. How it closed doors rather than opened them

She didn't like that.

But she didn't know how to explain why. The wrongness lived in her chest, not her head, and every time she reached for the words they slipped sideways, the way water runs off oilcloth. So she said nothing. She just held Rosa's hand tighter and kept her eyes open and waited for the shape of the thing to reveal itself.

Gemma noticed something else entirely.

She noticed how tired the adults were.

Not the bone-deep exhaustion of survival. She knew that kind. She'd seen it in the Jenkins cabin when Maddie hadn't slept in four days, in the hollow cheeks of families who showed up at the school with nothing but the clothes they stood in. That kind of tired lived in the body. It could be fed, rested, mended.

This was different. This was the fatigue of vigilance. Of choosing every word before it left your mouth. Of scanning a room for what shouldn't be there and scanning again because the first pass might have missed something. Of holding a line that never stopped asking to be crossed.

She saw it in the way Clare's hands paused over dishes, not washing but thinking. In how Marcus stood at the window with his coffee gone cold, eyes tracking the treeline like he expected it to move. In Gin's jaw, which never seemed to unclench anymore, not even when she laughed. The laugh itself had changed. Shorter. More deliberate. A thing performed rather than felt.

Gemma catalogued these symptoms the way she catalogued any others. Elevated tension. Disrupted sleep. Hyperawareness masked as competence. She'd read about it in one of the medical texts Tobias kept on the shelf above his cot, a chapter on prolonged stress in caregivers. The book called it compassion fatigue. She called it what it was: people loving too hard for too long without anyone checking on them.

She found Jo one evening sitting alone on the porch. The rocking chair barely moved. Odin lay at her feet with his nose between his paws, his brown eyes half-lidded. Jo's cane leaned against the rail within reach, and her hands rested in her lap, still for once. The light bled out of the birches in long amber streaks that made the bark look like old parchment.

"You okay?"

Jo's fingers curled once, then relaxed. She smiled, small but real. The kind that reached the lines around her eyes without quite filling them. "I am."

Gemma settled onto the top step, pulling her knees up. She didn't fully believe it, but she accepted the answer for what it was. An offering, not a shield. There was a difference, and she'd learned to honor it. Some people needed you to push. Jo needed you to sit.

So she sat.

The last of the light pooled between the mountains like something poured. A barred owl called from the ridge, two notes repeated, and Odin's ears twitched but his head stayed down. Jo's rocker creaked once against the boards. Neither of them spoke again, and the silence was enough.

Inside the shed, Buck and Gus worked side by side under the glow of a single lantern. Buck sharpened an axe head against the whetstone with slow, measured strokes. Gus sorted hardware into coffee cans, each nail and bolt dropped with a small metallic ping. They didn't speak much. Didn't need to. Grief had settled into them differently. Buck's ran sharp and restless, a blade that wanted to cut something. It showed in the set of his shoulders and the way his eyes narrowed at nothing. Gus's was dense and quiet, a stone swallowed whole that sat heavy behind his ribs.

But it no longer pressed outward. Neither man paced the porch at midnight anymore. Neither slammed a door or left a room when Zeke's name surfaced in conversation. The pressure had found its walls and held.

Buck set down the axe head and flexed his fingers.

Gus dropped another nail into the can.

That felt like progress.

On Tuesday, at Market, Edwin and Jake went to help Eve as they had an explosion of new lambs that needed care. When they reached Eve she immediately sent Edwin off to get water and Jake to get a bale of straw. Grabbing the bucket, Edwin headed to the pump. He pumped rhythmically and stared at nothing, his mind turning over a thousand things. When the water sloshed onto his foot he startled, frowned at the over filled buckets, and then lifted them with effort.

He walked along the edge of the yard toward the sheep pens. Suddenly, Edwin paused with a bucket in each hand.

The water sloshed against the tin sides and soaked through his gloves, but he didn't set them down. He stood at the edge of the yard where the path met the road.

Temperance stood on the road once again. Not close. Not intruding. Just present in the way she always was, like a fence post or a familiar tree, something you stopped noticing until you realized you'd been looking for it. She faced a woman Edwin didn't recognize, one of the newer families from the west-side houses. The woman held a toddler on her hip and spoke in a low, unsteady voice. Temperance listened with her whole body, her head tilted, her hands still at her sides.

"We all do the best we can," Temperance said. "Especially when we're afraid of making the wrong choice."

The woman's shoulders dropped an inch.

Edwin shifted his weight. The buckets pulled at his arms, and his fingers ached. He watched Temperance rest a hand briefly on the woman's elbow, then step back. She didn't glance toward the yard.

She didn't ask him to come closer.

She didn't need to.

The Lodge settled into its bones the way it always did after dark. Floorboards ticked as they cooled. The fire in the great room had been banked low, and the smell of woodsmoke and the remnants of bean soup lingered in the hall. Somewhere upstairs, Rosa murmured in her sleep, and Grace's voice followed, a low hum that smoothed whatever wrinkle had crept into the child's dreaming.

Edwin sat on the front steps with his elbows on his knees. The cold bit through his jacket, but he didn't go inside. Marisol appeared beside him without a word, folding herself onto the step below, her back against the railing. She pulled her knees to her chest and tucked her chin. Neither of them spoke for a while. The woods breathed around them, branches scraping and settling, an owl calling once from somewhere past the south ridge.

"They think it's working," Edwin said.

Marisol looked at him. "What is?"

"The rules. The watching. Everything."

Marisol hugged her knees tighter. "Is it?"

Edwin turned a sliver of bark between his fingers, pressing its edge into his thumb until it left a crescent mark. He thought about Temperance on the road that afternoon. The way she'd stood with that woman. No urgency, no performance. Just presence. The toddler had fussed and Temperance hadn't flinched, hadn't tried to take the child or fix the moment. She'd just been there, steady as a hearthstone. And the woman had softened.

He thought about the rules board at the school, the chalk lines Gin redrew every morning. The way vendors kept their distance now and the Harbinger children no longer drifted through the yard like dandelion seeds looking for soil. He thought about how good it felt when Temperance had called him observant, the word landing in a hollow place he hadn't known was empty. Nobody at the Lodge had asked him what he thought. Not since Zeke. They asked him to carry things, to split kindling, to help Eve with the lambs. They gave him jobs that kept his hands full and his mouth shut.

"I think it's helping," he said carefully.

Marisol studied his face. The porch light was long dead, but the moon threw enough glow to read by, and she read him the way she read everything these days. Slowly. With the feeling that the important part hid between the lines.

"Helping who?" she asked.

Edwin didn't answer right away. He set the bark down on the step between them and wiped his palms on his jeans.

In the distance, carried on the still night air from somewhere beyond the tree line, a voice drifted. Soft. Confident. Certain. The words reached the porch like smoke, curling and shapeless but unmistakable.

"Peace takes patience."

Edwin stood. His knees popped. He brushed off the seat of his pants and didn't look at Marisol.

"I should go," he said.

Marisol watched him pull open the screen door and disappear into the dark hallway. The door bumped shut behind him. She stayed on the step, arms wrapped around her shins, chin pressed hard against her kneecaps. The tightness in her chest had no name. It sat below her ribs and no amount of breathing moved it.

On the porch above her, the rocker creaked. Jo sat with a blanket across her lap and Odin's warm weight against her ankle. Her cane leaned against the armrest. She had been there the whole time, quiet as the house itself, her eyes closed as the last thin band of light slipped behind the western trees and the sky turned the color of spent ash.

They had chosen daylight. They were holding the line.

And somewhere between intention and outcome, something subtle had already begun to lean the other way.

Chapter Twenty-Two

Bought Time

By the end of the week, the Lodge began to breathe again.

Not deeply. Not freely. But enough that people noticed the difference and mistook it for relief.

The Market ran clean on Tuesday and again on Friday. Vendors arrived on time, traded within their chalk lines, packed up before the light turned amber. The Harbingers complied without complaint. Their children appeared at the designated hours, stayed within the designated spaces, and left when the bell sounded. No one challenged the rules. No children strayed past the fence line. No voices rose above the general hum of barter and small talk. The calm held, like thin as ice over a November creek, but holding.

Gin marked it on her internal ledger as progress. She stood at the south gate each Market morning with her rifle slung low and her eyes sweeping the yard in measured arcs. She counted heads. She noted who lingered and who moved with purpose. She watched the spaces between people, the gaps where trouble liked to root. The board stayed current. The chalk lines stayed crisp. When a vendor's eldest boy drifted six feet past his family's table to chase a dropped spool of twine, Gin didn't raise her voice. She walked over, handed the spool back, and pointed. The boy returned to his table. That was enough.

Clare noticed the way shoulders lowered a fraction around the dinner table. The way people lingered half a beat longer before leaving a room, as if the walls had stopped pressing inward. Mary laughed at something Ellie said during dishwashing one evening, a real laugh, full-throated and sudden, and the sound of it stopped Clare mid-step in the hallway. She stood there with a stack of folded linens against her chest and let the laugh wash through her like warm water. She didn't call it safe. She called it managed. And for now, managed was enough.

Jo said little. She didn't need to. The line had been drawn. The family understood it. The work now was keeping it visible, not shouting about its existence. She walked the perimeter once a day instead of twice, her cane tapping a rhythm against the ground while Odin padded alongside her, nose working the air. Not because she trusted the woods more. She'd never trust the woods. But because she trusted the people watching them. Hunter's patrol routes had tightened, his instincts sharpening into something that reminded her of Marcus at that age. Rowan checked the fence posts without being asked, her reports to Gus growing shorter and more precise each day. Quinn kept the barn in order with a quiet ferocity.

Father Tom mentioned to Jo over tea one morning, quietly, almost as an afterthought, that attendance at evening prayer had steadied. Not increased. Steadied. The same dozen faces appeared each night in the great room when he opened his worn Bible and read by firelight. They didn't come seeking answers. They came seeking the rhythm of something predictable. Grief, contained, tended to settle rather than spread. He'd learned that in seminary. He was learning it again now, the hard way, the only way that stuck.

Buck stopped splitting wood to exhaustion. His hands still shook some mornings, but the blisters had closed and the raw patches on his palms had begun to callus over into something that would last. He ate supper with the family three nights running and didn't leave the table early.

Gus slept through the night twice in a row. Jo knew because she lay beside him both times, listening to the slow draw of his breath, feeling the tension in his shoulders loosen one degree at a time until his hand unclenched on the quilt between them.

Small mercies. Earned ones.

At the school, Rita and Margaret stood shoulder to shoulder near the gate as the last vendors packed their tables. Rita tilted her head toward the yard where the Harbinger children filed out in their usual silent line. Margaret watched them go, then looked back at Rita. Something passed between them that wasn't quite ease but wasn't the taut wire of the weeks before. Rita uncrossed her arms. Margaret exhaled through her nose and turned back toward the building.

Zara stopped hovering. She'd spent the better part of two weeks circling the edges of every conversation, inserting herself into doorways, standing close enough to hear but not quite participating. By Friday she was back at her desk with maps spread flat and inventory sheets pinned under a mug of chicory. Jillian noticed first, said nothing, and simply slid a fresh pencil across the table.

Someone cracked a joke in the cafeteria line. Carefully. Something about George's cooking tasting like boot leather with ambition. A few people laughed. No one flinched.

"We've bought time," Gin said to Clare one afternoon as they watched the children finish chores in the yard. "Not solved it. Just... time."

Clare nodded. She believed it, too. Or wanted to.

"Time matters," she said.

"Yes," Gin agreed. "It does."

They watched Edwin carry a crate between Ty and Jake, careful and precise, the three of them moving in step without speaking. Edwin set it down gently at the storage shed wall, checked the corner where the wood met the frame, adjusted it so it sat flush against the one beside it. He straightened and caught Gin's eye across the yard. He nodded once, the way he did now. Quiet. Competent. Grown.

Gin felt a brief, unwarranted swell of pride.

Edwin liked that people trusted him.

He didn't talk about it. Didn't mention it to Jake or Marisol or even Gin. He just made room for it the way he made room for the extra weight in the buckets or the longer hours at the board. He held it carefully and tried not to drop anything.

That afternoon, Temperance did not come to the Market.

Edwin noticed the way he noticed most things now, without looking for them. Her usual spot near the south corner of the fence stood empty. No basket. No calm, unhurried hands folding cloth or sorting dried herbs. The space she normally occupied looked oddly bare, like a shelf missing a jar you'd grown used to seeing there.

Instead, a woman Edwin didn't recognize stood near the far fence, arranging jars with meticulous care. Small ones, brown glass, stoppered with wax. She worked alone, eyes down, movements practiced. Her hair was pulled back tight and her clothes were clean but plain, the kind of plain that looked chosen rather than worn into. No patches. No fraying hems. She set each jar in a line with the label facing outward, spacing them evenly with her fingertips.

When Edwin passed carrying an empty crate back toward the storage shed, she looked up and smiled. Not wide, not inviting. Just acknowledging. The way you'd nod at someone sharing a path.

"Could you tell Temperance," she said softly, "that the supplies arrived intact?"

Edwin slowed. His boots scuffed gravel. "I don't—"

"It's all right," the woman said. Her voice carried no urgency. No weight. She tilted her head slightly and returned her hands to the jars. "I can find her later."

She went back to her work. Steady. Unhurried. As if the question had already been answered and she was simply tying off loose thread.

Edwin stood there a moment. The crate sat light against his hip. Somewhere behind him, Ty called for Jake to grab the gate latch. The sounds of the Market filled the space around him, familiar and close. He watched the woman line up the last jar.

Then he nodded. "I'll tell her."

The woman glanced up. That same half-smile. "Thank you."

He didn't know why he said it.

He didn't know why it felt easier than explaining he wasn't supposed to.

Later, as the Market thinned, Edwin saw Temperance at the edge of the road, speaking with an older man. She wasn't looking for him. She never did.

The man had a gray beard cut close and a canvas coat patched at both elbows. He held a walking stick but didn't lean on it. Temperance listened the way she always listened, with her whole body angled toward the speaker, hands still, chin slightly dipped. Whatever the man was saying, she received it without interruption. When he finished, she placed one hand briefly on his forearm and said something Edwin couldn't hear. The man's shoulders loosened. He nodded twice, adjusted his stick, and walked north without looking back.

Edwin waited. He set the crate down beside the fence post and brushed his palms on his jeans. The chalk line Gin had drawn that morning was still visible on the packed dirt, a faint white arc marking where the vendor boundary ended and the common path began. He stopped just inside it.

"They said the supplies came in fine," Edwin said. "Nothing broken."

Temperance turned, surprised, pleasantly so. Her brows lifted and she folded her hands loosely in front of her the way she did when something small pleased her.

"That's good news. Thank you for remembering."

"It wasn't hard," Edwin replied.

She smiled, just a little. The corners of her mouth moved but the expression lived mostly in her eyes, something warm and unhurried settling there.

"It rarely is, for people who notice."

A gust rolled across the field and pushed the smell of woodsmoke toward them. Someone was banking a fire near the school. Edwin heard Ty's laugh carry from the gate, followed by the squeal of the hinge he'd oiled that morning and a giggle from Jenny. The Market was emptying. Families packed bundles into arms and wagons. A child somewhere called for a mother.

Temperance glanced toward the road where the man had gone, then back at Edwin. She didn't step closer. She didn't reach out or lower her voice or say anything that would have sounded wrong if repeated at the dinner table.

She did not ask him to do anything else.

She did not need to.

Edwin picked up the crate, tucked it under his arm, and walked back toward the gate. The chalk line passed beneath his boots without a sound.

That evening, Clare sat with Jo at the long table, the oil lamp casting a steady pool of light between them. The kitchen had emptied an hour ago. Dishes dried in the rack. A towel hung over the back of a chair where Mary had left it. The fire in the hearth had burned down to a bed of coals that ticked and shifted, throwing faint orange across the far wall.

Clare wrapped both hands around her mug. The tea had gone cold, but she held it anyway.

"The rules are holding," Clare said. "They're adjusting."

Jo nodded. Her cane leaned against the table's edge, and Odin lay beneath it, his broad head resting on her boot. Jo's fingers moved absently over the dog's ear, the swollen knuckles catching lamplight.

"So are we."

Clare turned the mug a quarter rotation. She watched the surface of the tea, dark and still.

"I think this might work. At least long enough to make the next right move."

Jo met her eyes. The laugh lines deepened, but the mouth didn't smile.

"Maybe."

It wasn't doubt. It was honesty. Clare recognized it the way she recognized her mother's handwriting or the particular creak of the third step on the porch. Jo had never once lied to make the truth easier. She wasn't going to start now.

Clare exhaled and set the mug down. The lamplight held them there, two women at a table, the silence between them full of everything they'd already said and everything they hadn't needed to.

Outside, the children played until dusk, their voices drifting through the windows in ragged, breathless bursts. Lucy chased Jake around the rain barrel. Max lobbed pinecones at a fence post and missed wide every time. Rosa crouched in the dirt, arranging pebbles in a pattern only she understood.

The laughter was cautious but real.

Marisol sat on the porch steps, knees drawn up, chin resting on her folded arms. She watched Edwin cross the yard with an armload of split kindling. He stacked it against the shed wall, neat and square, brushed off his hands, and stood a moment looking south toward the tree line. Then he turned and carried the last bundle inside without a word.

He seemed the same. Helpful. Calm. Thoughtful.

And slightly elsewhere.

The tightness came back to her chest, the one she couldn't name and couldn't shake. Not fear exactly. Not anger. Something quieter, lodged between ribs like a splinter too deep to reach.

"Come on," Rosa said, tugging her hand. "It's getting dark."

Marisol let herself be pulled inside.

The door closed behind them. The porch light guttered once and held.

In the quiet that followed, Edwin lay awake again. The ceiling beams stretched above him, familiar as his own hands. Jake breathed slow and even on the other bunk. Wind pressed against the window glass and fell away.

He thought about the woman and her jars, the careful way she'd arranged them along the table edge. He thought about Temperance, the way she'd received the message without surprise, like it was something expected, something already accounted for.

About how easy it had been to help.

He told himself he hadn't broken a rule.

He told himself he'd simply passed along information anyone could have shared.

He told himself adults didn't need one more thing to worry about.

The wind picked up again. A branch scraped the roof. Jake rolled over and muttered something about firewood in his sleep.

Edwin closed his eyes.

Outside, the woods held their breath. The pines stood black against a sky salted with bright stars, and nothing moved along the south trail.

Inside, time slipped forward all the same. Bought and carefully spent, it moved the way water moves under ice, silent, steady, impossible to hold.

And somewhere between vigilance and trust, the future adjusted its course by a single, unnoticed degree.

Chapter Twenty-Three

What Remains

The morning broke clean and clear. Spring had come on gently, the kind of day that felt borrowed from a world that used to hand them out for free. Sunlight cut through the trees in steady bands, warming the frost from the ground and setting the pines whispering to one another. Smoke rose straight from the chimneys, no wind to bend it. The air smelled like bread and woodsmoke and something close to ordinary.

That was the first mistake.

Jo noticed it and let herself feel, just for a moment, that maybe they had done it right. Not solved. Not fixed. But steadied. The way you set a broken bone and wait for the body to do its stubborn work.

She stood at the edge of the yard, cane planted in the soft earth, watching the children gather for chores. Odin pressed warm against her left leg, his head lifted to the breeze. They moved easily now, patterns reestablished, the rhythm of the place clicking back into something she recognized. Edwin checked the list pinned to the barn door twice before assigning himself to carry water. He hefted the first bucket without complaint and walked toward the pump with his shoulders squared, a boy trying on the shape of a man who hadn't arrived yet. Marisol stayed close to Rosa, her vigilance easing just enough to let her smile at something Merryn said. Rosa crouched by the garden row, pressing seeds into the dark soil with her thumb, humming that tuneless melody she'd carried since the Market began.

Life, stubborn and ungrateful, continued.

Across the yard, Quinn worked at the fence with a coil of wire and the prosthetic arm fitted with pliers. Grace handed up a post brace without being asked. Hunter walked the perimeter trail with his rifle slung low, and the watchtower flag hung limp in the still air.

Gin joined Jo at the fence rail, hands tucked into her jacket pockets. Her boots were already muddy from the morning patrol. She stood the way she always stood, weight balanced, eyes moving even when the rest of her was still.

"No incidents," she said. "Market yesterday was quiet."

Jo nodded. She watched a robin land on the garden fence and cock its head at Rosa.

"Quiet can be good."

"It can," Gin agreed. "And this time, I think it is."

Neither of them smiled. Smiling would have been a kind of spending they couldn't afford yet. But the silence between them was comfortable, the kind that comes from two people who trust each other's judgment enough not to fill it.

Jo didn't answer right away. She watched Edwin bend to pick up a dropped bucket, watched the way he glanced up instinctively toward the road before setting it right.

“That boy carries more than he should,” Jo said finally.

Gin followed her gaze. “He's handling it.”

“Yes,” Jo said. “He is.”

That, she thought, was the part that kept her awake.

Jo breathed deep. The cold still lived in the air beneath the warmth, the way it does in the mountains when spring is more promise than fact. Her knuckles ached. They always ached anymore. She shifted her grip on the cane and let the feeling pass through her like water through a sieve.

Down by the pump, Edwin filled the second bucket and paused. He looked south, the way he'd been looking south for weeks now. Just a glance. Quick and quiet, the kind a boy gives a thought he hasn't shared.

Then he turned and carried both buckets toward the barn, water sloshing against his shins.

Gin watched him go. Her jaw tightened a fraction, then released.

"He's a good kid," Gin said.

Jo's gaze followed the boy across the yard. She heard what Gin said and what Gin didn't say, the way mothers learn to hear the space between words the way a hunter hears the space between birdsong.

"He is," Jo said. She tapped the cane once against the fence post, a sound like a period at the end of a sentence.

Odin shifted beside her. His ears turned forward, then back.

The morning held.

At the school, Rita folded a letter and tucked it into a box marked *later*. The word had become its own kind of filing system. Not urgent. Not forgotten. Just not yet. She pressed the lid down and pushed the box to the corner of her desk where it sat with three others just like it.

Margaret came through the doorway with a cloth-wrapped loaf, still warm enough to fog the air around it. She set it on the edge of the desk without ceremony and pulled a knife from her belt.

"Eve's sourdough," she said. "Second rise finally took."

Rita tore off a piece and ate it standing. The crust cracked between her teeth, and the inside was soft and faintly sour, the way bread used to taste when people still had time to make it right.

Down the hall, Zara laughed. Soft. Surprised. The sound of someone caught off guard by a child's honesty. She didn't look around to see who had heard, didn't catch herself or tuck the sound away. She just laughed, and it stayed in the air like the warmth of the bread.

The fear had loosened its grip.

Not gone.

But loosened.

"We might have turned a corner," Margaret said. She leaned against the doorframe, arms crossed, hopeful despite herself.

Rita chewed slowly. She wanted to believe it too.

Edwin finished his chores early.

He hauled the last bucket to the trough, checked the latch on the south gate twice, and stacked the split kindling against the shed wall so tight a playing card wouldn't have fit between the pieces. Good work. Clean work. The kind that would have earned a nod from Eve at the school. Here he got a clap on the shoulder from Donovan, who was already moving on to the next thing.

No one questioned it. No one stopped him when he drifted toward the tree line instead of back toward the Lodge. The morning had that quality to it, bright and unhurried, where people trusted the rhythm and didn't count heads until lunch. He told himself he was just walking. Thinking.

Letting the morning settle into his bones the way Gus always said a person should before making any kind of decision.

He wasn't making a decision. He was walking.

The trail narrowed past the old softball backstop, where rust had eaten through the chain link in patches. A bramble full of thorns pushed up through the base. Beyond that, the birches thinned and the ground softened underfoot, carpeted with soft spring grass.

Temperance was there, as if the day had arranged itself around that fact.

She didn't greet him immediately. She stood with her back to the woods, gaze lifted toward the ridge where the morning light caught the tops of the hemlocks and turned them silver. Her hands folded loosely at her waist, the way they always did. No book, no basket, no prop. Just her. Patient as a stone in a creek bed.

When she turned, her smile carried no triumph. Only welcome.

"You seem steadier today," she said.

Edwin shrugged. "Things are calmer."

"Yes." Temperance drew the word out, tasting it. "Calm helps people hear themselves think."

He liked that. The idea that calm wasn't emptiness but space. Room to breathe without someone watching to see how deep the breath went. At the Lodge, even the silences felt supervised lately. Not here. The breeze moved through the birches and nobody was listening for what it meant.

"They're doing their best," Edwin said. A reflex more than a defense.

"I know," Temperance said gently. "So are you."

The words settled into him, warm and dangerous all at once, the way the first sip of hot cider burned and soothed in the same swallow. He looked at his boots. Mud on the left toe. A fraying lace on the right. Things he could fix, things he understood.

She didn't ask him to come closer.

She didn't have to.

"There will be a gathering soon," she continued, her tone conversational, like she was mentioning weather. "Nothing formal. Just families. Talking. Remembering what matters."

Edwin's jaw tightened. "I don't think—"

"You don't have to decide now." Temperance raised one hand, palm open, then lowered it. "Choice only means something when it's free."

She stepped back. One step. Two. Giving him space that felt like respect, that wore the shape of kindness so well he almost forgot to question it.

"We'll be there," she added. "If you want to listen."

Edwin nodded once.

Not agreement.

Not refusal.

Something in between that sat in his chest like a seed pressed into soil, unseen and waiting.

He turned back toward the school. The backstop appeared through the trees, and beyond it the Market fence, and beyond that the sounds of people building something worth keeping. He walked faster than he'd left. His hands hung loose at his sides, and the morning light fell clean across his shoulders, and he did not look back.

But he remembered the way.

Marisol felt it before she saw it.

That tightening again. That quiet alarm that never rang loud enough to justify shouting.

She stood at the edge of the yard, Rosa's hand warm in hers, and watched Edwin walk back from the trees. He looked the same. Moved the same. His stride carried the easy confidence he'd earned over the last few weeks, shoulders squared, chin level. The kind of walk that made adults trust you and stop checking your work.

But something in his face had shifted. Settled? Maybe. As if he'd placed something carefully inside himself and closed the lid.

"Edwin?" she called.

He turned, smiling easily. "Yeah?"

"Where were you?"

He shrugged. "Just walking."

She believed him.

That was the problem.

Rosa tugged free and ran to Edwin, wrapping her arms around his waist. He caught her, spun her half a turn, set her down. Rosa laughed and grabbed for his hand and started pulling him toward the garden where she'd planted marigold seeds in crooked rows that morning.

"Come see, come see, I did three whole lines and Rowan said they were almost straight."

"Almost straight is pretty good, Rosie."

Marisol watched them go. Rosa's braid swung against her back, already loosening. Edwin matched her pace without slowing or speeding up, a thing he did now that he hadn't done before. Matching. Adjusting. Reading the person beside him and becoming what they needed.

She couldn't say when he'd learned that.

She couldn't say where.

The garden gate creaked and Rosa pulled Edwin through. Marisol stayed where she was, bare feet on cold ground, arms folded across her chest. The yard hummed with the usual sounds. Declan and Jake hauling lumber past the shed. Somebody's hammer ringing off metal near the barn. Quinn at the fence line, prosthetic braced against a post while he worked a stubborn nail free. All of it ordinary. All of it exactly right.

She looked back toward the tree line. The birches stood pale and still, offering nothing. No footprints in the soft ground that she could see from here. No broken branches. Just the gap between the last fence post and the first trunk, wide enough for a boy to pass through without anyone noticing.

Wide enough for him to come back looking the same.

Inside the Lodge, Clare's voice carried through an open window, reading something aloud to the younger ones. Marisol caught fragments. Words about seeds and soil and patience.

She chewed the inside of her cheek.

Edwin wasn't lying. That was the thing she kept circling back to, the knot she couldn't pick apart. He wasn't sneaking. He wasn't hiding. He walked openly, smiled freely, answered questions without hesitation. Nothing about him screamed wrong.

But Marisol had spent her whole life before the Lodge reading rooms where nothing screamed. Rooms where the danger wore soft clothes and spoke gently and never raised a hand until it did.

She didn't have a word for what she felt. Not suspicion, exactly. Not fear. Something thinner. A thread pulled taut between what she saw and what she sensed, vibrating at a frequency only she seemed to hear.

Rosa's laughter rose from the garden, bright and unbothered.

Edwin's voice followed. Warm. Patient. Present.

Marisol uncrossed her arms. She walked toward the garden gate, bare feet pressing into the cool earth, and she did not take her eyes off her brother.

Not because he'd done anything wrong.

Because she loved him too much to look away.

The Lodge filled that evening the way a vessel fills with water. Slowly, then all at once. Bodies drifted toward the long table in ones and twos, drawn by the smell of rabbit stew and the last of the cornbread Grace had baked in the Dutch oven. Chairs scraped. Hands reached. Someone passed the salt without being asked.

Jo settled into her place at the end, Odin pressing his warm bulk against her calf. Gus sat beside her, his large hand resting on the table near hers. Close. The tip of their pinkie fingers touching. A bulwark against any storm that may arise. The way forty years taught a man to be.

The table was full. Every seat taken, every bowl claimed. The little ones wedged between the older ones, Rosa perched on a cushion to reach properly, Luke balanced on Mary's knee. Quinn sat between Grace and Boone, the prosthetic resting naturally against the table's edge as he tore cornbread with his good hand. Gemma and Hunter bookended the far side, their shoulders nearly touching. Edwin ate steadily, answering Jake's questions about fence posts without looking up.

Marisol sat across from her brother. She buttered Rosa's bread and listened and said nothing.

The stew was rich. Thyme and wild garlic. Jo had seasoned it herself, standing at the stove with her cane hooked over the counter, Odin supervising from the doorway.

Buck was the one who told the story.

He didn't mean to. He was reaching for the water pitcher when Jake asked about the time Zeke got his boot stuck in the creek mud, and Buck's mouth moved before his grief could stop it.

"Stuck so deep he had to leave the boot behind," Buck said. "Walked home with one sock. Told Emma Jean a bear took it."

Silence held for half a breath.

Then Gus laughed.

Not the careful sound he'd been offering for weeks. Not the measured chuckle meant to reassure the room. A real laugh. Deep and rough and startled out of him like a bird flushed from cover. It cracked something open in his chest, and Jo saw it happen, saw the way his eyes creased and his shoulders dropped and his hand finally covered hers on the table.

The sound moved through the room. Clare smiled. Grace ducked her head. Rosa giggled without knowing why, and that made Edwin grin, and Father Tom closed his eyes the way he did during a prayer he meant.

Jo watched it all.

Her knuckles ached. Her hip had been bad since morning. The cane leaned against her chair where she could reach it, and Odin's weight against her leg steadied the tremor she hadn't mentioned to anyone.

But her heart was so full it hurt in a different way.

This. This ordinary miracle. Rabbit stew and cornbread and a dead man's story making the living laugh.

This was what she had fought for.

When the meal ended, nobody scattered. Dishes moved from table to sink in a chain of hands. Boone washed. Beth dried. The children argued.

"It's my turn."

"You dried last night."

"That was Tuesday."

"It's still my turn."

Clare stepped beside Jo at the sink, rolling her sleeves above her elbows. They stood shoulder to shoulder, Clare seemed taller now, or maybe Jo a little less. The water ran warm from the kettle Ellie had heated.

"We did right," Clare said. Quiet enough that only Jo heard.

Jo looked at her oldest daughter. Saw the freckles she'd given her. The jaw she'd gotten from Gus. The steadiness she'd built herself, plank by plank, through a world that kept tearing things down.

The woman Clare had become. The one Jo would one day leave behind.

"Yes," Jo said. "We did."

She meant it.

Outside, the last light clung to the ridge as though the day couldn't bring itself to leave. The sky went amber, then copper, then the deep bruised blue that came before the stars. Odin shifted against Jo's leg, and somewhere down the hall, Rosa's laughter spiraled upward one more time, fading into the woodsmoke and the warmth and the breathing of the house.

The dishes were done. The laughter had thinned to murmurs and the soft padding of stockinged feet on old floorboards. Doors closed one by one down the hall. A child coughed. Someone hummed a lullaby that faded before it found its end.

Edwin slipped out the front door without a sound.

He sat on the top step with his knees drawn up, arms wrapped around his shins. The night air seeped through his flannel, but he didn't go back for a jacket. The air felt good. Clean and sharp, the kind that made his thoughts stand out like fence posts in snow.

The clearing held the last ghost of daylight along the western tree line, a pale ribbon dissolving into charcoal. Beyond the barn, the watchtower lantern swung in a lazy arc as whoever held the shift adjusted position. Crickets had gone quiet weeks ago. The silence that replaced them was bigger, wider, the kind of silence that made a boy feel both small and strangely important.

He thought about the gathering. The way Temperance had said it. Not an invitation, exactly. More like an opening. A space she'd held out the way you'd hold out your hand to a horse you hadn't spooked yet.

"A place where families share what matters. Where people remember together."

He rolled the words over. They didn't feel dangerous. They felt like the things Gran said at supper, like what Father Tom talked about during his homily. Remembering. Sharing. Holding on to what mattered.

He hadn't promised anything.

He turned that fact over too, the way he'd seen Owen turn a piece of wood on the lathe, checking every angle before deciding whether it was sound. He hadn't said yes. He hadn't said he'd come. He'd only listened, and listening wasn't a crime. Gran herself said that listening was the beginning of wisdom.

He hadn't betrayed anyone.

The word sat strange in his mouth even as a thought. Betrayal was a grown-up word. Heavy and sharp-cornered. It belonged to the conversations held behind closed doors, the ones he caught pieces of when he carried water past the kitchen window. He was eleven. He was a big brother. He carried buckets and stacked kindling and helped Eve with the lambs on Market days. He wasn't the kind of person who could betray anything.

He had simply kept a door in mind.

That was all. A door he could walk through or walk past. His choice. And choice was what the adults kept talking about, wasn't it? Gran had stood in the great room and talked about shining light and facing truth and letting people decide. She'd said the children were watching. She'd said it mattered.

So he was watching. And it mattered.

The stars came out in handfuls, scattered like grain across black soil. Edwin tipped his head back and tried to find the Dipper the way Gus had taught him. There. Steady and sure, pointing north. Always pointing north, no matter what happened underneath it.

Behind him, the door was open a crack. Warm light fell in a thin stripe across the porch boards.

Marisol stood just inside, one hand on the frame. She could see the back of his head, the way his shoulders had squared over the last few weeks, broader now, more certain. He looked like someone becoming. She recognized it because she felt it too, that strange pull between the child you were and the person assembling itself inside you, piece by piece.

But Edwin was leaning forward. Toward the dark. Toward something out past the clearing that she couldn't name but could feel, the way she felt weather changing before the clouds showed themselves.

She did not call his name.

Not yet.

She stood and she watched and she held the door.

Inside, Jo turned the iron latch, and the back door closed against the night with a sound like a period at the end of a long sentence. Odin settled at her feet. Gus's hand found her shoulder. The fire ticked and sighed in the hearth.

The Lodge stood firm. The line held. The light remained.

And somewhere past the clearing, past the fence posts and the watchtower lantern and the tree line where the dark pooled thick and patient, the future waited. Not to be inherited. Not to be handed down like a rifle or a recipe or a name.

To be chosen.

Core Cast

Children of the Pines

The Lodge – (Callahan Homestead)

The Callahan Family

- Jo Callahan
- Gus Callahan

Marcus & Deb's Household

- Marcus
- Deb

Clare & Tobias's Household

- Clare Callahan
- Tobias
- Gemma
- Leah

Cole & Ellie's Household

- Cole Callahan
- Ellie
- Declan
- Donovan

Franklin & Mary's Household

- Franklin Callahan
- Mary
- Lily
- Ruth
- Ian

Boone & Beth's Household

- Boone Callahan
- Beth
- Quinn
- Rowan

- Fiona

Judith & Owen's Household

- Judith Callahan
- Owen
- Merryn
- Luke

Other Lodge Inhabitants

- Grace
- Zeke
- Buck
- Father Tom
- Jake
- Sadie
- Max
- Lucy
- Edwin

- Marisol
- Rosa

Lodge Security / Military

- Gunny
- Gin
- Doc
- Harlan
- Morrow
- Tessa
- Yaz
- Riley
- Maddox
- Morales
- Jamisen
- Kosinski

School/ Market Community

- Zara
- Ty
- Eve
- Jenny
- Aiden
- George
- Lori
- Meg
- Rita
- Margaret
- Jillian
- Anna

The Harbingers

Leadership

- Oracle
- Devotion
- Serenity

Enforcers

- Ash

Children of the Harbingers

- Willow
- River
- Thorn

About the Author

KELLY SCHWEIGER lives tucked among the hills, fields, and trees of upstate NY, where stories grow wild and the seasons write their own poetry. A lifelong lover of

quiet places and fierce characters, she writes fiction that explores resilience, family, and the unbreakable thread between land and heart. When not writing, Kelly can be found relaxing with her loving husband, Fred, playing with her grandchildren, foraging for 'lawn salad', reading, or drinking too much coffee with her cats curled at her feet. This is her debut novel, although she has published several cookbooks and children's books in the past.

Acknowledgements

I am forever grateful for all of the love and encouragement of the people who kept believing in this book, and in me, on the hard days. To my family, both by blood and by bond: thank you for your strength, your stories, and your endless supply of patience. Thank you for sharing your knowledge and the small bits of your personality that made it into my characters.

I want to especially thank my husband for standing by me and loving me, through all of my adventures, projects, and my endless chaos. I love you forever, and ever, amen

Most of all, thank you, dear reader, for walking this path with me. Thank you for loving these characters as much as I do. Thank you for come back, again and again to read the stories that live in my head.

I'm so glad you're here.

www.ingramcontent.com/pod-product-compliance
Lightning Source LLC
LaVergne TN
LVHW100522110826
845146LV00002B/747

* 9 7 9 8 9 9 9 0 9 9 8 6 0 *